LAKE OSWEGO JR. HIGH SCHOOL
2500 SW COUNTRY CLUB RD
LAKE OSWEGO, OR 97034
503-534-2335

Lpromised

CARAGH M. O'BRIEN

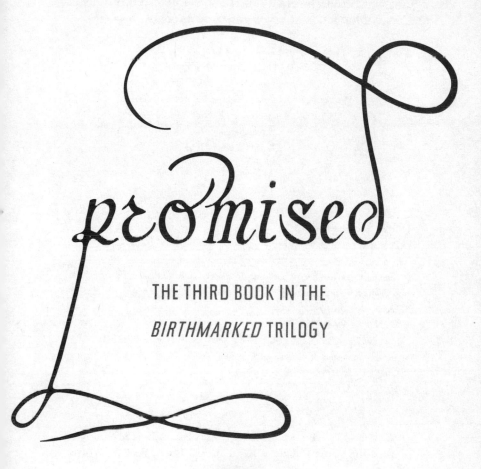

promised

THE THIRD BOOK IN THE
BIRTHMARKED TRILOGY

ROARING BROOK PRESS
New York

The author is donating a portion of the proceeds of this novel to the Global Greengrants Fund, a non-profit, international, grassroots organization that provides small, pivotal grants to people dealing with environmental destruction. Interested readers may find more information at www.greengrants.org.

Text copyright © 2012 by Caragh M. O'Brien

Published by Roaring Brook Press

Roaring Brook Press is a division

of Holtzbrinck Publishing Holdings Limited Partnership

175 Fifth Avenue, New York, New York 10010

macteenbooks.com

Library of Congress Cataloging-in-Publication Data

O'Brien, Caragh M.

  Promised / Caragh M. O'Brien.—1st ed.

    p. cm.—(The birthmarked trilogy ; bk. 3)

  Summary: Gaia succeeds in leading her people to Wharfton and the Enclave, but rebellion there threatens them all just when everything they have dreamed of seems to be at hand.

  ISBN 978-1-59643-571-1 (hardcover)

  [1. Midwives—Fiction. 2. Sisters—Fiction. 3. Survival—Fiction. 4. Genetic engineering—Fiction. 5. Parents—Fiction. 6. Science fiction.] I. Title.

  PZ7.O12673Pro 2012

  [Fic]—dc23   2011047115

Roaring Brook Press books are available for special promotions and premiums. For details contact: Director of Special Markets, Holtzbrinck Publishers.

First edition 2012

Printed in the United States of America

1 3 5 7 9 10 8 6 4 2

To William, Emily, and Michael LoTurco

contents

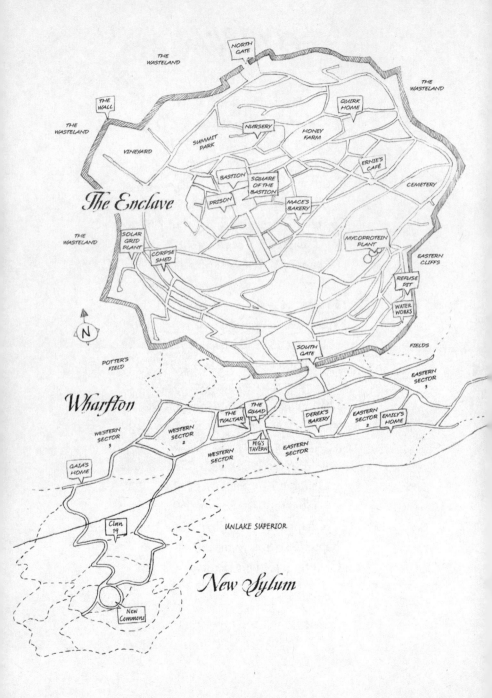

CHAPTER 1

exodus

GAIA NOTCHED HER ARROW and drew back the taut string of her bow.

"Don't move," she said. "At this range, I can't miss, and I'm aiming for your right kidney."

The spying nomad lay belly-down, with goggles pushed up and binoculars pointed down the cliff toward Gaia's clans. An old rifle was propped within easy reach. At Gaia's voice, the spy lowered the binoculars a centimeter.

"That's right. Now slowly move away from the rifle," Gaia said.

Instead, the nomad rolled over, threw the binoculars at her, and grabbed for the rifle. Gaia released her arrow and dodged sideways. She reached to notch a second arrow even as the first one pierced the nomad's hand, knocking the rifle wide to bounce over the cliff into silence. Before the spy could recover, Gaia stepped down hard on the arrow to pin the skewered hand to the ground.

"I said don't move," Gaia said.

She aimed her arrow point-blank at the nomad's face, and saw

1

for the first time that below the goggles, the features belonged to a young girl.

Startled, Gaia eased up and lifted her foot off the girl's hand. She wrenched a dagger from the girl's belt and shoved back away from her. A quick look over her shoulder showed Gaia they were alone on the ridge, which annoyed her to no end. Where were her scouts? Overhead, the sky was an effulgent canopy of pinks and oranges, but the wasteland was washed in the ashy shadows of dusk, making visibility sketchy at best. Gaia notched her arrow again, ready.

"You can't be out here alone," Gaia said. "Where's your tribe?"

The nomad girl curled over her wounded hand. Blood dripped red onto the rocks, and the feathers of the arrow blossomed like a pernicious flower out of the back of her hand.

"Speak up, girl," Gaia said.

The nomad girl hunched up her shoulders instead, and cradled her pierced hand to her chest. Ringed with dirt from the circles of her goggles, her dark eyes glistened with pain. If Gaia didn't know the girl had just been armed, she'd have thought she was the most vulnerable, helpless-looking thing she'd ever seen.

"Are you understanding me?" Gaia asked.

The girl still didn't reply, but from her alertness and the way she'd initially responded, Gaia was convinced she did understand.

Gaia had a bad feeling about this. She scanned the ridge top again, peering around boulders through the brush and shadows. Sending a girl this young to spy implied that the girl's tribe was a bare-bones operation, but that didn't mean it wasn't dangerous. Down below, within easy range of a rifle shot, the nineteen clans of the caravan were setting up fires and cook pots, digging out their carefully rationed supplies of food. They had nothing extra to spare to raiders.

2

The girl couldn't be alone. Gaia noted critically that she was wrapped in layers of dusty cloth rather than sewn garments. Her worn boots looked like they'd crossed long kilometers, and a red fringe around the ankles, evidence of loving craftsmanship, was now dark with dust. The girl turned startled eyes toward the brush, and in the same instant Gaia heard rustling. She crouched low, lifting her arrow again and pointing it at the girl.

"Don't move," Gaia said, her voice low. "You'll be the first one I shoot if someone gives me trouble."

"Mlass Gaia?" came a low, familiar voice.

Relieved, Gaia straightened again and lowered her bow. Chardo Peter and five of her other scouts closed in on them, the women and men moving lightly over the rocks.

"We've been looking for you," Peter said to Gaia. "Are you all right?"

"Of course," Gaia said. "I expected forty scouts along this ridge. Where are they all?"

"Out further," Peter said. "They're moving inward now. Look."

Gaia glanced across to the next promontory and saw a hint of movement. Two scouts were highlighted briefly against the sky-line before they shifted out of sight. Gaia slung her bow over her shoulder and put the arrow back in her quiver.

"Warn them we're not alone. I want another full search of the perimeter, starting now," Gaia said, and a pair of scouts slipped into the shadows. Gaia stepped nearer to the girl, "Who else is out there?"

The girl, alarmed, shook her head.

"Can't you talk?" Gaia asked.

"Need help," the girl said in a barely audible, guttural voice. She pointed to the west.

"Who's out there?" Gaia pressed. "Your family?"

3

The girl shook her head again and conspicuously swallowed, working her throat. "My friend is hurt," she said. "Please."

Gaia stooped beside her. "Let me see your hand," she said. "Peter, look around for some binoculars. She threw them at me. And there's a rifle over the cliff. I want that retrieved."

Gaia reached for the girl's small hand, examining where the arrow shaft pierced her palm. The wound was ragged, and she couldn't staunch the bleeding until the shaft was removed. Gaia's stomach went light and queasy, but she focused, positioning the girl's hand on a wide, flat stone. She took a bandana out of her pocket and folded it in a square to be ready. Then she pulled out her knife.

"Hold still," she said.

The girl watched her solemnly.

Gaia braced the arrow against the stone, cut sharply to sever off the tip end, and then leaned close to examine it for slivers. It was a clean, blunt cut.

"I need your bandana, Peter," she said without looking at him. "Fold it long on the diagonal, please." She met the girl's gaze. "I'm pulling the arrow back through now. You ready?"

The girl nodded, shutting her eyes tightly. Gaia pulled the arrow out with a slick sound, then held the girl's hand up high and packed her bandana into her palm.

"Peter."

Peter passed her the makeshift bandage, and she secured his black bandana carefully around the girl's bloody hand. "Keep it up here, by your neck, and apply pressure to both sides. See?" she said, guiding the girl's other hand into place.

The girl opened her eyes and tentatively examined the arrangement.

"How's that feel?" Gaia asked.

4

The girl nodded. She cleared her throat, but instead of speaking, she pointed west again and started getting to her feet.

"It needs to be properly cleaned," Gaia said. "I'll take you down to camp."

The girl shook her head and pulled at Gaia's sleeve, clearly indicating she wanted her to go with her away from camp.

"Is your friend far?" Gaia asked.

The girl raised five fingers.

"Five minutes?" Gaia asked, and the girl nodded.

"Mlass Gaia, you can't go," Peter said. "It could be an ambush."

Gaia knew he was right, but something about the girl's stoic demeanor with her wound had tempered Gaia's suspicions of her. She put a hand on the girl's shoulder and studied her eyes, seeing hunger there, and wary desperation.

"Will I regret trusting you?" Gaia asked.

The girl shook her head once, and her voice was little more than a croak. "Please. It's safe."

"I'll go with her," Peter said. "You belong back in camp. There must be fifty people down there with questions for you right now."

Gaia's duties were precisely what she'd wanted to evade for five minutes when she'd set out for a walk on the ridge, and here was the perfect excuse to do it.

"No. I'll take you with us," Gaia said, and turned to her other scouts. "The rest of you be careful. If this girl had been hostile, she could have picked off any number of us from here, but I suppose you all realize that." She put her knife away. "If we're not back in thirty minutes, tell Chardo Will he's in charge."

Without waiting to see her orders followed, Gaia headed off into the wasteland with the little nomad. The girl led her through the brush, moving quickly and silently in the fading light. Her outfit was exactly the brown-gray color of the land, so watching her was like seeing a piece of the landscape itself shifting through the shadows. Gaia could hear Peter following behind her.

They'd gone only a short distance before Gaia felt her queasiness again, only worse. She kept on, hoping it would pass, but in a matter of seconds, she was shaking and clammy. "Wait," she called.

Grimly, Gaia put her hand out against a boulder, waiting while nausea hit her full force. She buckled over with her guts clenched and grit her teeth, hoping she wouldn't actually throw up. For an instant longer, she thought she could control her stomach, but then she heaved into the shadow of the boulder.

Lovely, she thought. At least she avoided drooling on her trousers.

"You shouldn't still be nauseous," Peter said. "Everyone else was finished two weeks ago. Have you been sick all along?"

She closed her eyes, waiting for her stomach to settle.

"Mlass Gaia?" he said more gently, nearer.

She didn't want Peter's gentleness. She waved him back and spat. "I'm good."

The girl was staring at Gaia, her eyes wide with concern. She tilted her face and made a gesture for a big round belly in front of herself before pointing to Gaia.

"No, I'm not pregnant," Gaia said, acutely aware that Peter was listening. "The problem is, I can't shoot things. Living things, that is. I get sick afterward, every time." No amount of training had ground that out of her.

The girl looked surprised, and then she waved her wounded hand and laughed with a husky, musical sound.

"I know. Real funny," Gaia said.

Peter was not amused. "Who else knows?"

6

"Leon, obviously, and a few of the other archers," Gaia said. "It's not a big deal. I'm not usually the one shooting things. That's what my scouts are for."

"If you'd take them with you."

Being around Peter compelled her, annoyingly, to be truthful. That much hadn't changed. "All I wanted was five minutes to myself. Just *five minutes*," she said. "I didn't ask you to worry about me."

"It's my *job* to worry about your safety."

"Then you should have had the scouts on the ridge like you were supposed to."

The instant she spoke, she regretted her sharpness. In silence, she wiped her lips with her sleeve.

"You still can't even look at me, can you?" Peter asked.

Gaia turned slowly, bracing a hand on her hip. Peter hitched at the strap of the arrow quiver that cut vertically across his chest, and gave his bow an impatient jerk. He'd let his light brown hair grow out, and the ends had turned lighter, almost blond with his endless days in the wasteland, planning the route of the exodus. It was true. She was uncomfortable around him still, even though it had been more than a year since their decisive exchange on the porch of the lodge.

"Is there something you want to say?" she asked.

He watched her quietly. "Are you ever sorry for what you did to me?"

Their broken relationship had ripped her up longer than she cared to consider and had caused her no shortage of unspoken friction with Leon over the past year. "Of course I am."

His eyebrows lifted in surprise. "Then why didn't you say so?"

"What good would it do either of us?"

She regarded him across the distance and felt an invisible

7

boulder materialize between them to ensure they stayed apart. The nomad girl was watching curiously.

"It would make a difference," he said. "Even now."

Gaia briefly pressed a hand between her eyes. "In that case, I'm sorry for what I did," she said. She hadn't deliberately misled him when they'd kissed so long ago, but that was what had happened, and she'd made it worse by getting in the stocks with him. "I thought you must know I was sorry. I feel terrible about how I treated you, but I'll never regret that I chose Leon. You and I can't be friends. It isn't possible."

Peter's aloof posture melted slightly. "I'm not asking to be your friend."

"What do you want, then?" she said.

"Just don't *ignore* me," Peter said. "Just look at me like you look at other people, like I exist. I deserve that much." He took a step nearer, into the invisible boulder, which cracked and began to disintegrate into painful shards.

With an effort, Gaia met his gaze. His blue eyes were as discerning and vivid as ever, but the generous humor that used to brighten his visage was gone, replaced by stark, wary reserve. As their gaze held, she could feel herself knowing him, understanding him, and it hurt because deep down she knew his transformation was her fault.

He took a half step nearer, waiting her out.

It wasn't friendship he wanted, she realized, or even the closure of forgiveness. He wanted something harder: honesty without intimacy.

"I can try," she said.

In the stillness, he nodded. The girl made a snapping noise with her fingers and pointed impatiently ahead, but Gaia kept her focus on Peter.

"Enough said?" she asked.

"Yes," he said. His voice dropped, and he was the first to turn away. "Enough."

Gaia turned then to the girl. "Lead the way, Mlass."

The girl took off into the shadows again.

A ping of conscience mixed with Gaia's relief, and she wondered what Leon would think of her new truce with Peter. Shoving it back, she strode rapidly after the girl.

Already the heat of the wasteland day was switching over to the coolness of evening, and in another hour it would be lightless and cold. Gaia could smell dry sage and the ubiquitous dust of the wasteland, layers of it, like the opposite of water. The terrain dipped into a ravine of deeper shadows, and the girl slowed as they reached the bottom. The next moment, she vanished.

"Where'd she go?" Gaia asked. There had to be a hidden passage or cave, but for the life of her, Gaia could see no way through the rock wall of the ravine.

Then the girl's head peeked up about knee-high, several yards away, and she reached toward Gaia. Gaia moved cautiously forward, peering into the shadows, and it was only when she was right on top of the girl that she saw a crevice in the rock, dim with dusty shadow. It looked too small to conceal anything, but Gaia could hear breathing. She squinted as the girl drew her in, and then slipped the strap of her quiver off over her head to duck down farther.

A slumped, prone man lay in the back of the crevice. The smell of blood was a metallic, sweet taste in the air. The girl drew close to him, snuggling against his heart, and the man put a limp arm around her.

"Silly Angie," the man mumbled. "What did I tell you? You have to go join the caravan. I'll catch up with you."

There was a flicking noise behind Gaia, and Peter leaned in as far as he could with a lit match. The injured man frowned, wincing. His eyes were feverishly bright in the sepulchral space, and his expression turned to wonder. Gaia took in his gaunt cheeks, his pale hair and darker beard, the strangely youthful angle of his eyebrows even as he suffered, and recognition hit her gut before it reached her consciousness.

"Jack?" she asked, disbelieving.

Gaia's brother quirked his mouth in a half smile. "Wouldn't you know," he said, his speech slurred. "Now, if only I were pregnant, you'd be a big help."

clan nineteen

Peter's match went out.

"Light another, quickly please," Gaia said. "It's my brother." She was as delighted to find Jack as she was horrified to see him in such dire shape. "Where are you hurt? How long have you been like this?"

Peter struck another match and kept them coming. Jack blinked slowly, watching Gaia with his oddly lustrous eyes. His shirt was dark with caked blood.

"Just take care of Angie," Jack said. "She's had a bad time of it. I'm glad I got to see you once more. I kept hoping I might."

"Tell me how you're hurt."

"I got knifed in my side here," Jack said. "I didn't think it was that bad, but it's wiped me out. The blade must have been poisoned."

"When was this?" Gaia asked.

"A couple days back, when we ditched our band of nomads," Jack said. "Angie's mother just died, and the kid has no other family. It's a long story, but her mom asked me to get Angie to the Enclave so she could have a shot at a future, and I owed her, so that's what I was trying to do. Gaia, promise me you'll take care of her. You're headed back, aren't you?"

The girl had slid her fingers into Jack's hand and looked like she would never let go.

"Take care of her yourself," Gaia said. "We Stones don't die easy."

"Odin Stone. Right." He mumbled his birth name as if it were still unfamiliar.

"Where's your tribe now?" Gaia asked.

"They were two days west of here and heading south. They're long gone by now."

In the poor light, Gaia saw that layers of cloth were stuck against Jack's wound. Tugging at the fabric would make it worse and start him bleeding again before she could treat him properly. There was no point staying here talking.

"You ready, Peter?" she asked.

"Yes."

Carrying her brother back to camp was like hauling a limp block of granite between them, and the going was so slow that the sky was a rich violet by the time they reached the last ridge. Several scouts intercepted them and took over carrying Jack. The campfires of the caravan spread before them in the valley below as they made their last descent.

"You never said you had a brother," Peter said.

"I have two, both older," Gaia said. "We didn't grow up together because they were both advanced inside the Enclave. Just before I left, Jack helped me escape, and then he left for the wasteland, too."

Gaia glanced at Angie and wondered what the full story was there. The little Gaia knew of nomad culture was harsh and brutal, which fit with Jack getting knifed. The girl, still cradling her wounded hand in the makeshift bandage, kept close to Gaia as they wove through the ordered chaos of the camp.

Eighteen hundred people were noisily settling in for the night. Since leaving their home beside Marsh Nipigon in early September, Gaia's people had had over three weeks to establish their routines on trail. Each clan had a central hub of cook fires, with clusters of families surrounding them. True tents were few, but dark tarps were rigged over poles to shelter many of the families. Packs, baskets, and cages of chickens added to the jumble. Somewhere a clear tenor voice started up a ballad, and smoke brought the scent of chicken cooking with honey and curry.

"Welcome to our caravan. We're from Sylum originally," Gaia said to Angie. "Like it?"

The girl nodded, glancing ahead toward the men carrying Jack.

"I'll do what I can for you and Jack," Gaia said. "Try not to worry."

In the center of the activity, clan nineteen was laid out in neat circles around three fires, and Norris Emmett, drawing on his skills as the cook for the lodge back in Sylum, was overseeing the feeding of a hundred people. He glanced up as Gaia approached, and his gaze swept over Jack and the girl before he called something over his shoulder. Farther behind him, Josephine was feeding two toddlers: her daughter Junie and Gaia's sister Maya.

Gaia stopped to give the little girls hugs and kisses. Maya tried to feed Gaia some bannock by pressing it against her lips, but Gaia laughed. "No, that's for you. Eat up, squirt." Gaia looked up at Josephine. "Has she been good?"

"Good enough," Josephine said with her normal good humor.

"I've got her. Looks like you're busy." Josephine had cut her dark curls shorter for convenience on trail, and they were held back from her face by a jaunty red headband. Gaia's little sister had a bit of the same red in her hair.

With a pang of guilt, Gaia couldn't help thinking Josephine was in some ways a better mother figure to Maya than she was herself. "I'll try to come back to tuck her in," Gaia said, and gave her sister another kiss on top of her soft curls before she continued on.

A smaller, fourth campfire was burning to one side where Dinah, the former libby, had a tarp and supplies laid out in readiness for medical emergencies. She'd turned to healing in the past year, assisting Gaia and proving to have a steady hand with everything from childbirth to single sutures. Dinah's white, pleated shirt had remained spotless during the entire exodus, defying all logic and now, as they approached, she straightened, swinging her braid over her slender shoulder.

"Only you could wander off into the wasteland and come back with two more mouths to feed," Dinah said. She nodded toward the men carrying Jack. "Do you want help with him?"

"Let me get started," Gaia said. "See what you can do for Angie's hand."

The scouts lowered Jack to the tarp, where he lay still. Gaia was already reaching for the soap.

Peter lit two extra torches and arranged them nearby. "I'll get back to the ridge," he said.

"Right. Good." Gaia heard the perfunctory note in her voice and made a point of looking up to meet his eyes. The faintest irony tinged his expression. "I mean, thanks, Peter."

"You're welcome, Mlass," he said evenly, and with a brief smile at Angie, he was gone.

Dinah's gaze followed Peter and turned back to Gaia. "What was that?" she said.

"What?"

Dinah pointed her thumb after the retreating scout, then stopped. "Okay. Never mind."

Gaia sank down beside her brother and reached for his shirt. "I need an update. Have the scouts who went ahead to the Enclave returned? Munsch and Bonner?"

"No. Not yet."

"It's getting to be too long. What else do you have for me?"

Dinah filled her in about some bickering between the miners and the fishermen, a woman's persistent fever, a shortage of corn meal, and a broken travois. "Chardo Will is mending the travois. Otherwise, nothing major."

"Has Leon come in with the crims?"

"Not yet. He sent word they'd be in around sundown."

Then he's late, Gaia thought.

Gaia would not relax until all the clans were settled in for the night, including and especially the crims. Leon was in charge of a dozen prisoners who accompanied the exodus, working to earn their freedom by the time they reached Wharfton. In a concession to safety, the crims were chained by the ankle in pairs, which meant they were always the last ones into camp each night, along with Leon.

Dinah was working over Angie's hand, and Gaia could see from the child's glassy gaze that Dinah had given her a lily-poppy draught for the pain. Gaia started on Jack's wound. With scissors, she cut away the looser fabric, then used a sponge to wet the caked blood and carefully peel the rest away. The wound was ten centimeters long, and deep, scraping along his lowest rib. The edges were ragged and pink with infection.

"Bad, huh?" Dinah asked.

"Yes." Gaia glanced at her brother's face, considering carefully. Jack was out cold.

In the past year, there had been dozens of times when a medical situation needed more expertise than she had, and she'd come up with a policy. She was brutally honest, always, with her patient, and she let the patient decide what she would try. Sometimes it had been deemed best to do nothing, and the patient had died. Other times, she had done nothing, and the patient's body had healed itself. Most times, the patients had wanted her to try cleaning, stitches, compresses. Once she'd amputated a man's crushed hand, and he'd survived. But digging around in people was not something she excelled at, and she was loath to do it without their consent.

"Any ideas?" Gaia asked Dinah.

Dinah left Angie for a moment and came nearer, holding her braid back as she leaned over Jack's wound. "It isn't bleeding too badly anymore," she observed.

Gaia narrowed her eyes as she inspected the wound again. "I'm going to irrigate it." She poured some of the boiled water into a separate bowl, dropping in three leaves of cohosh and a twig of witch hazel. She swirled it to let it cool before she poured half of the solution into Jack's wound. It bubbled a little coming out.

"That can't be good," Gaia muttered.

With her scalpel she evened off the roughest edges of the wound, then stretched the opening a bit wider, trying to see further in. A black, triangular sliver of knife tip was briefly visible in the deepest layer of the cut before oozing blood obscured it.

Gaia worked carefully with her tweezers to extricate the sliver, then irrigated the wound repeatedly until the bubbling stopped

16

and the water washed out smoothly. She put in a drain, drew the muscle tissue together again, and wrapped a bandage to keep the wound closed. She wished they had some antibiotics.

"What's your brother like?" Dinah asked when Gaia at last sat back.

"I hardly know him," Gaia said. She glanced over to see Dinah had finished with Angie's hand. "We've only talked a few times. I know he's brave, though, and selfless. He saved me from the Bastion once. He was an Enclave guard, like Leon."

"How old is he?"

Gaia calculated. "Twenty, now. Leon's age. Why?"

Dinah was regarding him thoughtfully. "He just looks older."

Gaia thoughtfully regarded her brother's face, seeing it faintly flushed in the firelight, his lips dry and cracked. Her gaze lingered over the planes of his face, seeking and finding a resemblance to her mother in the lines of his eyebrows and the curves of his closed eyelids.

"It's going to be interesting, meeting some new men," Dinah said.

Gaia glanced up. "You've never had a shortage of men liking you."

"Doesn't mean I'm not curious," Dinah said.

"It isn't going to be easy," Gaia said. "Our women won't be special in Wharfton the way they're used to. It's going to be an adjustment."

"I'm not worried."

Gaia took a second look at her friend, and guessed she was probably right to be confident. Certain women would always be prized, no matter what society they landed in, and Dinah was lively, smart, and uncommonly pretty. What Gaia was going to miss was the closeness she had with her women friends in Sylum. She missed Taja and Peony, who had stayed behind with their families in Sylum. Already, with the responsibilities of the exodus, Gaia saw little of her nearest friends, like Josephine, and she hoped she wouldn't see them even less once they reached Wharfton.

"I've always sort of wondered if you might hit it off with Chardo Will," Gaia said cautiously.

Dinah gave her an odd look. "I don't have a chance with Will."

"Why not?"

Dinah laughed. "Very funny. I'm not stupid." Her eyes went warm with teasing humor.

"Don't, Dinah," Gaia said.

"I'm not blaming you, but I know a hopeless case when I see one. Poor Will. Unrequited love seems to be his specialty. Or maybe it runs in the family. No, I think I'll just see what Wharfton and Enclave men are like.

They're different, Gaia thought. *They aren't as polite.* All kinds of things could go wrong.

"You look so anxious," Dinah said, laughing. "You've warned us plenty, Gaia. Different cultures and all that. You go ahead and take care of the big diplomacy. Leave the one-on-one to the rest of us. We'll be fine."

As Dinah moved off to other chores, Angie came drowsily nearer, sliding onto the tarp to cuddle beside Jack. Firelight reflected off the goggles she'd lowered around her neck.

"You're just happy to have a warm fire and a safe place to sleep, aren't you?" Gaia asked.

Angie glanced up and pointed a finger to Gaia's scarred cheek.

"It's a burn from when I was a baby," Gaia said. "It doesn't hurt now."

The girl pointed next to Gaia's necklace.

Gaia lifted it from the neckline of her blouse to show her, turning the small, weighty objects in the firelight. "The locket watch is from my parents for timing contractions when I'm a midwife. The monocle is from my grandmother, the last Matrarc of Sylum, for leadership and heritage, I guess," she said. She remembered how reluctantly she'd accepted the monocle at first, and considered how familiar it was now. "So, what's the story of your voice? Care to tell me?"

The girl watched her groggily, then shook her head.

"Didn't think so," Gaia said. "Can you sit up a bit? Take off your goggles."

The girl complied, and Gaia tilted a torch nearer so she could examine her throat and neck. "Does it hurt?" Gaia asked gently.

Angie slowly nodded her head. "When I talk."

Gaia shifted behind Angie so she could line her fingers softly all around the girl's warm neck. "Try to say 'Ah.' Nice and steady now."

With the sound, Gaia could feel Angie's neck muscles tense unnaturally, fighting to trap her voice instead of releasing it. Gaia handed back Angie's goggles and began making up a cure as she went along.

"Here's what I want you to do," she said. "Take a big drink of water every hour, whether you're thirsty or not. And put your hand to your neck, like this, and think about keeping those muscles loose and calm. No one can hurt you." Gaia smiled, watching to see that the girl was listening closely. "Pretend the inside of your voice is just cool and open, like water going down. All the time, whether you're talking or not, even when you're falling asleep. Will you try that?"

The girl looked slightly hopeful. She nodded again.

Gaia lifted the dressing on Angie's hand to inspect what Dinah had done, and judged she could do nothing better. She rested Angie's small, splinted and bandaged hand lightly on the girl's chest, and thought of a wounded bird, fragile and hollow-boned. Gaia knew what it was like to be motherless.

Angie's eyes closed, and she rolled slightly, turning her cheek to rest on Jack's shoulder. She put her fingers to her throat.

Gaia sat back and reached to wash her hands again.

"There's a story there," Leon said quietly, stepping into the firelight. "Unbelievable."

Happiness shot through her at the sight of him.

Leon dipped his head to take off his hat, and putting a strong hand on her shoulder, he leaned near for a kiss.

"Best part of the day," he said, and chucked his hat on a blanket near the fire.

CHAPTER 3

a promise

"ARE YOU GOOD?" LEON asked.

"Yes," Gaia said. "And you?"

He smiled and started to roll back his sleeves. "Good. Where'd you find Jack and the urchin? They look pretty beat up." He reached to take the bar of soap from her hand. His arms and hands were filthy, and she guessed he'd helped to carry the crims' loads.

"Back behind the ridge west of here," she said. "Peter helped me bring them in. Jack said they left a band of nomads two days west of here."

"How old do you think she is?" he asked.

Angie stirred, and blinked up at Leon.

"I don't know. Not more than eight or nine," Gaia said. "She's tough, though. I shot her hand before I realized she was a kid and she never even cried.

"Shot her yourself?" Leon asked. "How was the aftermath?"

"Normal," she said and checked to see that no one was within earshot besides Angie and sleeping Jack. "I threw up, but I was able to delay it a little. That's progress."

"Face it, Gaia. You'll never get over it," Leon said. "You're not meant to hurt people."

"I need to be able to protect our people," she argued.

"I don't mean you won't do what you have to," Leon said. "I'm just saying you'll always pay for it somehow. Were you embarrassed?"

"Only Peter and Angie saw me. She thought I was pregnant."

Leon's smile turned amused. "Are you?"

"No," she said. "You'd be the first person I'd tell."

"We've been careful, but things can happen."

"As if I didn't know." She made big warning eyes at him and inclined her head slightly toward Angie. "We are *not* talking about this here."

He laughed. "Have you eaten any dinner?" He leaned over the basin to splash water on his face, drenching his three-week beard, and then he flicked the excess water away. A drop sizzled in the fire.

"I was waiting for you," Gaia said.

"You mean you forgot."

"I'm not exactly hungry," she said.

"You ought to be. Have a seat. I'll get you a plate." He lifted another woolen blanket from a pile and dropped it next to the fire. Norris's cat darted over from the other campfire and circled Leon's boot. As Angie's gaze followed the cat closely, Leon picked it up and subjected it to a nonchalant rub that flattened its ears and elicited a purr.

"Hey, kid," Leon said. "Do you like cats?"

Angie cleared her throat. "Yes," she said. "What's an urchin?"

"A very brave girl," Leon said. "Can you watch Una for me? I need to feed the Martrarc here." He passed over the cat and pointed at it sternly. "Stay put, Una."

Angie smiled sleepily, curling her good hand gently into the cat's fur. Gaia shouldn't have been surprised. Naturally, the girl would struggle to talk to Leon when she talked to no one else, just as the cat would obey his commands.

"Be right back," Leon said, and gave Gaia another kiss. "Don't fall asleep on me. We have some planning to do."

She sank down onto the blanket, settling in comfortably up-wind of the smoke, and soon Leon was back with a couple of steaming bowls. He passed her one and tossed a couple more sticks heavily into the fire before he sat down beside her. They had no real privacy, but at least they were together, and the part of Gaia that responded only to him expanded a little.

His knee pressed into hers, and he clinked his bowl to hers. "To Jack," he said. Will he make it, do you think?"

"I don't really know. Antibiotics will help once we reach Wharfton, if we can get them. Angie ought to have them, too," she said. It was amazing to think they were so close to medica-tion that could save someone's life. The proximity reminded her of her missing scouts. "Munsch and Bonner haven't returned from Wharfton yet. I'm getting worried."

"Want me to go after them?" Leon offered.

"No," she said. "You've got enough to do."

"When are you ever going to let me be in any danger?" he asked, spooning up his stew at a steady rate.

"You're in danger every day," she argued. "Who else could handle the crims?"

"You know they're loyal. It's their only charm."

"Loyal to you. Not to the rest of us. What you do is in-valuable."

"No gratitude, remember," he said.

"Right." She'd discovered he had the quirk of not wanting to

23

be thanked for anything he did for Sylum. To him, it was his job, but it was hard for her to remember because it felt like her people were an extension of herself, and any service or kindness to them felt personal to her. "I'll just thank you for bringing me the stew, then," she said.

"You're welcome," he said. "I'll get you more." He held out a hand for her bowl.

"I'm not finished with this," she said. Carrot chunks were mixed in with the meat, sweet and orange in the brown gravy, and she pushed one aside to save for last. Suddenly, her stomach clenched again, this time for a different reason, and she lowered her spoon.

"What is it?" he asked.

"We're almost there," she said. "Just two more days."

"Scared?"

Terrified was more like it. There were so many things that could go wrong once they reached Wharfton and the Enclave, and the responsibility weighed on her like a leaden mantle. The people of Wharfton might reject them. The guards of the Enclave might turn their guns against them. Her people could all be dead in forty-eight hours. She drew up her knees and curled her arms around them.

"Gaia," he said gently, drawing out her name. "Tell me."

"What was I thinking, bringing us all here?" she said. "This is insane."

"It wasn't all your decision, remember? And it's not insane," he said. "It's less insane than staying to watch us all die off in Sylum. Not one girl was born this past year. Not one."

"I know."

"Haven't you seen how excited people are getting? We'll be

able to see the obelisk rising over the Square of the Bastion by the day after tomorrow. They've never seen a city or even a working light bulb. The men cannot believe there'll be enough women for them to meet."

"But see? Right there. That's a problem," Gaia said. "It's not like the women of Wharfton have been eagerly awaiting us. They're not all single women ready to wave welcome banners to our men."

"The women don't have to wave any banners. They exist in sufficient numbers." He smiled slowly. "You watch. The men will make inroads, and it won't take long."

She looked past the nearest campfire to one farther on, where Norris was dishing up the last of the stew to a couple of men while a third reached for a beat-up, blackened teakettle. They had to be exhausted, but there was an air of optimistic happiness about them, an undercurrent of anticipation that Gaia had been sensing for days, while her own anxiety had increased in reverse proportion.

She glanced again at Leon. "All our blueprints and charters to build New Sylum won't come to anything if we can't get the Protectorat to give us water."

"You'll convince him."

"How can you have so much faith in me? Honestly," she asked. "Aren't you afraid of your father?"

He set aside his bowl. "No."

"And there. That," she said, watching his profile in the flickering light. "I don't like what happens to you when you think about him, and now we're actually going to have to negotiate with him."

Leon shifted slightly, allowing a gap of space to widen between them. She hated that.

She softened her voice. "Why don't you talk about him?"

He pushed a hand back through his hair. "Why do you bring him up? We know he's ruthless. He's also politically astute, which is in our favor. He can't afford to look as ruthless as he is, so outwardly, he'll have to be diplomatic."

She uncoiled and reached for her stew again, then swallowed another spoonful. She didn't have to be looking at the scars on Leon's back to know they were there. "It's what he can do to you privately that worries me," she said.

Leon tossed a bit of a stick into the fire. "You don't need to worry about me. There's nothing left there, Gaia."

She doubted the Protectorat felt equally neutral about Leon. "What about your mother?"

"I left on decent terms with Genevieve. There won't be any reason to see her much, not when I'm living outside the wall with you."

Gaia suspected that was an over-simplification, too. Uneasy, she glanced down at her monocle and locket watch, glinting in the firelight. Somewhere ahead, in a grave in Potter's Field, her father lay decomposing, if he wasn't dust in the dry earth already. She had no idea if her mother was buried beside him, though she hoped so. Complicated as Leon's family was, at least he had people to return to. His sister Evelyn would welcome him, and his brother Rafael, too. He had a birth father outside the wall. By contrast, Gaia had no family to return to, beyond her newfound brother Jack and another brother in the Enclave she'd never even met.

A spark snapped in the fire, and the logs shifted, letting out a new burst of heat. "Do you think you'll get to know Derek better?" Gaia asked.

"He's a good man. I'm not sure how much he'll want me

involved with his new family, but I'll certainly look him up. He'd want that much, I know." Leon smiled, studying her attentively. "You don't need to worry about my family liking you," he said. "It's not like we need anyone's approval."

"I know."

He drew her hand into his so she could feel the warmth in his fingers. "Marry me," he said. "Don't make me wait anymore."

She'd known this question was coming again. He'd been patient for a whole year. But knowing the moment was here didn't mean she was ready.

"Gaia, we're starting a new life. We should do it together," he added. "You know we should. You can't still have doubts about us."

"I don't about you," she said. "I'm sure about you." And she was. No one would ever love her as deeply as Leon did.

He almost sounded hurt, and she couldn't stand that.

"Then what's left?"

"I'm afraid," she said. "I don't care if it's not rational. I'm afraid the Protectorat will go after you deliberately because I'm the Matrarc. He could try to hurt you to manipulate me if we're married."

"You're too late, then," Leon said. "He'll know we love each other whether we're married or not. All he has to do is ask anyone who's seen us together this past year."

"We could pretend we've argued," she suggested.

"And then you'd what? Pretend to start up with someone else?" His voice turned deceptively light. "One of the Chardos?"

She could tell he wasn't buying it, but she kept trying anyway. "Or someone else. You could pick the guy. It wouldn't matter to me."

"This isn't amusing anymore," he said. "You've had a year to think about marrying me, and any time along the way you could have told me it wouldn't work. You promised you would decide about us, remember? You weren't supposed to decide *no*."

"I've had doubts. You know I have."

"You've also been happy, and loyal, and loving. Don't forget that," he said.

"Not so loyal. I talked to Peter just today," she said.

"Nice try."

"No, I really did. Up past the ridge, when we were getting Jack," she said.

"That's hardly sneaking off to be alone with him," Leon said, watching her closely. "It probably couldn't be helped. What did you say?"

"We agreed never to be friends," she said.

Leon relaxed. "See? That's not breaking a promise to me. It's making it stronger. I know you, Gaia. I'd trust you forever. Why are you resisting me on this? I feel like I'm fighting you, and this is supposed to be a proposal."

She slowly shook her head. "There's Will, too."

Leon laughed. "Now you're really stretching it."

"He loves me, Leon. He hasn't said it lately in so many words, but I can tell."

"Obviously," he said. "But that doesn't mean you care for him the same way. Don't you think I'd know? Think I haven't watched you with him? I have to hand it to the guy. He never crosses a line. His devotion would be funny if it wasn't so awful to see."

"I keep hoping he'll fall for someone else," she said hopelessly.

"So do I. Both of those Chardos." With strong hands, he pulled her closer and shifted her onto his lap so he could wrap his arms

28

around her. "What's with all these excuses? Tell me what you're really thinking," he said tenderly. "What's really the matter?"

She felt a crumpling sensation around her heart. Why did Leon always see into her so perfectly?

"It hurts to love someone this much," she said finally. "I feel each place where our minds meet, and each little place where they don't, until we talk things over and line up again. Like now when you won't let this go. I feel the other, muddled places we leave alone, like with your parents. But even those places are ours. I've never had anything like this with anyone else. Now I'm never fully happy anymore unless you're with me. I'm teetering in this stupid place where I want to keep you selfishly with me every minute, but I can't. And what if I ever lost you? This isn't strength. It's weakness. It's not supposed to feel this way."

"You're amazing," he said, and nudged her chin up with his thumb.

"But do you know what I mean? Does it actually hurt for you, too?"

"Of course it does. And it doesn't matter what it's *supposed* to feel like. It's ours."

By the soft, flickering light of the fire, his eyes gleamed. A tiny corkscrew of expectancy twisted in her gut. His face tipped until she felt his beard skim near, then his mouth, and then everything else vanished. She held on to him tightly, afraid and hungry and sweetly happy all at once. They had never let their kisses go too far in public, but when finally she had to pause to breathe, she glanced around anxiously. People were still moving around the fires, but no one was watching.

"So shy," he muttered. He was smiling easily, and then he surreptitiously ran a finger along the neckline of her blouse.

"Not here," she said. She ducked away so his chin tickled her ear, but she was ridiculously pleased.

"Okay, hold still," he said. "I have something for you." He shifted his weight but still managed to keep her on his lap. Then he pulled a thin, braided band of red wool from his pocket.

"What is it?" she asked.

"Hold out your hand," he said. With both arms still around her, he tied the strings of the band around her left wrist. "I had Mlady Roxanne teach me how to make the stitches. See here?" He lightly touched a strand of gold that threaded through a wider part of the fabric bracelet. She frowned, holding her wrist toward the firelight so she could see the tiny characters.

"It says 'orange,' " she said, awed. "When did you make it?" It was the loveliest thing she'd ever seen, both strong and delicate, with work as fine as any her father had ever done. She could hardly believe Leon had made it for her.

"Last fall," Leon said. "It took me about ten tries to get it right."

"And you've been carrying it around all this time?" she asked.

"I was waiting for the right moment," he said. "I have the feeling this will have to suffice."

She stilled her hand on the bracelet. "You were going to give it to me as an engagement present, weren't you, like a ring?"

"It's yours, Gaia. I just want you to have it."

She felt her eyes misting.

"Just take it." He kissed her cheek, and then her lips again. "You'll say yes to me someday," he said. "I know you will. As far as I'm concerned, we're engaged."

A last, spindling thread of reservation unraveled inside her, allowing her heart to leap blindly forward. "Me, too. Of course I'll marry you. Nothing would make me happier."

His eyes grew warmer and deeper than she'd ever seen them. "You mean this? You won't take it back?"

She laughed. "Yes. Really. You're right. It's ours, and I just have to learn to live with it."

"Like a curse or something." He was nodding, and then he was shaking his head, too, like he could hardly believe her. Then he laughed. "When?"

"I don't know," she said. "Whenever we get settled. Okay?"

"We're pretty settled tonight. Right now, actually, come to think of it."

She laughed again. "You'd have to shave."

"I can shave. I'm very good at shaving." He toppled slowly sideways to the blanket, bringing her with him and half squashing her.

"We agreed not to tease each other on trail," she reminded him.

"We agreed not to tease each other *too much*," he said. "You're mine now." His voice dropped soft and close to her ear. "You've made a promise."

"I know. You have, too."

Leon shifted her more comfortably in his arms, and she snuggled near, feeling the warmth where her clothes met his and inhaling the warm, smoky scent of him. He somehow reminded her of cinnamon, even though she hadn't tasted any in over a year. The idea of him being with her always, just like this, for the rest of her life, brought her a kind of wondering joy. Then, with an awful sense of premonition, she hugged him more tightly, peering past his shoulder to the black void of sky beyond the drifting

31

campfire smoke, as if she might not get the chance to hold him again for a long time. *Ignore the fear*, she thought.

She felt his finger move lightly along the chain of her necklace.

"Finally," he said tenderly, and for the first time, Gaia heard a new, ineffable sweetness in his voice.

CHAPTER 4

the crims' deal

THE PACKED, WIND-SWEPT DIRT was parched and
gray beneath Gaia's boots, and the little clumps of sage and oat
grass had turned almost colorless in their wasted, spindly grip
upon the earth. *Like us*, Gaia thought. She was climbing up a
long, gradual hill of dusty rock and scrub two days after picking
up Jack and Angie when she noticed the people in the caravan
stopping ahead, on top of the next ridge. She glanced down at
Maya, whom she carried straddled on her hip, supported with a
sling. The little girl had her fingers in her mouth, and she made
a petulant noise, tugging at her cloth hat.

"You have to keep your hat on," Gaia said. "Look! Look up the
hill. See Josephine and Junie? We're going to catch them."

The people kept spreading out in a knobby line along the
ridge top, and Gaia knew it could mean only one thing: the
Enclave. She looked back eagerly for Leon, and moved aside with
Maya to let others pass. Several girls and boys, her messengers,
paused conveniently nearby, and over their heads rippled her
standard: a yellow oval ring on a green background, reminiscent
of the commons back in Sylum. Mikey, Dinah's son, was in charge

of bearing the flag, which made it easy for anyone in the caravan to locate Gaia.

"What is it?" Norris asked her. The cook leaned heavily on his crutch to rest his peg leg.

"We must be close," she said, smiling. "They're stopping to see. Go on. I'll be right there."

Adjusting the angle of her hat brim, she scanned back along the caravan, where every able-bodied person was heavily loaded. Men and women carried food, clothes, poles, and rolled tarps, sometimes in huge loads on their backs. Where there were no roads, they could use no wheels, but they'd rigged travois for the horses to drag. Angie was carrying a pole with two cages of chickens balanced over her shoulder, keeping it steady with her good hand as she followed Jack's stretcher. Other children drove a small herd of close-shorn sheep, and far in the back, trailing slowly behind, came the crims with extra loads of water.

Wanting to see the Enclave for the first time again with Leon beside her, Gaia automatically hitched Maya higher and started walking back along the line of travelers, with Mikey in her wake.

In the distance, one of the crims stopped to wait while his chainmate maneuvered their ankle chain around a rock, and then they came forward again. The next pair of prisoners, each carrying a heavy skin full of water on his back, was impeded at the same place, and managed the same clumsy dance. She watched it twice more before she dragged her gaze away, looking for Leon, and found him in the back. Leon was helping to carry a platform laden with water sacks and spelling one of the crims who trailed behind, head bowed, hands on his hips, moving his legs in exact mimic of his chainmate so as not to disrupt his chainmate's stride.

Gaia had never been happy about the crims. Back in Sylum, after she'd been elected Matrarc, many of the prisoners had been

34

retried and their sentences commuted. Others had been released to their families, leaving incarcerated only the forty who were convicted of the most violent crimes.

The families who had elected to stay behind in Sylum, a minority of two hundred people, had not wanted to be burdened with running the prison. Their leader, Mlady Maudie, had argued vociferously that Gaia should take all the crims with her on trail, and after weeks of negotiating, they had ended up one night at a table in the lodge, dealing out the files of the prisoners into two piles and trading to see which crims would stay and which would go.

Mlady Maudie had offered to swap a murderer for five of Gaia's lesser criminals.

"We need to keep our numbers down," Leon had said quietly, turning aside to confer with Gaia. He had once been unjustly imprisoned with the crims himself, and he'd been running the prison since Gaia had become Matrarc.

"We won't be able to guard them forever," Gaia had said to him, considering. "What if he breaks free and kills us all in the night? What if he kills us when we reach Wharfton?"

"He won't," Leon had said, explaining what he knew of the men's characters, and Gaia had trusted Leon's guidance on the matter.

In the end, Leon took charge of twelve crims for the exodus. Those twelve traveled the first three-quarters of the trail many times over, carrying stockpiles of water and supplies for replenishment stations along the route. Their thankless labor had been critical for setup long before the huge exodus ever began.

"Come on, Mlass Matrarc!" a youthful voice called from the ridge. "You can see the Enclave from here, with the towers and the wall! It's amazing!"

35

"Wait for me," Gaia called back. "Just wait there. Break for lunch. I'm taking care of the crims."

Leon looked up at her voice. "Hold up there," he said to the crims, and coordinated with his team to lower their platform.

The other crims lowered their heavy water skins and stood panting under the bright sun, their gray and tan clothes saturated with sweat. Leon took off his hat to brush back his sweaty hair as he approached, and Gaia met the piercing blue of his eyes when he put the hat back on.

"What's up?" he asked.

"It's time. We can't go over the ridge with the crims in chains," she said. "I don't want Wharfton or the Enclave to see us like this."

She watched his gaze shift skeptically up the ridge. The travelers had put down their packs, and many were lounging on boulders amid the dry grass, passing canteens and resting their feet as they broke out their midday victuals. In contrast to their sturdy wholesomeness, the chained crims appeared even more depraved and vicious. What was more, the segregation of one small dangerous group cast an unsavory pall over everyone else, too.

They couldn't afford to look disunified.

"I see your point," Leon said. He turned to the crims, unclipping an iron key from his belt. "Malachai, you first."

The tallest crim and his chainmate left their burdens and made their way forward. Malachai was a stiff, deep-chested man with a rough, dark beard and gnarly knuckles who had killed his wife. Claiming self-defense and defense of his children from her abuse had not convinced the jury to release him. He had a way of regarding Gaia with an unblinking concentration that made her uneasy, and yet she knew Leon trusted him completely.

"What's going on?" called a burly man, strolling back down the ridge toward them. Bill, a thick-headed, well-liked miner from the rowdy end of Sylum, worked a lump of chaw in his cheek as he spoke. "I don't remember anything about freeing the crims. What are you doing?"

Behind Bill came several of the miners from his clan.

"It was part of the deal," Gaia said. "The crims staged our supply drops and carried extra water for us in exchange for their freedom once we arrived. We've essentially arrived."

"Nobody asked me about this deal," Bill said.

"It was part of negotiations back in Sylum, weeks ago," Gaia said. "You maybe don't recall."

"I don't like it," Bill said. "You there, Vlatir, hold up a second."

Leon had already undone the shackles on Malachai's and his chainmate's ankles. He looked briefly at Bill, then moved pointedly to the next pair of crims.

"Hey!" Bill said. "I'm talking to you!"

Leon straightened. He gave no overt command, but as fast as their chains would allow, the twelve crims circled defensively around Leon, Gaia, and Maya. Positioning himself between Gaia and Bill, Malachai picked up his chain and gripped it in one hand, silently prepared to swing it into savage motion.

The only one more surprised than Bill was Gaia herself.

"What's this?" Bill demanded.

"Leon, stop them," Gaia said.

"They aren't doing anything," Leon said.

"I said stop!" Gaia commanded.

"Drop the chain, Malachai," Leon said.

"He can't threaten Mlass Gaia," Malachai said.

"Nobody's threatening me," Gaia said. "It was a misunderstanding. Drop your chain. Now!"

Malachai did, slowly setting his fists on his hips, still facing Bill.

"Did you see that? They're savages!" Bill said.

Others were coming rapidly down from the ridge. Several of the archers readied their bows. On Gaia's hip, Maya began to whimper.

"Put up your bows," Gaia said. "No more of this. You'll treat the excrims with respect. They're citizens of New Sylum now, and they have the same rights as anyone else. Yourself included," she added to Bill.

The archers lowered their bows but remained on alert. Gaia reflexively smoothed a hand around Maya's back, and she watched as Bill's gaze shifted to the little girl.

"You're scaring the baby," Bill said.

"Are you done?" Gaia asked.

Bill turned once more to the crims, then to the others who had gathered around, and he gave out a loud, aggressive laugh of disbelief. Maya began to cry in earnest, and Gaia slid her up out of the sling to cuddle her close to her neck. "You're okay, baby," she said softly, still watching Bill. Maya's wail subsided into a little hiccupping sob, and the tiny girl wrapped her soft hand around Gaia's neck. As Gaia kept her gaze zeroed on Bill, demanding his concession, she felt the prickling, volatile silence of the others around them.

"Tell me you understand," Gaia said.

"All right," Bill said. "But if they harm any one of us, so help me, I'll personally rip them apart."

"And you'll face the consequences for vigilantism if you do," Gaia said.

"Is that so? Are you and your boyfriend going to run the courts in Wharfton when we get there?" Bill asked.

Gaia took a step nearer. "You'd better hope I'm still in charge when we get there," she said darkly. "You mess around in Wharfton or the Enclave and you'll get strung up fast with no questions asked."

Bill's eyebrows lifted. "What kind of place are you taking us to?"

"It's brutal," Gaia said. "We've discussed this. Do you want to go back to Sylum to die there? You still can. We'll give you enough water to go back," she said. She shifted Maya to her other shoulder. "That goes for anyone else, too." She faced up the hill to where the others waited. "Once we go over that ridge," she called, "there's no going back.

Uneasiness rippled tangibly through the crowd.

"None of this is going to be easy. Life outside the wall is hard, and in some ways it's even worse inside. But if we stay together," Gaia said, "if we can count on each other, no matter what, I know we can build our new home in New Sylum, just as we've planned. That means we can't start out divided, with some of us already second-class citizens. Do you all understand?"

She picked out the clan leaders, one by one, to be sure they were with her. Dinah represented the libbies and the fishermen families from down by the shore; Norris's cousin, a cobbler, headed up the trade workers who had run shops side by side in the center of Sylum; Mlady Beebe represented many of the homeowners from around the commons; Mlady Roxanne, the teacher, led a large group of loosely connected laborers; and the morteur, Chardo Will, who was Gaia's second in command and Peter's brother, led the largest clan of hardworking, quiet men who had never married.

One after another, eighteen clan leaders nodded to confirm their loyalty, and then Will nodded toward Bill the nineteenth and final leader.

"How about it?" Will asked in his calm, steady voice. "Where do the miners stand?"

Bill shouldered his pack again and sauntered a couple steps toward the ridge. "I already said it. If any crim messes with me and mine, I'll break his neck. But I wanted to get out of that death trap back home my whole life. The miners aren't going back. That's where we stand on that."

A couple of the other miners chimed in. Gaia gave Maya another pat on her back and exhaled in deep relief as the crowd began to move again. Leon turned to unlock the remaining chains. One excrim peered down at his ankle and lifted his foot as if testing the unaccustomed lightness. Beside him, Malachai was hugging a young boy. Gaia had expected more of a celebration, but aside from a few smiles and back slaps, the excrims seemed content to stand together, patiently waiting instruction.

Gaia glanced at Leon. "We still need the rest of this gear."

"We've got it, Mlass Gaia," Malachai said, nodding respectfully. "Your dad's free now, son," he said softly to his boy. "None of that now. Not to worry."

Leon dumped the chains on the water platform with a heavy rattling, and took a place alongside the platform. Three of the excrims took up the other places, while the remaining men picked up their burdens, no longer forced but voluntarily.

Gaia met Leon's gaze, wondering.

He smiled at her, as if he'd expected all along that his men would continue to operate as a unit. "Go ahead," he told her.

She took a few steps, pausing to look back. Apparently, she wouldn't be going over the ridge with Leon beside her.

"Ready?" Leon asked. "On three."

The four men lifted the platform of water sacks as one, and

started forward. One of them said something Gaia didn't catch, but she heard the genuine warmth in Leon's responding laughter.

"He has them more in control than ever," Will said.

Gaia turned, surprised to see he'd fallen in beside her. Will's face and hands had gained extra color during his weeks in the wasteland, and his tan strengthened his resemblance to Peter, his younger brother. He had a beard now, too, like all the other men who hadn't shaved on trail, and she decided the darkness delineating his jaw suited him.

"It's a little frightening," she agreed. "Like he has his own mini army of loyal followers now."

"I expect their loyalty extends to you," Will said. "I'm not sure how much farther."

She smiled, and as she walked, she peered up under the brim of his hat to his kind brown eyes. "How've you been, anyway?"

"Good. I haven't had the chance yet to congratulate you on your engagement."

"Thank you." She glanced at her red bracelet.

"Be happy, Mlass Gaia. You deserve it."

She laughed. "Thanks. So do you."

He settled his thumbs under the shoulder straps of his heavy pack. "Will Vlatir mind if we're still friends?" he asked.

"He hasn't minded so far," she said. "We've worked so well together."

"That's true."

Beyond Will, along the ridge top, people were sorting themselves out, preparing to move on.

"I've been wondering what's best," Will said mildly.

She glanced up at him. He was smiling, but some faint guardedness hinted that their friendship might be at a turning point.

Her heart felt a twitch of alarm. If she knew a friend was in love with her, but he never asked for anything and accepted he could never have more, was she responsible for any heartache he might suffer?

"I don't know what to say," she admitted.

"I guess we'll see, then, won't we?" he said.

I guess, she thought.

Gaia continued to carry Maya up the weather-beaten slope with Will silent beside her. Her heart began to work in her chest, as much from eagerness as exertion. A couple of boys went by with a pack of goats, their bells tinking in the dry heat.

With each step, the horizon of the ridge grew nearer, until finally Gaia breached it and the last expanse of wasteland stretched before her, a great, shimmering landscape of brown and white and gray. In the distance, the Enclave rose on a majestic hill. Its towers and white roofs and the spike of the obelisk cut a distinct skyline against the blue above, while below, the great, impregnable wall divided the city from the tumbling gray structures of Wharfton, her home. Farther below, the sweep of the vast unlake fell away toward the south.

Gaia took a long, deep breath. "That's it, Maya," she said to her sister.

Will paused beside her. "It's bigger than I expected."

"Yes," she said simply.

"Who's that?" he asked, pointing, and passed her a pair of binoculars.

Small in the distance, rippling in the heat waves, a figure was walking toward them: a woman moving with a steady but unhurried gait.

Gaia zeroed in on the motion. There was no mistaking the woman's purposeful bearing, nor the black medical bag she clutched at her side. "It's Myrna Silk," Gaia said. "One of the doctors from the Enclave. She was in Q cell with me. In prison."

"Apparently she's out," Will said.

Gaia scanned through the binoculars along the top of the wall, picking out the tiny figures of the guards, and her pulse kicked up a notch. Far in the distance, the Enclave was fully armed and waiting for them.

the backward siege

"A**T LEAST THEY AREN'T** sending out forces to attack. So far." She handed back the binoculars.

"Keep them," Will said. "What happened to yours?"

"One of my messengers has them," she said. "Thanks." She slung the strap around her neck and Maya began to inspect them. There was nothing to do but continue onward and keep an eye out for an aggressive move.

The caravan veered south, skirting wide of the Enclave and Wharfton to approach along the old shoreline of the unlake. If Gaia's judgment was correct, they were a couple of hours away from the wall when they met up with Myrna Silk. Her black eyebrows contrasted vividly with the white hair fringing out from the edges of her hat, and there was an acerbic, no-nonsense quality to her features even when she smiled.

"Exile agrees with you, I see," Myrna said, clasping Gaia's hand warmly. "Who's this delightful creature?" she added, lifting the brim of Maya's hat.

"My sister, Maya."

"Of course," Myrna said. "Did Leon ever find you?"

"He's here," Gaia said, gesturing behind her. She drew Myrna aside on a wide, sunny ledge of rock while the caravan continued, stretching out in a long line to their left as they faced the Enclave. She waved for the vanguard to progress along the shoreline without her, and they trudged onward. "I sent two scouts to Wharfton four days ago and they haven't returned. Do you know anything about them? Munsch and Bonner?"

"They were taken in for questioning. That's how I heard you were coming with an army." Myrna glanced around and set down her bag. "Looks like that rumor was a bit off the mark. Unless those are attack chickens."

Gaia laughed. "We're not an army. We're coming to relocate permanently. We're peaceful."

Myrna looked amused as she shook her head. "Only you."

"What?" Gaia said.

"Things have changed since you left," Myrna said. "There's even more hostility across the wall now than there used to be. Listen, I came to talk to your leader to see if I can persuade you all to leave. What are the chances?"

Gaia shook her head. "We can't leave. We've come too far, and our old home is a death trap. We'll do whatever it takes to survive here."

"Even so. Who's in charge?"

Gaia felt a certain ironic delight. "I'm our elected leader. You're looking at the Matrarc of New Sylum."

Myrna's gaze went from Gaia to the caravan of walking people with their burdens and back to Gaia. "That figures."

Gaia offered Myrna a canteen, but the doctor had brought a bottle of her own, and while the older woman drank, Gaia lifted Will's binoculars again. The wall, with its massive blocks of limestone, appeared taller than before, and now that she was nearer, she inspected a new wooden layer that had been built along the

45

top. A parapet connected the towers so soldiers could walk along the continuous top length, at least along the legs of the wall that overlooked Wharfton.

She adjusted the focus on a soldier who had his own pair of binoculars aimed back toward the caravan.

Gaia lowered the binoculars and turned to the doctor. "Are you spying for the Protectorat?"

"Why? Do you have something to hide?"

She had a point. Gaia glanced over her shoulder to where her young messengers waited discreetly for orders. "Tell Leon Vlatir and Mx. Dinah to join me, please," she said to one. "They're both behind me a ways." She gestured to another. "Chardo Will went ahead. Find him and k him to come back, too."

The messengers sprang off.

"My scouts were supposed to ask a couple of my old friends in Wharfton to start stockpiling water for our arrival," Gaia said. "Would you have any idea if that's happening?"

"I don't know. Derek Vlatir is the one who told me your scouts had been taken in. He always knows what's going on."

"How do you know Derek?" Gaia asked, puzzled. "He still lives outside the wall, doesn't he?"

"So do I, now," Myrna said, and jogged up her chin. "I told you things have changed. I took over your old house on Sally Row. I hope you don't mind, but it didn't look like you were com-ing back. I'm running a blood bank there."

"But isn't that illegal? How did all this happen?" Gaia asked, amazed.

"Outside the wall the blood bank isn't illegal," Myrna said. "You began it all by stealing the birth records. It took the Enclave a few days to realize you gave them to your red-headed friend, Emily."

46

"Emily! How is she? Is she all right?"

"Didn't Leon tell you? The Protectorat took Emily's baby to persuade her to give the records back, which she did, of course. But then the Protectorat accused her of having copies made. When the Enclave still didn't give Emily's son back, she and her husband went berserk."

"They *would* go berserk. Especially Kyle," Gaia said. "Leon left around then, so I don't know what happened after that."

People kept streaming past on Gaia's left, glancing over curiously. Her standard made a rippling noise in the wind, and its shadow flicked in the dust.

Myrna took another sloshing swig from her bottle. "Enclave parents were afraid that birth parents from outside the wall would track down their advanced children to steal them back," she said. "There was a panic, so when Emily's husband was caught coming under the wall to try to get their son back, there wasn't much sympathy for him. I imagine you recall the punishment for breaching the wall."

Gaia hugged her sister closer. "Execution."

"Exactly," Myrna said.

Gaia couldn't believe it. She touched a hand to her forehead, horrified.

Leon arrived then and slid a hand around her waist. "What is it?" he asked quietly.

"Emily's husband Kyle was executed," Gaia said, her voice tightening. "Did you know that?"

"No," he said. "Don't think it was your fault."

But it was, she thought. She was the one who had brought the ledgers to Emily's family and started the trouble in the first place. As Leon's arm tightened, Myrna tilted her face, regarding them frankly.

47

"How did your back heal?" Myrna said. "And your finger."

"Well enough, thanks to you. I'm in your debt, Masister," Leon said. He reached out a hand to shake with her. "What happened after Kyle's execution?"

Myrna dabbed at her neck with a handkerchief. "Apparently, Emily garnered a lot of sympathy from people outside the wall, and she built on that. She united all the pregnant women of Wharfton for the first baby strike. They refused to advance any more babies, and they sent a message to the Protectorat demanding that he return Emily's baby. They claimed it was the right of every mother to keep her own child."

"A baby strike," Gaia said, amazed. She'd never guessed that Emily would be the one to organize such a protest.

"I expect that didn't go over well," Leon said.

Chardo Will and Dinah arrived then from different directions. They unobtrusively joined the circle on the rock ledge as Myrna continued.

"The Protectorat doesn't play games," Myrna said. "He didn't reply to Emily's demands. He simply turned off the water to Wharfton."

"Every spigot?" Gaia asked.

"Even the irrigation water for the fields," said Myrna.

Gaia tried to imagine the panic that had hit Wharfton as people discovered they had no water. "It was like a backward siege, wasn't it? With the people inside the wall controlling the people outside by cutting off what they needed," Gaia said. "Did the strikers give in?"

"Actually it got complicated," Myrna said. "The people of Wharfton united behind the mothers, and inside the wall, the Protectorat's hard-line policy backfired." She glanced briefly at Leon. "People in the Enclave are not all as cold as you might think, and some of the very wealthy, influential families formed a consortium and spoke up on behalf of the people outside the wall. It became a humanitarian issue."

"I'll bet," Leon said dryly. "Those same families are probably the ones who own the fields outside the wall. They didn't want to lose their investments."

"Did the Protectorat's own people persuade him to turn on the water again?" Gaia asked.

"No," Myrna said. "But he was forced to negotiate. On the third day of the siege, the Protectorat named two conditions to turn the water back on. He wanted all of the people of Wharfton to register their DNA into one database."

Gaia was confused, trying to remember. Hadn't she and Mabrother Iris once discussed such a possibility? She thought he'd said it wouldn't be practical.

"But that must be fifteen thousand people or more," Gaia said.

"Sixteen thousand, four hundred, and twelve, to be exact," Myrna said. "The Protectorat wanted cheek swabs collected from everybody, in family groups. That way he would have a record of everyone's DNA, once and for all."

Gaia looked at Leon. "What good could that possibly do him?"

Leon was watching Myrna. "It's an overabundance of information, certainly, but he likes to plan ahead. It fits."

Gaia shifted her weight, repositioning Maya on her hip. "What was the second condition?"

"He wanted Emily to come live inside the Bastion, as his permanent guest," Myrna said. "She could have her son back, but inside the wall, in the Protectorat's own home."

"To control her," Gaia said, with instinctive understanding. It was practically the same thing that had happened to her in Sylum when the Matrarc had confined her for a period of reflection in the

49

lodge, only Emily's status as a guest would never end. "Did she go?"

"By day six, Wharfton was completely out of water," Myrna said. "They'd drunk every last drop of cider and distilled wine just for the liquid. Pets were dying, and people were pressuring Emily. She said she'd never signed on for a rebellion. She just wanted to see her son again, so she went."

"But is she all right?" Gaia asked.

Myrna frowned thoughtfully. "She appears to be. She's risen to a position of some importance. She's been there over a year now, and her second child, a boy—that's the only home he's ever known."

Gaia turned to Leon, whose gaze was directed toward the Enclave, as if he could penetrate the mind of his father just by observing the city where he dwelled.

"So there's a full DNA registry," Leon said.

Myrna nodded. "It took us a month, but we swabbed every single person. That's when I moved outside the wall, and I found, to my great surprise, that despite the rampant ignorance of your old neighbors, life in Wharfton suits me just fine."

"He'll want us to register our DNA, too," Chardo Will guessed.

"Yes," Myrna said, turning to him. "That's a given. And you are?"

Gaia made quick introductions.

Unexpectedly, Dinah laughed. "I wonder what the Protectorat will think of our expools."

Myrna glanced at Gaia.

"Many of our men are sterile," Gaia explained. "We suspect .they're XX-males. I suppose now we'll find out for certain from their DNA."

50

Myrna looked surprised. She took another look at the line of people in the caravan. "How about the women? Are they fertile?"

Dinah nodded, still smiling. "I'd say. Our mothers have, on average, eight children each. Many have over ten, and the children are almost all boys. We hope that will change now that we're here, away from the water that poisoned us in Sylum."

"There does seem to be quite a preponderance of men," Myrna said.

"We have nine men for every one woman," Gaia said. "And there were no girls born in the past year."

Myrna was clearly interested. "Very odd. Is there any hemophilia in your population?" Myrna asked.

"None," Leon said.

Myrna crossed her arms, plainly considering. "Interesting," she said finally, and turned to look speculatively at Leon. "Your father will be very interested."

"We're counting on that," he said.

Gaia was still worried about her old friend. "Does Emily ever come outside the wall? What happened to advancing the babies? I can hardly believe there are no more quotas."

Myrna's gaze narrowed slightly, and she adjusted her hat brim over her eyes. "Emily came out briefly for a recruitment. She works for Leon's father now. For the Vessel Institute."

"What's that?" Gaia asked.

"It's in its pilot phase," Myrna said. "Essentially, the Vessel Institute is a baby factory."

homecoming

"THE PROTECTORAT WOULD NEVER describe it so crudely," Myrna added. "But that's what it is."

"You can't mean what I'm thinking," Will said. "Women would never allow themselves to be used that way."

"Maybe not where you come from," Myrna said.

"How does your baby factory actually work?" Dinah asked.

"The Vessel Institute hires women to bear children for childless couples in the Enclave," Myrna said.

"How many?" Gaia asked. "What does it pay?"

"There are twelve women in the pilot program, and I'm not aware of the particulars of the stipend," Myrna said.

"Is Emily one of these women?" Leon asked.

"Emily is the spokeswoman for the Vessel Institute," Myrna said. "Whether she's also pregnant, I don't know. Her second son is only a few months old, but I suppose it's possible. I guess she'd be the thirteenth."

"You just said Emily led the baby strike. How could she become the spokesperson for a baby factory?" Gaia argued. "It doesn't make sense. How is this system any better than advancing babies?"

"These mothers have a choice," Myrna said. "They sign on with their eyes wide open."

"Wait. You approve of this?" Gaia asked Myrna.

"I'm just telling you how it works," Myrna said coolly.

"Listen, I don't want to interrupt," Dinah said, "but we've got some practical problems of our own right now. Shouldn't you be at the head of the caravan, Gaia?"

Gaia lifted the binoculars again and realized the vanguard was approaching the first, poorest houses of Western Sector Three. Soon they would reach the dip where she wanted them to turn down into the unlake. After all their planning and their weeks in the wasteland, they had reached the brink of arrival.

Gaia turned to find Mikey behind her and gestured to the boy. "Red flag," she said, and the boy lifted one high into the air. Within moments, other red flags went up along the line ahead of and behind them, and people stopped where they were.

"If you'll excuse me," Gaia said to Myrna. "Leon, please take Myrna to Jack to see what she can do for him."

"I'm coming with you," Leon said.

"I want you to stay out of sight for now," Gaia said, absently adjusting Maya on her hip once more. "I'm hoping your presence is still a secret from the Protectorate. For that matter, I'd just as soon he doesn't hear about Jack yet, either."

"He'll find out soon enough," Leon said.

"But not now. Not right from the start," she said.

He came a step nearer. "Gaia. Be reasonable. I want to be with you. This is important."

Gaia glanced around at the others and then dropped her voice. "You'll distract me," she admitted. "I don't want to have to worry about you. Stay back, with Jack and Myrna."

Leon's eyes flicked oddly. "That's insulting, you know. I'm

perfectly capable of taking care of myself. Are you asking me as the Matrarc or as my fiancée?"

She gave a slight, apologetic smile, already backing away from him. "Which way will you argue with me less?"

He watched her a silent moment, his mouth set, and then he turned to Will. "Go with her. Don't let her leave you. Don't let her do anything stupid."

"Will do," Will said. His teeth flashed in a grin before his voice turned solicitous. "Keep yourself safe, buddy."

"Shove off, Chardo," Leon said. He gestured at the toddler on Gaia's hip. "You want me to take Maya?" he asked Gaia.

Gaia hesitated, and glanced at the load he already carried. "No. I've got her."

He clearly thought that was a poor decision, too. "Fine," he said, and turned back with Myrna.

Gaia knew she'd annoyed him, but at the same time, she was relieved that Leon wouldn't be in the lead with her. She had a secret fear that he would take some risk in the Enclave that she'd be helpless to prevent. She turned, beckoned to Will and Dinah, and began striding the length of the caravan toward the vanguard.

"All right, green flag," she said to Mikey when they eventually reached the low rise where Peter was waiting with a corps of archers and scouts. The caravan of people shifted, collected itself, and began moving again.

Peter tipped his hat brim as she fell in beside him. "I'm finally seeing where you came from, Mlass."

She glanced up and felt the natural pull of a smile. "Yes." With Peter's beard and the dust of the trail, he looked much like he had when she'd first met him. She would have died if he hadn't rescued her, and she wondered if he ever remembered that night. "So much has happened since I left."

54

"For all of us," Peter said.

"It's so big," Mikey said.

Gaia glanced over at the boy and smiled. "It is, isn't it?"

She tried to see Wharfton from his perspective, considering he'd never known anything bigger than the sylvan village of Sylum, and the clusters of buildings magnified before her eyes, especially the bright ones inside the wall that glistened in the sun. She needed no binoculars to perceive a boy on the path to the water spigot above Western Sector Three. Brown and gray garments hung on clotheslines, and across Wharfton, thin lines of dingy smoke rose from chimneys. A colorful pot of pink flowers stood on the porch of the closest little home. The first sound she heard was a blacksmith's bang, and suddenly she was home.

"What if I get lost?" the boy said.

Gaia laughed. "We'll keep you safe. If you lose your way, just head downhill, toward the unlake. You'll always find us then." She made a gesture for the Chardo brothers and the others. "We'll turn off here."

Gaia started down into the great blue bowl of the unlake, and when a grasshopper leapt past her trousers, Maya squeaked in surprise. Soon, Gaia intercepted a trail she knew from her childhood when she, Emily, and Sasha used to explore. She'd drawn from her memories of the unlake to create a terrain map the planners had used for deciding where to lay out New Sylum, but she didn't realize how sweet it would be to actually retrace the old paths. It felt like signals were reawakening in the dormant corners of her brain, making her senses even more acute. Her heart lifted. This was going to be home again, but better than before.

"See?" Gaia said, turning to Will. "It's just like I remember."

"Your two lives are finally meeting up," Will said.

She looked up, surprised. "Yes."

His profile was aimed ahead, to where a flight of swallows careened through the clear air. "It's beautiful," Will said. Then he added, "We're a long way from the marsh."

"That's the point," Peter said.

"I'm just saying it's different," Will said.

"Are you going to get homesick?" Peter asked.

Will adjusted the shoulder strap of his pack and regarded his brother. "Not before you do."

Peter forced a smile. "I won't."

Gaia glanced at Peter again, picking up on his mood. "Everything all right?"

"Get it over with," Will suggested.

"What?" Gaia asked.

Peter shook his head. "It's nothing."

Will laughed at him. "He wishes you and Vlatir all the best."

"Thanks, Will. I can speak for myself," Peter said.

"It's really okay," Gaia said, her cheeks warming.

"I do, of course," Peter said stiffly. "Congratulations."

For goodness' sake, she thought. "Thanks," she said abruptly. She gestured forward. "Shall we?" she said, and continued on.

Around the next bend, the bay of boulders descended into a wide, flat shelf of bluegrass, wildflowers, and low brush. Stands of aspen promised firewood. Farther along, angling northeast, a path led directly back up toward Wharfton and her old neighborhood on Sally Row.

Her gaze traveled up toward the towers of the Bastion and the obelisk. She lifted her thumb, measuring its height against the obelisk's as she used to do with her father, and a poignant longing for him touched her heart. Then she shifted her thumb toward the wall. Leon had told her that as long as the soldiers were no taller than her thumbnail, she would be out of rifle range, and the guards on the wall were still smaller than that.

Views change, she thought. She was no longer a kid.

Maya held her thumb up, too, puzzled.

Gaia laughed. "We're home, bug," she said. She turned to Dinah, Peter, and Will, opening her arms wide. "This is the place."

Dinah compared it to the site plans she'd pulled out and nodded. "I see. It's good. Will?"

He absently hooked a hand around the back of his neck as he looked over Dinah's shoulder. "Yes."

"We'll secure the perimeter," Peter said.

In no time, the clan leaders began filing people to their predetermined areas, adjusting in a fluid, flexible way now that they were confronted with the actual terrain. Archers appeared on three outcrops of rock that provided a clear vantage of the entire area. Mikey propped Gaia's standard in the place where clan nineteen would settle, and Gaia set Maya on her feet as Josephine came up with Junie. The two little girls gave each other hugs.

"Cute," Josephine said. "I'll watch them. You sure you want us setting up here, under the gun, so to speak?"

"Yes, closest to the path up to Wharfton," Gaia said, indicating a boulder that marked where the trail rose.

She took another look at the organized chaos around her. Norris was directing several expools to lay out his kitchen gear along a shelf of stone, and Angie, with a serious expression, was letting the little girls take turns with her goggles.

"Angie," Gaia said. "I thought you were staying with Jack."

"She's no trouble here," Norris said.

"I know, but I want it settled who's in charge of her, and I expect Myrna to take Jack up to the house on Sally Row." Gaia considered the girl. "Would you rather be here with Norris, or with Jack?"

"Jack," Angie said.

Gaia agreed. "Then I want you to stay with him and not wander. You can help out Myrna, at least until we're settled. Is that clear?"

The girl stood slowly and retrieved her goggles from the toddlers. She nodded.

"I have to go see about Munsch and Bonner," Gaia said. "They need to be released and I want to check on getting some fresh water for tonight, too. It's strange that no one has come down to see what's up with us," she said, thinking of Emily's parents and Leon's birth father.

"I'll get Peter to put an escort together," Will said.

"I'll take Peter and some archers," she agreed. "I'd rather have you stay here. You're in charge in case anything happens to me."

"And have Vlatir slit my throat for letting you go without me? No, thank you," he said. "Meet us up ahead." He started up the trail.

She took off the sling she'd used for Maya and checked to make sure she had her knife in her boot. Then she glanced back at the stream of people still winding their way down into the unlake. Jack's stretcher was coming, and she caught a glimpse of Leon giving Myrna a hand down a steep chute. Below, people were spreading out, clearing stones and setting up campsites.

She turned her back on New Sylum and trod up the familiar path, past the places where her mother had first taught her about motherwort and where her father had taken her to pick early morning blueberries. With each step, she was closer to home, closer to all she'd left behind, and it felt like time was reversing, too. Absently, she stroked her fingers along her scarred cheek, and wondered if she would find herself in her old skin.

As she came over the last ridge out of the unlake, she saw that Sally Row was deserted.

"It's not right," Gaia said. "It's too quiet."

"This isn't necessary, you coming up here," Peter said.

"I have to see what happened to Munsch and Bonner. Besides, now that I'm here, I'm curious. Aren't you?" Gaia said. "We'll be careful."

"Stay together," Peter said, and motioned the others to surround Gaia.

Most of the archers were women of the cuzines who'd been shooting since they were children, though a few, like Peter, were men who'd trained daily for the past year. Now all of them nocked their arrows in readiness.

Gaia walked up the middle of the quiet dirt road. The once familiar houses looked small and dusty, so much more weather-beaten than she remembered. She wondered if they'd deteriorated, or if they'd always been this dilapidated and she only noticed now. She was nearing her family's cottage when a clatter came from up the road.

A dozen Enclave guards marched toward them. Their black uniforms and hats stood out sharply against the mottled grays of Wharfton, and their rifles glinted in the sun.

"Gaia Stone!" called their commander.

She came to a stop. "I'm Gaia Stone," she said. "Who are you?"

"You're under arrest for treason," he said. "Tell your people to stand back."

Quicker than speech, Peter stepped in front of her and aimed his arrow at the captain with deadly precision. Will drew his sword. The rest of her guard packed in tightly around her with their arrows aimed at the Enclave force.

At the same time, the Enclave commander raised his hand in a signal to his men, who spread out to either side of him, dropped to their knees, and aimed their rifles with loud cocking noises.

"Don't be foolish. We'll shoot you to ribbons," the commander said.

"Not before half of you die," Gaia said. "You've lined yourselves up like target practice, and my archers don't miss at twice this range."

The commander stilled his hand and paused, plainly reconsidering the distance.

"What's happened to my two scouts?" Gaia demanded. "Why haven't they been released?"

"Come see for yourself," he answered.

"Not unless you put your guns down," she said. "We'll talk."

"You disarm first," the commander called.

"Mlass Gaia, I have his Adam's apple, easy," Peter said quietly.

Thinking fast, Gaia scanned the line of Enclave soldiers with their barrels pointed toward her. She knew her archers would not hesitate to shoot, but many of her friends would die defenseless in the exchange. Her heart jumped. If she made a mistake, Will and Peter could be dead within seconds.

"Disarm," she said quietly.

"No," Peter said.

"Now," she said, even more softly. "I insist."

She heard the creaking around her as bows, taut with strain, were carefully lowered. If possible, her archers tightened in even more closely around her, providing defensive cover for her with their own bodies. She had to peek over Peter's shoulder to see. On a command, the Enclave guards put up their rifles, and Gaia took a deep breath.

"I have to go with them," Gaia said. "I need to talk to the Protectorat anyway. I might as well start negotiations now."

"It's a mistake," Will said beside her, his sword still drawn. "Don't be reckless, Mlass Gaia."

"I'm not interested in exchanging bloodshed with some trigger-happy underlings," Gaia said.

"I'm not leaving you," Will said.

"Suit yourself. But sheathe your sword. I'm not giving them an excuse to shoot you," Gaia said.

"I'm coming, too," Peter said.

"Chardos," she muttered. She glanced at the other scouts. "Tell Vlatir and the others. I'll be back as soon as I can. Vlatir's in charge in my absence."

She stepped cautiously forward, with Will and Peter beside her.

"We don't want them," the Enclave commander said.

"It's all three of us or nothing," she said. "There's nothing in your orders against bringing extra hostages, is there?"

The commander nodded curtly. "All right. But no trouble, understand?"

Gaia took another step nearer.

"What's your name, Mabrother?" she asked.

Everything about the commander was medium: his height, his build, his age, his brown hair. If his intelligence was, too, she couldn't underestimate how dangerous he might be. She'd never trusted people who followed orders to the letter.

"Sergeant Burke." He gestured to his men. "Let's go."

61

Gaia glanced back at her archers one last time. Then she and the Chardo brothers were surrounded. They started through Wharfton. The dirt roads and small, scorched yards were empty.

"It's not normally like this," Gaia said in an undervoice to Peter and Will. "There are usually people out." She couldn't tell if they were hiding now because of her arrest, or if this was a permanent change, but she didn't like it.

When they reached the quadrangle, several people were talking before the Tvaltar, and though they stopped when they saw the soldiers, they held their ground. *At least the whole place isn't a ghost town*, she thought. A boy ran across the packed dirt, heading toward the eastern sectors of Wharfton. An upstairs shutter opened on squeaky hinges, and eyes peered from behind a rattan curtain.

They rose up the sloped road toward the south gate, and as Gaia glanced up at the new ramparts on top of the wall, a full compliment of soldiers looked down at her, rifles in hand. The south gate stood tall before her, its doors open like a great maw to expose the vacant space below the arch, and her courage began to fail her.

"Look," Will said, nudging her arm.

Along the rooftops of Wharfton, half shielded behind crooked stovepipes and chimneys, several sturdy young men crouched. Some held stones. One had a slingshot. He nodded at Gaia and held it up defiantly toward the guards on the wall, clearly ready to risk their retaliation.

"They'll help us," Will said. "We can still run."

Sergeant Burke prodded them forward. "Keep moving."

Gaia next saw Derek Vlatir, Leon's birth father, standing tall on a rooftop ridge. He held one knife in his hand and had a row of extra knives laid out on the chimney beside him with their hilts visible in silhouette. His solid stance and the set of his shoulders were unexpectedly familiar to her now, resembling Leon's. Slightly behind him stood a younger, pink-cheeked woman holding a slingshot in one hand and a stone in the other.

"You say the word, Gaia Stone," Derek called fearlessly.

A couple of the guards on the wall laughed.

Anxious for how vulnerable the rebels were, Gaia shook her head. "Don't do it, Derek," she called.

Sergeant Burke shoved her again.

The next instant, she stepped under the heavy shadow of the arch into the Enclave. Commotion erupted around her. The doors closed shut, and she spun back to discover Peter and Will had been blocked outside with half of the Enclave guards.

Before she could protest, rough hands grabbed her arms and she was lifted nearly off her feet by Sgt. Burke. Peter's and Will's voices called from the other side of the massive doors, then went silent. Half a dozen guards came running down the steps of the wall to surround Gaia.

"Search her, Jones," Sgt. Burke said.

A tall, big-nosed guard leered as he reached for her.

"Don't you dare touch me," Gaia said.

But Sgt. Burke spun her to pin her arms tightly behind her and she was unable to jerk away. She remembered Jones and his leering from a long-ago morning when she was delivered to the Bastion, and it sickened her now to have him pat along her torso and legs, making no effort to handle her with respect. He pulled the dagger out of her boot and tossed it to another guard.

"She's good," Jones said.

The commander loosened his grip, and Gaia whipped around to face him.

She was fierce in her controlled fury. "You filthy bastard," she

63

said. "I'm not some friendless girl from outside the wall anymore," she said. "I'm the Matrarc of New Sylum, and you can't treat me this way."

"Make no mistake. You're a traitor and you deserve to hang," Sgt. Burke said. "You can come nicely, or we'll tie you and haul you along. Choose."

Still recoiling from the sensation of Jones's rough hands, Gaia searched tensely around the entrance to the Enclave for any allies. As before, the buildings were whitewashed and clean, and warmed now by the golden light of afternoon, she had to squint. She was surrounded by gracious order: neatly cobbled streets, window boxes brimming with flowers, and awnings that cast their deep rectangles of shade on the shopping pedestrians.

A girl in a yellow dress, half hidden behind her mother's white skirt, poked up her hat to watch Gaia, and then craned her neck as her mother hurried her into a shop. Others were likewise backing away, as cautious as ever. Gaia was on her own.

"Just don't touch me again," Gaia said, detangling her hair from her necklace and straightening her blouse.

"Right this way, then," said Sgt. Burke, and her escort closed in around her.

The broad street rose steadily between the rows of shops and eventually opened into the Square of the Bastion, where the obelisk rose high against the blue sky, and the tower of the Bastion, where her mother had been kept, rose on the right. A gallows was set up before the terraced steps of the stately Bastion, which implied that someone had been hanged lately, or was due to be.

A vision of an executed pregnant criminal surfaced from the dregs of Gaia's mind, along with her old outrage at the injustice. Yet now her dread of the gallows was overlaid with a strange guilt, a weird sympathy for those in power, because she, as Matrarc, had sentenced her share of criminals to the stocks back in Sylum. On which side of a gavel did she belong?

A group of young women dressed in vivid red crossed the square diagonally. Other memories of people who had once helped her flooded back: the sloe-eyed, lively maid Rita, and the Jackson family who had owned a bakery around the corner.

"Here we go," Sgt. Burke said, and veered toward the prison.

When she saw the arch that led to the heavy doors, she instinctively recoiled. She had too many memories of her bleak existence in Q cell, and her instincts told her that if she entered again, she would never come out.

"I don't belong in there," she said. "I want to see the Protecorat. Take me to the Bastion."

"Grab her," the sergeant said.

"I'm not—!" Gaia screamed.

Jones grabbed her unceremoniously from behind and clamped a heavy hand over her mouth. She lodged her heels in the cobble-stones, struggling, and bit down on his hand.

"Let me go!" she yelled. "Help!"

Two guards lifted her off her feet, and she twisted, trying to get free, as they maneuvered her under the arch toward the prison.

"I *can't* go in there," she said, her voice breaking. "Please!"

"Gaia Stone?" asked a loud, feminine voice.

Gaia stopped struggling for a second. The guards caught her more securely between them, but Gaia craned around to see Leon's sister Evelyn peering through the arch.

"Stop!" the girl called.

Evelyn had grown taller, more slender, and her candid eyes appraised Gaia with genuine surprise. Gaia tried to escape from the guards, but they held her tightly and her right shoulder wrenched with pain.

65

"Evelyn, help me!" Gaia said.

"What are you doing here?" Evelyn asked. "Is Leon with you?"

Gaia decided impulsively that it was better to tell than to keep his arrival secret.

"He's with the caravan in the unlake," Gaia said. When the girl looked confused, Gaia wondered how many in the Enclave had not yet realized that hundreds of refugees were amassing just below Wharfton. She hadn't thought such oblivion could be possible. "Haven't you seen us outside the wall? You have to help me. I need to talk to your father, now!"

Evelyn took a step closer, her white dress and bright hair dimming as she passed under the arch. "Sergeant Burke, what on earth are you doing? Bring her to the Bastion at once."

"I have my orders from Mabrother Iris directly," Sgt. Burke said.

"Iris," Evelyn said, almost on a hiss, though the man's name had an obvious impact. Evelyn paused, biting her lips in a cautious line. "Don't worry. I'll speak to my mother."

"No, please!" Gaia said, resisting again. "Don't let them take me!"

But the guards lifted her bodily and swept her into the prison.

the vessel institute

SERGEANT BURKE AND HIS men delivered Gaia to a small office, strapped her to an examining table, gagged her, and shoved up her right sleeve. A young doctor entered with a tray. Wordless, he pushed her sleeve up a bit more, swabbed the skin at the crease of her elbow, and inserted a needle into her vein, flicking a little glass vial as it filled with her blood. When she tried to protest, he ignored her and, with indifferent efficiency, fit another vial to the needle in her arm. She watched the purple blood gush into it, and then, with quick fingers, he capped off the vial, pulled the needle from her vein, and put a cotton swab and bandage over the wound.

He pushed her sleeve up still farther, swabbed a new area, and injected her arm with a syringe. *What are you giving me?* she tried to ask, despite the gag. He simply bandaged that place, too. He set his thumb on her chin. Curiously, clinically, he inspected her scar without ever meeting her eye. Then he loosened the neckline of her blouse, set the cold circle of a stethoscope to her chest, and tilted his head, listening. Gaia tried again to protest, but as before, her words were muffled.

One of the guards laughed. "She's a chatty thing."

"Enough of that," the doctor said, and the guard went silent.

The doctor listened another long moment, moving the stethoscope twice more, then he twitched her blouse back into position, picked up his tray and left.

"That's one way to handle her," said Jones, grinning.

"You're a sick one, Jones," Sgt. Burke said.

Sergeant Burke and his guards released her from the examining table only to bind her hands together before her and carry her struggling down the dim hallways of the prison. At the end of a short corridor stood a thick wooden door, with a large V carved into its heavily bolted surface.

She recalled sharply that V cell was where Leon had been tortured, and her eyes rounded with fear. She turned desperately to Sgt. Burke, but he signaled for the men to dump her inside.

"I don't know how long you'll be here," Sgt. Burke said. "It could be a minute, or weeks. When they want you, they'll send for you."

As the door closed behind him and the lock clicked, Gaia scrambled to her feet and backed against the cold masonry of the wall. With her tied hands, she clawed to pull her gag loose so she could suck in a big breath. She bit the strap that contained her wrists, ripping at it until it came loose, and then she hugged her arms around herself, panting, breathless.

It was a stone-walled room with no furniture, and at first, she thought it was empty. A drain, covered with a black grate, lay in the center of the floor, which was damp from recent washing. The air smelled faintly of wet stone and cleanser. Above, two barred windows let in the cool light of the late afternoon, and she saw, hanging from the ceiling, a long black chain, ending in a pair of cuffs just below her eye level. On the far wall, loosely coiled on a hook, was a black whip.

The chilling simplicity of the cell pierced to some primal, unreasoning core of her and ignited vicarious pain: this was the exact place where Leon had been whipped, where they'd cut off the upper knuckle of his ring finger. She pressed back to the farthest corner of the cell, but there was no escaping the nightmare.

As silent echoes of Leon's pain barraged her and she heard the whip sting into his back, she covered her ears and crouched down on her heels, curling into a tight ball. *Not Leon*, she pleaded, and flinched. He'd never fully told her. He'd never explained the details of how he'd gotten his scars. So how did she know, how could she feel it now herself?

She lifted her chin for a big breath and in the top corner of the cell, she saw a small white box with a red pinpoint of light. A camera. She was being watched, just as Leon once must have been watched, and even at this moment, someone knew she was sitting here, unglued, prey to her own imagination.

"Why are you doing this to me?" she whispered. "I haven't done anything wrong." If the Protectorat could treat her like this, knowing she was the ruler of her people, which he must have learned from her scouts, there was nothing to stop him from being even worse to her people. *I've already failed*, she thought.

She folded her fingers over the bandage on her arm, squeezing. Why did they take her blood? What had they injected into her? Her gaze returned to the chains, black and motionless, and a fly buzzed slowly around the metal, circling higher, as if seeking a trace of old meat. Again Gaia pictured Leon there, suffering because he'd protected her. Because his father hated him and could hurt him again. She cringed, pressing her hands to her face.

"He's all right," she said aloud, to make it true. "He's not here. He's all right."

She struggled to remind herself that no one was hurting her

right now. No one was wielding the whip. Her only torture was her own terror, and that was all in her mind, if she could only stop it. She took a deep, ragged breath and tried to draw on the inner strength she'd learned as the Matrarc. She strove to visualize the marsh back in Sylum with its calming blues and soothing greens, and the sweetness of the wind on her lips.

When she finally heard a noise beyond the door, she listened, attentive, and nearly cried with relief when a click came in the lock.

She pushed herself to her feet, keeping her hands on the wall.

The door opened, and Mabrother Iris stood on the other side. Dressed in his customary white, his urbane appearance contrasting sharply with the rough hallway, the man seemed completely at ease, as if accustomed to visiting V cell. The overhead light glared in the lenses of his tinted glasses, concealing his eyes. In his arms, he cradled a small, white animal with a pale snout: a baby pig.

"Had enough, my dear?" he asked.

She wanted to puke. "Take me to the Protectorat."

He lifted an eyebrow. "It is so, so tempting to leave you here, just as you are. You're far more satisfying to deal with than Leon ever was. Or your mother. You care so much more, like a finely tuned instrument. I can't decide which one. A viola, maybe."

She could feel him wanting her to beg him to release her. She wiped at her face, feeling the smudges of tear tracks.

"Just let me out," she said. "You've had your fun."

"A taste of it," he agreed.

"The Protectorat didn't order me here, did he?" she said. She could not believe how odious the small man was to her, with his gray hair and slumped shoulders. "This was your idea."

"Naturally, but we had to keep you somewhere while we waited."

"For what?"

A banging noise came from the corridor and she flinched in alarm.

Mabrother Iris smiled slightly. "Your blood work. I felt it would be wise also to remind you who's in charge here, especially considering your past record with us. It's a very poor record. The Protectorat would prefer to deal with you himself, but cross the line, and he'll pass you along to me. I get results. Are we clear on that?"

Gaia glanced again at the whip. "Is that what happened with Leon?"

"Leon was a very special case." Mabrother Iris stepped back and gestured in four guards. "Tie her hands," he said. "We won't need another gag, will we, my dear?"

She shook her head. Strong hands pulled her arms together before her, and she winced as the strap was bound tightly around her wrists again.

They left V cell, and at the end of the hall, turned down a staircase. At the bottom, a musty, narrow tunnel led farther down, and caged bulbs came on automatically as they progressed single file. In places, the guards ducked to avoid the low ceiling. Wooden joists bracketed the walls and ceiling, reminding her of the old mine tunnels she'd traveled once with Leon, and at last they came around another corner to an old door.

The quality of the air changed when Mabrother Iris shoved open the door to a small, private wine cellar. Black bottles had turned pale under a coating of fine gray dust that conveyed not neglect, but precious wealth. In the opposite corner, a staircase, cleanly swept and bordered by a gleaming wooden banister, ascended upward.

Gaia knew without being told that they were under the Bastion now.

"That's convenient," she said. "To have a secret link between the seat of government and a torture cell."

"You'd be surprised how convenient," Mabrother Iris agreed, discounting her irony. "On we go. Marquez, see that she doesn't trip."

The youngest guard, a stout, short man with pale eyebrows and hair, guided her elbow and stayed beside her up several flights. At the top, Gaia looked down a long hallway, recognizing the tall ceiling and patterned carpet that ran its length. They'd reached the second floor of the Bastion, and if memory served, the head-quarters of the Enclave was ahead on her right.

"Marquez, remain," Mabrother Iris said, opening the door. "The rest of you may go. After you, my dear." He gestured Gaia in before him, and with a sense of foreboding, she walked into the familiar room.

The four tall windows looked out on the Square of the Bastion, where evening sunlight sharply illuminated one taper-ing side of the obelisk. Just as before the desk with the glowing screen-top still dominated the room, with upholstered chairs and small tables in groupings to her right. The air smelled fragrantly of tea that she knew would never be offered to her. The only thing missing was the canary's cage, which had been replaced by a low glass box containing a blanket and paper shavings. Mabrother Iris leaned over to put the piglet inside, and it snuffed into the blanket.

As a man turned from the window, Gaia was face-to-face with the Protectorat, her future father-in-law. His salt-and-pepper hair was trimly cut, and his black mustache was shorter then he'd previously worn it. His white suit gleamed, and his trousers fell crisply to shiny black shoes.

She measured him in wary silence. Knowing Leon more closely

as she did now, she discovered her feelings for the Protectorat had gained secret layers. She had already distrusted and feared him, but now, on Leon's behalf, she resented him for his failings as a father, too. It somehow made him more human, but in the worst sense.

The Protectorat did not smile. His cool eyes scanned her trenchantly from head to toe and back up again.

"The blood work?" he asked.

"As we've hoped," Mabrother Iris said. "In every possible way. It's a miracle. She's even O negative." He stepped to the computer desk and touched his fingers over the surface. "Dr. Hickory checked everything twice. He's ecstatic."

"What did you test me for?" Gaia asked.

"You carry the anti-hemophilia gene," the Protectorat said calmly. "Like your mother did."

The information at first confused her, and then fury coursed through her. He'd mention her mother so casually, as if she'd been nothing more than an experiment to him. "You *killed* her," she said. "You confined her until she was so weak and sick at heart she couldn't live!"

The Protectorat crossed the room, took the strap that confined her, and coiled it around his hand. She tried to withdraw, but he drew her wrists inexorably against his chest. With his other hand, he reached toward her face, and when she ducked away, he took her right ear and pinched inward with his thumbnail. The pain was so sharp that Gaia gasped, cringing, but trying to twist away was impossible.

"Actually, I believe you had the honor of killing her," the Protectorat said. "We were caring for a fragile pregnant woman as best as we could. Feel that?"

"Yes."

"You sure?"

The pain increased, piercing and radiating.

"Yes! Please, stop!" she said, gasping.

"You will not speak rudely to me," he said.

"I'm sorry!"

"I didn't hear you."

"I'm sorry, Mabrother!" she repeated. "I'm sorry!"

He released her abruptly, and Gaia lifted her hands to her pulsing ear, feeling blood where he'd gouged into her tender skin. Her heart was racing, and a rushing noise filled her head. The Protectorat took a handkerchief from his pocket, wiped blood from his fingertips, and held out the handkerchief to her.

She had to step near to him again to take it, and as she did so, she found she was shaking, so thoroughly intimidated she was. Her episode in V cell had shaved away all her reserves, and now she, the Matrarc of New Sylum, had been reduced to a frightened girl in a matter of minutes.

"And what do you say when a gentleman hands you a handkerchief?" he prompted her.

"Thank you, Mabrother," she said softly, and pressed the white cloth to her ear.

He regarded her dispassionately. "What's this about you bringing my son back?"

She was too rattled to reply. She was still trying to figure out the significance of the anti-hemophilia gene. It even seemed like they'd been planning for her, but they couldn't have known she was coming until they'd arrested her scouts. Did having the gene put her in more danger or make her more valuable, or both?

"Speak up, girl," the Protectorat said briskly. "Do you have Leon with you or not?"

"We do."

"And how many others? Two thousand? Answer my questions. Don't act stupid."

"There are eighteen hundred of us. We want to set up a new community, New Sylum, just below Wharfton. We'll need a supply of water to survive."

"Let me correct you," he said. "You've brought me a political nightmare. An army of rats, swarming outside my walls. In the last hour, I've had a dozen do-good busybodies pounding down my door and insisting we open the gate for you, and twice as many others clamoring to know how I'm going to protect them from your diseases and criminals."

"We just need some time for your people to become better acquainted with ours," she said. She kept her voice respectful and quiet. "We're not criminals, or unhealthy."

"Your scouts gave me the same hogwash. I'm not buying it."

"Where are they now?"

"In the prison. They're of no use to me anymore, now that their information has proven accurate. I can release them. You see, I'm a reasonable person," the Protectorat said. "You, on the other hand, are not. You came here needing our help, yet you didn't even have the courtesy to give us a warning. I'm sure you'll understand if we're not prepared to be generous."

"I didn't send envoys earlier because I was afraid you'd refuse to let us come."

He smiled slightly. "But now that you're here, we have no choice. You're forcing my hand. Is that correct?"

She hesitated, knowing it was true. "We can't go back, Mabrother," she explained. "The environment in the Dead Forest was poisoned. My people have been dying off by generations until we reached a critical point. Now we just want a chance to survive. We want to see our children survive. It's the same thing you want here, isn't it? The Enclave has more than enough resources to share."

"We only have resources because we planned and sacrificed. People always seem to forget that."

"We'll pay for what we need."

The Protectorat paced away from her, and then turned.

"How do you think you could pay?" he asked. "I'm curious. For eighteen hundred of you, that's four thousand, five-hundred liters of water a day, not counting bathing or crops. Water costs, Masister Stone."

"We can work for it," Gaia said. "We bring craftsmen and artists and farmers. We're not helpless."

"Artists?" the Protectorat said, plainly amused. "I didn't realize you had a sense of humor."

Gaia fell silent. She refolded the handkerchief and pressed a clean area to her ear again, trying to think how to persuade him. "You must still be concerned about the problems of inbreeding," she said.

"Interesting you should mention that," he said. "It so happens I am quite concerned."

"Diversification is the best long-term solution," she said. "Your hemophilia and infertility inside the wall are a direct result of inbreeding. Open the gate, encourage the people of the Enclave, Wharfton, and New Sylum to get to know each other, and intermarriage will solve your problem. In the meantime, we can irrigate—"

He waved a hand, cutting her off. "Your idea of intermarriage does have merit, I concede," he said. "Don't think I haven't considered it, but aside from how distasteful the concept is, it's a long-term solution that would take generations to be fruitful. It can't help our acute problem right now, and just as your people can no longer wait, we in the Enclave are no longer willing to wait for an answer. I wonder how much you, personally, would be willing to sacrifice for your people."

"What do you mean?" she asked.

He moved slowly around the room, setting his hand on the back of one chair, and then another, observing her. While she'd been on trail, she'd hardly noticed the unavoidable grime that had settled into her clothes, but now, surrounded by impeccable elegance, she realized how dingy her blouse and trousers had become, and she could only guess how wild her hair must look. She straightened, meeting his scrutiny with her own unapologetic dignity, and saw a hint of respect register in his eyes.

"I am caught in a delicate position, the sort you might appreciate as a leader yourself," he said. "Additional cases of hemophilia this past year have brought unspeakable anguish to certain families, and we've been helpless to do anything for them. Myrna Silk's blood bank is a stopgap at best before her patients die from the disease." His gaze met Gaia's. "We have no cure, but we have found a way to prevent hemophilia. At least, in theory, we have. To put it in practice, we've just needed one more key piece."

"Which is what?"

The Protectorat tilted his head slightly, and idly smoothed his mustache. "I'd like you to consider an interesting dilemma. Suppose one person could sacrifice something that would help a handful of people, and then that handful of people went on to help an entire community. Should that one first person make the sacrifice?" He regarded her closely. "Should the community compel the first person to make it?"

"It depends on what the sacrifice is, and the benefit to the community," Gaia said. She wasn't stupid. He obviously wanted something from her.

The Protectorat patted his hand on the back of the nearest chair and straightened taller. "I'd like to reacquaint you with a very important, pivotal person. She's a fine, peace-loving young woman to whom I am deeply indebted," he said, and glanced at Mabrother Iris. "Please ask Masister Waybright to join us."

A side door opened softly, and Emily stepped in.

"Emily!" Gaia cried. She was so happy to see her old friend that she impulsively started forward, but Emily's quiet smile remained aloof.

"Untie her, please, Mabrother," Emily said politely to the Protectorat.

Gaia stopped where she was, shocked. Who was this calm, genteel girl? Her auburn hair was neatly swept back in a soft bun, setting off her wide cheekbones and jawline. A white, high-waisted dress draped gracefully over her slender form and fell to below her knees. An unusual bracelet adorned her left wrist, and Gaia had to look twice to realize it wasn't simply reflecting light, but emanating a soft, blue glow. Emily's formerly expressive eyes were as intelligent as ever, but now gently calm. What surprised Gaia the most was the assurance with which Emily spoke to the Protectorat, the most powerful man in the Enclave, as if expecting her command to be obeyed.

Even more startling, the Protectorat nodded to the guard by the door. "Release her," he said.

Gaia held her wrists up and felt the little jerks as the young guard undid the strap. She couldn't take her eyes off her girlhood friend.

"Are you all right?" Gaia asked. "Where are your children? Are your boys well?"

"They're in the nursery," Emily said. "They're quite well,

thank you." She turned to the Protectorat. "Have you told her anything?"

"I thought you could explain things best, seeing as you're old friends," he said.

"Are you offering her a position?" Emily asked.

Gaia rubbed at her wrists, attending closely.

"It's not the usual position. Just bring her up to date on the institute as it now stands," the Protectorat said.

Mabrother Iris cleared his throat, and Gaia glanced over to find him following the exchange with interest, but he said nothing.

"As you like, Mabrother," Emily said. "The girls are in the back courtyard breaking for tea. It would be easiest to take Gaia there to explain."

"Take her to one of the overlooking balconies," the Protectorat said. "Have you seen Genevieve?"

"Your wife was in the kitchen half an hour ago," Emily said.

The Protectorat gestured to the guard, who opened the door. "Stay with them."

The guard inclined his head, holding the door, and in a moment that seemed strangely surreal to Gaia, she walked out behind the elegant girl who had once been her best friend in hardscrabble Wharfton, and followed her down the hallway of the Bastion.

"Emily!" Gaia said urgently in a low voice. "What's going on? What's wrong?"

Emily glanced over her shoulder as she kept walking. "I'm sure this is all rather a surprise to you."

"You're my *best friend*. I haven't seen you in over a *year*, and you're treating me like a stranger!" Gaia said.

"Well, then. If you put the clues together, you can probably guess I'm not your best friend anymore," Emily said.

Gaia came to a stop. "What is this?" she demanded.

Emily paused, too, crossing her arms as she turned to face Gaia. She flicked her gaze toward the guard, who was obviously within earshot and showed no inclination to leave. "My old life is over. All of it. I'm going forward, and difficult as it is to greet you with civility, I'm doing my best. Please don't ask me for more. Now if you'll turn here, you'll be able to see into the courtyard."

Gaia stared at her. "You can't be serious. This is *me* you're talking to!"

"Believe me, I am fully aware of who you are. Now if you please, come along here," Emily said.

A popping noise burst in a bright rhythm, went silent, and then began again, growing louder as they approached. When Gaia and Emily came around another corner, the corridor opened into a covered balcony that overlooked a square courtyard, and Gaia recognized that she'd been there once before with her mother, although perhaps on one of the other tiers. She hadn't had time before to appreciate how the graceful, arched openings surrounded the courtyard on all four sides, stacked four levels high, but now she found the harmonious effect decidedly inviting.

Emily raised a hand in greeting over the balustrade. The popping noise, Gaia saw, came from a pair of young women playing ping pong at a table below, their collars loose and damp with sweat. Five other young women were resting with their feet up on lounges and chairs. Two more were pouring tea at a dainty, wheeled cart, and two others were playing chess. Potted ferns in the corners added touches of green, and several pale orange awnings were unfurled to provide wide swatches of shade, but the overriding color was white, from the whitewashed columns of the surrounding balconies to the flowing white fabric of the women's dresses and the porcelain sugar bowl on the linen-covered tea cart.

One of the women reached over to retrieve the ping pong ball, bracing a hand to her back. A luminescent bracelet identical to Emily's gleamed on her wrist. All of the women, Gaia saw, wore the bracelets on their left wrists, and all of them were visibly pregnant. She had found the baby factory.

"Hello, Gaia!" one of the women called up, waving. "Come have some tea with us!"

Gaia recognized her from her days in Wharfton, playing in the quad, though she'd never known her well. A couple of the others looked vaguely familiar, too, and she saw from the way they looked at her scar that they knew who she was. She lifted a hand in polite greeting.

"I want to know everything," Gaia said to Emily. "Are you pregnant, too?"

"Yes. Just two months," Emily said. "I'm not showing yet. The others are much farther along. Trixie is due any day. What do you know of the Vessel Institute so far?"

"Only that you're surrogate mothers in a pilot program."

"That's not strictly accurate," Emily said, crossing her arms. "A few of us are surrogates, carrying children that are not biologically our own, but most of us have been artificially inseminated with the father's sperm. Either way, we're carrying promised babies for other parents, and our part is over when the babies are delivered."

"You make it sound so simple. Like it's a job," Gaia said.

"In a way, it is," Emily said. "We've been hired for one year, with the option to continue a second and third year if we satisfy. Anyone who delivers three healthy babies is entitled to stay in the Enclave for life, with a pension."

Emily trailed a hand along the banister as they began a lap around the balcony. Gaia glanced back to see the guard discretely following them.

"What if you change your mind?" Gaia said. "What if you don't want to give up your baby?"

"It isn't my baby," Emily clarified. "It doesn't matter if we've been implanted with a blastocyst or inseminated with sperm. When we signed on, we agreed to give up any rights to the babies."

"You lost me. What's a blastocyst?"

"Sorry. It's a little package of cells that forms about a week after fertilization," Emily said. "It has everything you need to develop into a human embryo, so if it attaches well in the woman's womb, it can eventually grow into a baby."

Gaia glanced down to where two women leaned over a large book, and one laughed. They made a picture of health and peacefulness, and she couldn't help contrasting it to what she knew of life back outside the wall.

"Do you actually sign a contract or something?" Gaia asked.

"We get this." Emily held out her left wrist, where her bracelet shimmered around her skin. It was made of some material Gaia had never seen before, both delicate and strong, elastic enough that Emily could push the band comfortably up her arm yet snug enough that she couldn't slide it off over her hand. A golden clasp attached the ends together, and fine strands of gold laced a filigree on the surface. Most unusual was the soft, blue glow.

"It's beautiful," Gaia said.

"This is the contract," Emily said. "It's a matter of honor. When you agree to join the Vessel Institute, you agree to stay until your promised baby is born. You keep this on until the birth ceremony, when the parents receive their child and cut the bracelet. Until then, it emits a signal so the Protectorat always knows where you are. The parents know, too, anytime they want to check on you. They find it reassuring."

"So it's a security device?" Gaia asked.

Emily looked at her oddly. "If you want to be cynical."

"I'm just trying to understand. Are you saying you're not captives?"

"Of course not," Emily clarified. "One girl has already broken her promise and left. Do you remember Sasha? From back home? She left."

"Sasha was in on this?" Gaia rarely thought about their other girlhood friend.

"She isn't anymore. You can cut off your bracelet any time you like," Emily continued, "but if you do, the contract is null and void. You won't be paid and you won't receive any more medical care. You'll prove yourself a liar. Worst of all, you'll give unspeakable grief to the disappointed couple that trusted you and paid for your care all this time. You'll be stealing their child."

Gaia was increasingly uncomfortable with Emily's use of "you."

"But, Emily," Gaia protested. "How can you possibly carry a baby in you all those months, knowing you have to give it up? How could you do that? You've had your boys."

"I still have my boys," Emily said. "I'm staying with them here forever. I'm doing this for them."

Gaia stared at her, shocked. "So you'll give away their *sibling*?"

Emily closed her eyes and took a deep, visible breath. Gaia suddenly realized that she'd crossed a line. When Emily opened her eyes again, she had herself firmly in control.

"Of course we grow attached to the babies," Emily said. "That's a natural part of it, and if you ask me, babies need to feel they're loved and wanted long before they're ever born. But that's why being a vessel mother is such an amazing, sensitive job. It takes a special person to do this, Gaia. A completely selfless, generous woman. But it's worth it. Have you ever met a couple that wants desperately to have a child, but can't? Your heart goes out to them."

"I thought that's why we used to have advanced babies. So they could adopt," Gaia said.

"But those Wharfton mothers never had a choice. You saw that firsthand. Isn't this better? We vessel mothers see where our babies are going. They aren't just lost to some void."

Gaia was surprised. "You know the parents of your babies?"

Emily's profile was aimed toward the courtyard below, and she smiled once more at one of the women who looked upward. "We aren't supposed to know, specifically, which couple's child we carry, but some of us have guesses," she said. "The couples know. They picked us, and some of them can't help seeming to have favorites. We meet them socially. They like to take us to events and give us cute little gifts. They're so grateful. We're invited to all the nicest parties. We're like royalty here."

"For a year," Gaia said.

Emily turned to her. "Yes. For a year. Maybe longer."

"And then what? The mothers go back outside the wall, like nothing ever happened and leave their pampered lives behind? What happened to Sasha?"

"I haven't heard from her. I'm not surprised." Emily paused beside a corner pillar and leaned a shoulder against it. "We'll have to see about the rest. Some will have a chance to stay on, as I said. For the ones who go back outside, their lives couldn't possibly be as hard as they were before they came because they'll have sizable payments. And memories. They'll have memories of living here that they never could have had. Look at them." She glanced sideways at Gaia. "Don't you remember how amazing this all was to you the first time you saw it?"

Gaia regarded her friend. "Yes. But it changed. And it changed how I see things outside the wall, too." Gaia wondered uneasily what role in this scenario the Protectorat saw for her. "How were the women chosen in the first place?"

"The Protectorat chose the women. We invited forty initially. We ended up with twelve who agreed to be vessel mothers, plus me."

"But why the original forty? I want to know how they were chosen," Gaia pressed. "Was it for genetic reasons? Didn't you say that the couples picked you?"

"I only meant that each couple picked a vessel mother to carry their child once we'd joined the institute." Emily's expression grew puzzled for a moment. "I don't know how the forty women were originally selected. I mean, they were all healthy, single women from Wharfton. They had to be intrinsically generous to even consider joining. No one's doing it purely for greed, that's for sure." She met Gaia's gaze directly. "Frankly, Gaia, you don't need to worry. The institute only takes women who actively want to do this, and you obviously don't. The Protectorat won't want you on board."

"He has some other plan for me," Gaia said. "I don't know what. I could have told him already that I'd never sell a baby of mine, not for any price."

Emily's face closed as completely as if a shutter were drawn. "Harsh, Gaia."

Gaia couldn't help herself. "I'm telling you, Emily, this isn't going to work. This is heartache just begging to happen."

"I'm not naïve," Emily said, moving toward the hallway that led back to the Protectorat's headquarters, snapping her fingers to signal the guard to follow. "Heartache's a given, isn't it? At least this is chosen heartache."

"*Emily,*" Gaia said, her voice hushed.

Emily managed two more steps and then spun around again. With her cheeks flushed and her poise gone, she looked once more like the girl Gaia remembered. "How dare you judge me? How dare you accuse me of selling my child? You left. You went off into the wasteland with your sister. If I had known what was going to happen, I'd have taken my family and gone with you. But I didn't. And I've had to survive just as much as you have."

"I'm sorry," Gaia said. "I heard how the Protectorat took your son, and I heard about Kyle. I miss him, too."

Emily took a step nearer, dropping her voice.

"I don't want to hear you say his name," Emily said.

"No. I won't. I'm sorry."

"And I don't want your pity, either."

Gaia felt an awful burst of emotion rising through her. She couldn't stand to be fighting with her oldest friend. It felt like the last good thing from her childhood was exploding in her face. "Please don't be like this," Gaia pleaded.

Emily's expression turned dismissive. "You were always so immature."

CHAPTER 8

cameras

Emily pushed open the door to the office, and the guard hurried to catch it and hold it wide for Gaia. Gaia stood riveted to the carpet, stuck between shame and hurt. The guard made a soft humming noise, and she glanced up. He'd obviously heard her entire exchange with Emily, but his expression was impassive.

"What?" she said quietly.

"You might tell Leon that Marquez says hello. That's all," he said. "After you, Masister."

His calm voice and kindness gave her just the reprieve she needed to regain some of her composure. She inhaled deeply. "Thanks," she whispered, and stepped into the room after Emily.

The Protectorat and Mabrother Iris were standing together over the desk, discussing something, but they looked up as Gaia entered.

"Your people know better than to attack, don't they?" the Protectorat asked.

Gaia moved forward, alarmed. "What do you see?"

She didn't think they'd attack without her, not this quickly, but she realized she had no idea. Who was running things out

87

there? Will? Leon? The Protectorat tapped an enlarged screen on the desktop, and the quad before the Tvaltar came into startlingly clear view. Will, Peter, and Dinah were huddled in a tight conference with Derek Vlatir and several other leaders from Wharfton. Two dozen of the female archers from New Sylum were poised on the Tvaltar steps, and a rough-looking lot from Wharfton had gathered with shovels, pickaxes, and clubs.

Gaia scanned each face for Leon, but couldn't find him. *Something's wrong,* her gut told her. *He should be with them.*

"Call up reinforcements for the wall guard," the Protectorat said. "They're not getting anywhere with arrows, but keep an eye on them."

At that moment, the door opened forcefully, and Genevieve, the Protectorat's wife, charged into the room. "Miles!" she began, then stopped as her gaze met Gaia. "You!" she exclaimed. "Do you know where my daughter is?"

"I don't have the slightest idea," Gaia said.

Genevieve flew to her husband. "Evelyn's gone! I sent a girl to look for her an hour ago, and it turns out no one's seen her. She's nowhere to be found."

"Iris?" the Protectorat said.

"I'm looking," Mabrother Iris said, typing rapidly. "South gate? Did Masister Evelyn pass through today?"

Genevieve braced both of her hands on the computer desk, leaning over it as she peered closely at the screen. Her white dress reflected in the black glass, and when her golden hair slipped forward over her shoulder, she shoved it back with distraught fingers.

A crackle came from a speaker in the desk, and then a man's voice. "Yes, she passed through about two hours ago. She hasn't returned. You want us to go looking for her?"

"If they hurt one hair of her head, you're dead," the Protectorat said to Gaia.

"Find her! Please, Miles, we have to find her! What if these new people have kidnapped her?" Genevieve said, then spun toward Gaia. "You must know something."

"How could we possibly kidnap her?" Gaia said. "She saw me being arrested. That's all I know. I asked for her help, and she said she would talk to you."

Genevieve frowned. "Arrested?" she asked, and turned to the Protectorat. "Isn't she the leader of the new people?"

"She's more like collateral at this point," he answered. "If they have Evelyn, we'll get her back."

"Please, Masister," Genevieve pleaded, approaching Gaia. "Did Evelyn say anything else? Anything at all? She never came to see me. Do you have any clue why she'd go outside the wall?"

Gaia glanced at Emily, who was remaining silently observant in the background. "She probably went out to see her brother," Gaia said.

Genevieve went still. "Leon's back?" she asked, her voice suddenly quiet. After her frenetic worry, she now turned deliberately toward her husband. "How long have you known this?"

"Since yesterday," the Protectorat said. "One of Masister Stone's scouts saw fit to mention it."

The tension between him and his wife became a live thing that Gaia could sense, coiled between them like an invisible snake. Genevieve gave a nearly imperceptible shake of her head, and the Protectorat pushed his coat back to prop a fist on his hip.

"I think you should see this, Mabrother," Mabrother Iris said, gazing down at the desktop.

The Protectorat stepped nearer to the screen, and then gestured to Gaia. "Get over here."

Across the slick surface, a row of new rectangles showed different views from security cameras. With a brush of his fingertips, Mabrother Iris expanded a dozen of the rectangles: the quad by the Tvaltar again, plus the approaches to the south gate, the paths to the six water spigots, the fields, the shoreline ridge of the unlake, and several key roads. The surveillance in Wharfton was even more pervasive than she'd realized before.

One of the rectangles went black, and only then did Gaia notice there were four other screens already dark, too. Next, two other screens went black almost simultaneously.

"Mabrother Iris," came the voice over the speaker. "Are you seeing this?"

Mabrother Iris brushed his fingertips again, and a dozen more screens appeared showing shots of the wall, and a close-up of a guard's face with the south gate behind him.

"I'm here," Mabrother Iris said.

"They're shooting out the cameras with arrows," the guard said. "Fine shots they are, too."

The Protectorat nodded wordlessly to Mabrother Iris.

"Take them out," Mabrother Iris said.

There was motion as the soldiers on the wall took aim.

"No," Gaia said. "You can't kill them. They're not hurting anybody."

"Enclave security is not negotiable," the Protectorat said. "Pick them off."

"Yes, Mabrother," the guard said, and stepped out of the rectangle.

"Don't!" Gaia called.

She rapidly scanned the other screens. Her ears were primed to hear the sound of rifle shots either from the speakers or in the distance. A fraught silence stretched out for a long moment. Another one of the views went dead, and then, slowly, three more. She nearly laughed with relief. Her archers knew how to avoid exposing themselves. Despite a flurry of activity along the top of the wall where the guards were aiming their rifles, screen after screen was being eliminated until there were only three of Wharfton left, then two, and finally only one.

The last view was an angle she'd seen once before: a stretch of dry shore by the unlake, directly downhill from the south gate. The Protectorat had ordered the shooting of a raven in just that place, demonstrating the reach of his power to Gaia. Now a man and a woman were walking into the frame of the picture.

"Hold your fire," the Protectorat said. He skimmed his fingertips over the desktop, and the rectangle enlarged to fill the screen. "See there, Genevieve. There's your precious boy."

Leon and his stepsister Evelyn stopped mid-screen, turning forward, and Leon raised an arm to point out the camera until Evelyn nodded to indicate she saw it, too. He had to know that he was now standing within easy range of the rifles on the wall. It was a ridiculous risk.

Gaia glanced quickly up at the Protectorat. "You wouldn't shoot him," she said.

"I'll see what he has to say first." The Protectorat was staring at the screen as if fascinated, a look of merciless concentration transforming his features into a hard mask.

Emily slipped nearer to Gaia and looked over her shoulder. Gaia shifted to allow Emily a better view and heard the soft intake of Emily's breath. On the day the raven was shot, Emily had stood only a meter away from the bird, and Gaia guessed she was remembering it, too.

In her filmy white dress, Evelyn looked as fresh and delicate as a gardenia bloom, while Leon was still covered in the grime of the trail, unshaven and darkly strong. Evelyn casually put her arm around Leon's waist, smiling. Leon ruffled the top of her hair and then slung an arm around her neck, rocking her in a kidding, brotherly way.

As he looked up again at the camera, his arm tightened a notch farther so that he was mock strangling her for an instant, and his smile didn't reach his eyes.

Leon had looked that cold in Gaia's earliest days of knowing him, and then again for a brief time after he'd been released from prison in Sylum, but she'd thought that side of him was gone. Now she was shocked at how passionlessly ruthless he appeared. If she didn't really know him, she might think he was capable of anything.

Genevieve made a gulping noise. "Oh, Miles! I'm so sorry."

"Don't talk to me," the Protectorat said.

Mikey came running into the shot, looking more gangly than he did in person. Leon took a paper out of his pocket, handed it to Mikey, and pointed toward the south gate. Then he looked back at the camera and said something to Evelyn that made her laugh. Together, brother and sister blew kisses to the camera, and then, holding hands, they descended rapidly into the unlake and vanished.

Across the desktop, the Protectorat's gaze grew hard. "You think you're running New Sylum?" he asked Gaia, his voice cutting. "Who's running you?"

Leon is not running me, she thought.

"We just need water," she said. "We just want to survive."

"Is that your ransom for my daughter?"

"It's just the truth."

"I don't bargain with animals. Tie her up and take her back to V cell," the Protectorat ordered Marquez. "Mabrother Iris, call up the captains. We're getting Evelyn back and eradicating the refugees. Now."

"You can't!" Gaia protested, her eyes darting to Mabrother Iris.

"Miles, you cannot put this girl in V cell," Genevieve said.

"Stay out of this. It's your fault he's even alive," the Protectorat said to his wife.

Genevieve clicked her nails sharply on the desktop. "I will not stay out of this. Let me remind you that I have saved your political neck more than once. *They have Evelyn.* Would you get that through your thick head? Where's your diplomacy?" She gestured to Gaia. "You need to start treating this girl properly."

"Wrong," he said. "There's no need to pretend any compassion for her whatsoever. We can move forward immediately, consent be damned."

"Have you forgotten the consortium entirely?" Genevieve said.

"I am thinking of them. Rhodeski will be delighted."

"*Miles!* He will *not!*" Genevieve said, shock and disapproval blatant in her voice.

The Protectorat controlled himself with visible effort.

"He had his hands on her," the Protectorat said quietly.

"I know," Genevieve said, dropping her voice, too. "I saw. It's going to be all right. It won't happen again."

The Protectorat clenched his hand into a fist, and Genevieve moved slowly closer to him.

"It'll be all right. We'll get her back," she added soothingly.

Leon's move with Evelyn was a mistake. Gaia could see that. It had escalated the Protectorat's animosity in a way that could only make things worse. She traced the fading red lines on her wrists again, and knew Marquez was hovering behind her with the strap. She glanced at Emily, who stood patiently, regarding the scene as if it hardly concerned her.

"Do you still want me to call up the captains, Mabrother?" Iris asked.

"Hold that order," the Protectorat said. "We'll see what his note says."

"Should I bind her, Mabrother?" Marquez asked.

The Protectorat glanced at his wife. "Hold that, too."

"Mabrother, you can hardly want me here," Emily said.

"You're excused, of course. Thank you, Masister," the Protectorat said, and Emily slipped out without another glance at Gaia.

"What do you want from me?" Gaia asked. "Why don't you just tell me?"

She looked from the Protectorat to Mabrother Iris, and then to Genevieve, who was regarding her husband intently. When he moved toward the desk and began talking curtly to Mabrother Iris in low tones, Genevieve turned to Gaia.

"It's a delicate offer and we're not going into it while Evelyn's safety is uncertain," Genevieve said, and then hesitated. "You won't be forced into anything," she added, and turned to join the others.

Gaia was far from reassured. She strode to the window to watch for the arrival of Leon's note, and the square of the Bastion spread out below with fan patterns in the pavers. The gallows, she saw, had been disassembled and removed. White-clad people congregated near the Bastion, talking earnestly in twos and threes. More colorful groups of merchants and workers gathered farther out, naturally segregating into the hierarchy of the Enclave, like pieces on a game board. Though the adults appeared tense, children played marbles at the base of the obelisk, and a boy rode by with a basket of bread on the back of his bike, weaving sharply around a toddler with a red ball.

Beside Gaia, the piglet made a rummaging noise in its blanket. To her surprise, Mabrother Iris came to stand beside her, and she instinctively recoiled a step from him.

"I haven't told you about my piglet," Mabrother Iris said. "He's the first of his kind, born to a surrogate pig mother via implantation, with a donated egg. Interesting, don't you think?"

She declined to comment.

Mabrother Iris took a bit of potato from a cup on a shelf and tossed it into the bin. The piglet trod over to start gnawing on it, tail high. "We've done a number of experiments on pigs lately," he added. "It's safer than experimenting on humans. More humane."

He took off his glasses and regarded her openly. His black pupils were as dilated as ever, reducing the surrounding irises to the thinnest rings of blue. Now that she was familiar with the effects of rice-flower and lily-poppy, she wondered what drug he took that changed his eyes that way.

"Did it work out for you two, for you and Leon?" Mabrother Iris asked, lifting his eyebrows slightly.

The last thing she wanted to do was talk to Mabrother Iris about her private life with Leon, and she suspected Mabrother Iris knew this. When she didn't answer, he put his glasses on again and tossed the pig another chunk of potato.

"I would love to see his face when you tell him I had you in V cell," he said softly. "I promised him that I'd get you there some-day. I like to keep my promises."

Gaia was goaded too far. "You disgust me."

Mabrother Iris tsked his tongue, but he seemed pleased.

"Remember," he said lightly. "Remember who handles unpleasantness for the Protectorat."

A soldier came running across the Square of the Bastion, skirted the base of the obelisk, and sprinted up the steps. Mabrother Iris returned to the desk. In the next minute, there was a knock on the door and the messenger stepped in. He saluted and passed over the note, then stood panting audibly beside Marquez.

Genevieve peered over the Protectorat's arm while he broke the seal, unfolded the note, and read it.

"The rube still can't spell," the Protectorat said, passing the note to Genevieve. "Iris, I need a camera on the front steps now. I want you to broadcast us live to the Tvaltar." The Protectorat pushed a button on the desktop and spoke to the guard at the south gate. "Deliver a message to Leon. Tell him to look for my response in the Tvaltar. Immediately."

"Yes, Mabrother," the voice answered.

"Hurry, Miles," Genevieve said.

"What do you think I'm doing?" the Protectorat snapped.

"Let me see," Gaia said, reaching for Leon's note. Genevieve passed it over.

> Miles,
> Convince me Gaia is alive within the next
> five minutes or I poisin Evelyn.
> You'll get my sister back when you release Gaia.
> Leon Vlatir

Genevieve took the note back, clearly agitated. "What's this new name?" she asked Gaia.

"Vlatir is his birth father outside the wall," Gaia said.

"Not even 'Grey' is a good enough name for him anymore,"

the Protectorat said. "That would break Fanny's heart. Come, girl." He motioned Gaia toward the door and Marquez opened it for them. "Let's see how good you are at making nice for the camera."

"I want a guarantee of water for my people," Gaia said, as they hurried down the hall. "We can strike the deal live on camera. I'll get my people to register their DNA, like the people of Wharfton did. In exchange, we need our own water pipeline so we're not drawing off Wharfton's supply."

Gaia glanced back at Genevieve, who raced along behind them.

"Out of the question," the Protectorat said.

"You know you're going to have to do it," Gaia said. "You can't just let us die. Why not save face now? It'll look like it was your idea, right from the start. Pure diplomacy."

"No one will buy it, not after they know we had you in V cell," the Protectorat said.

She thought rapidly. "I'll tell only Leon about V cell. It won't get around. I'd keep it quiet so we can appear to be allies. I'll say I was visiting my scouts in the prison."

The Protectorat let out a laugh. "Interesting possibility. You've learned a thing or two."

They reached the top of the great double staircases that descended to the entryway of the Bastion, and Gaia could see the white-and-black tiles of the floor below as she quickly descended. Gardenias bloomed in large pots, releasing their fragrance to lightly tang the air, and through open French doors, she glimpsed the lush greenery of the solarium.

"Evelyn's already gone out to welcome Leon," Gaia said. "Build on that. People will be happy to see your family reunited, won't they?"

The Protectorat regarded her shrewdly. "All right. If your people are lined up, ready to register their DNA in the quad tomorrow morning, I'll see about the water." He turned sharply to the butler. "Open the door, Wilson."

"Is that a promise?" Gaia said.

Genevieve dabbed a tea napkin rapidly at Gaia's face to clean her up, and with a clip taken from her own bright locks, she arranged Gaia's hair over her wounded ear. Genevieve's eyes were near and pleading as she gave Gaia a tremulous smile. Then the Protectorat guided Gaia outside.

"Do you promise?" Gaia repeated.

"Just get Evelyn back to us unharmed. Stand there," the Protectorat said, guiding her to the front of the terrace. "Straighten your blouse. A smile, please." Putting on an easy, welcoming expression, he pointed to the cameraman. "We're going live. Now. Yes?"

"You're on," the cameraman said, and positioned the large, black lens of the camera in front of her and the Protectorat.

Genevieve hovered behind the cameraman, and though she wore a practiced smile, Gaia guessed she was high-strung underneath. Gaia didn't want to be like her, faking it and nervous. *This is who I am*, she thought, and quietly straightened.

"In an unlikely turn of events," the Protectorat began, "the girl many of you know as the scarred midwife from outside the wall, Gaia Stone, has become the leader of the refugees who are now setting up camp in the unlake. Welcome, Masister Stone. Did you say your people came from across the wasteland? You must have had a long journey."

Gaia focused past the camera lens to the people in the square. Dozens had stopped to gather near and watch, and on instinct, she addressed herself to them as she would if they were her own people. She picked one stranger, a sober old man, and spoke first to him.

"We've been traveling nonstop for four weeks to start a new home here, just outside your walls," she said. She filled her voice with unhurried confidence and warmth, and focused on more specific faces in the crowd, one by one. "We're calling it 'New Sylum,' and any of you are welcome to come out and visit us anytime. Before I say one word more, I must thank the people of the Enclave for providing us with the water we'll need. We couldn't survive without you, and we are *so* grateful."

The Protectorat smiled and nodded. "Of course, our plans are still developing, but I can say that we're equally honored that you appreciate the importance of registering your people in the DNA directory. It should be quite the exciting morning in the Wharf-ton quad tomorrow."

She extended her hand to the Protectorat with steady grace. "Will I see you there?"

He grasped her hand in both of his. "Of course. I wouldn't miss it."

A young woman's voice called out from the people below the steps: "But I heard the midwife was arrested. What was that about?"

Gaia tried to see who asked the question, but no one stepped forward.

A muscle clenched in the Protectorat's jaw, but he continued to smile. "As you can see, Masister Stone is perfectly fine. She was never arrested. She wanted to check on her two scouts as a top priority, and since they were being detained in the prison as a precaution, my guards escorted her there first. Her scouts have been released, of course."

"Who's going to pay for all that extra water?" called another voice. "Where's it supposed to come from? Our purification plant is already at capacity."

"I have a team working on it right now," the Protectorat said. "There will be no water shortages here in the Enclave. Now, if you'll excuse me, Masister Stone is needed outside the wall." He pointedly offered Gaia his elbow. "Let me take you down."

Gaia slid her fingers over the soft fabric of his sleeve, and this time, she aimed her gaze directly at the camera. "Masister Evelyn, if you're watching, I hope to see you at the south gate," Gaia said, and tried for a sisterly smile.

A receptive murmur circulated around the crowd, and then the people backed up to afford them room as Gaia descended the terrace steps with the Protectorat. She glanced back to see Genevieve greeting several of the elite who gathered to speak to her. The cameraman was panning the square. Gaia lengthened her stride to match the Protectorat's.

"Well played," he said, sotto voce. "Keep smiling."

Give me some credit, she thought.

Evening had fallen. As they walked briskly down the cobblestone streets toward the south gate, people who had watched the coverage on television came to their balconies and doorways. The Protectorat kept up an easy patter about the Enclave's vineyard and how his vintner was experimenting with certain grapes, but Gaia barely attended. She could feel the people watching her with new interest. Some of it was distrustful, but a few people even waved.

When Mace Jackson, in his baker's apron, appeared with his daughter Yvonne at one corner, Gaia could barely contain her pleasure.

100

"Mace! Yvonne!" she called.

The little the girl smiled prettily. "Welcome back, Gaia!" Yvonne said. She began to step forward, but her father put a hand on her shoulder.

"Come visit us soon," Mace said, and nodded respectfully at the Protectorat.

Gaia broke away to give Yvonne a quick embrace. "I'll come as soon as I can," she said. "Give my love to Pearl." She squeezed Mace's hand before she rejoined the Protectorat.

"You have fans," the Protectorat observed, offering his elbow again.

"Friends. There's a difference," Gaia said.

"He had another daughter, I believe," the Protectorat said. "One of the hemophiliacs."

"You know that?" Gaia asked, surprised.

The Protectorat glanced down at her, his expression ironic. "You think I have no concern for my citizens?"

"I just didn't realize you knew details about individual families."

"What other kind of family is there?" he said.

Gaia frowned, thinking of how she'd made a point of getting to know as many of her own people as she could, family by family. She'd never guessed the Protectorat made a similar effort.

"Tell me something," the Protectorat said, as they came within sight of the south gate. "How long did it take my son to find you?"

"A few weeks," she said.

"So he's been with you this whole time, more or less. Has he ever mentioned his sister Fiona?"

"Quite a few times," Gaia said, newly alert.

"Are you aware of what he did to her? Has he ever had the guts to admit it?"

Gaia tried to pull her hand out of his arm, but the Protectorat caught her fingers.

"I pity you," she said.

"Me? He molested his sister and drove her to kill herself," the Protectorat said. "Nothing will ever change that. He should be branded with a warning label. Keep him away from your young girls." He was still smiling for anyone who might be witnessing the conversation.

She shook her head. "You can't honestly believe he ever deliberately hurt his sister, not if you know him. Search your own heart," she said. "You're the father who neglected to see what poor Fiona really needed. What gave her the idea to come on to her own brother? Didn't you ever wonder about that?"

His grip tightened and his dark eyes flashed. "You have a perverted mind. No wonder he likes you."

She pulled away hard. "You nearly ruined him for good, and I don't mean just the torture in V cell. You should beg his forgiveness for all you've done to him," Gaia said.

The Protectorat closed his eyes briefly and shook his head. When he looked at her again, his gaze was penetrating, attentive.

"Leon never asked you to say that," he said.

"No," she said. "But if you did apologize, maybe then you could start to forgive yourself for failing Fiona."

"Think you're deep, do you? Think you've got us all figured out?" the Protectorat asked. His voice lost its edge and grew softer. "Have you ever dreamed what it is to lose two children at the same moment? Come see what we're really like, without the frills and Leon's lies. Your future lies here inside the wall, with us."

She took a step back, staring at him, while a creeping shiver ran up along her arms. Only one of the Protectorat's children, Fiona, had physically died, but the Protectorat was implying that he suffered the loss of Leon at the same time. He grieved for his son, too. She shook her head, not able to process it fully.

He nodded, his smile grim. "Tell him his mother would like to see him."

CHAPTER 9

peg's tavern

GAIA LEFT THE PROTECTORAT and hurried through the massive gateway. Down the sloped road, she could see Evelyn approaching from Wharfton to exchange places with her. Leon waited with the Chardo brothers and a dozen others below, alongside a stone dwelling which served as a shelter from potential gunfire. One of the guards above audibly shifted his rifle along the parapet to adjust his aim. To Gaia's left, along the rooftops, dozens of Wharfton men and New Sylum archers were similarly primed.

From a distance, Evelyn had a carefree air and a loose gait, as if she'd gone visiting for a picnic. Her white blouse had short, scalloped sleeves, and a graceful white wrap draped through her elbows. Her soft blond hair touched her shoulders in a tidy way, and her cheeks were bright with color. As she came nearer, however, and Gaia could see her refined, delicate visage, lines of strain bracketed Evelyn's eyes and mouth.

The younger girl held out both her hands to clasp Gaia's.

"How mad is my father?" Evelyn asked.

"He's livid, but not at you," Gaia said. "I can't thank you enough for helping us."

"Going out seemed like the surest solution. Besides, I couldn't wait to see Leon. He's so different!" Evelyn said.

"Not in a bad way, I hope."

"He's happy," Evelyn said. She had fluid, expressive features, and a quicksilver quality to her smile. "I mean, aside from how furious he is that you got yourself arrested." Her fingers found the red bracelet at Gaia's wrist. "So cute!" She sighed. "My brother's gone all crafty. When will you choose a date?"

"He told you we're engaged?" Gaia asked.

She glanced down the road to see Leon waiting, his arms crossed, impatience visibly emanating from him.

"Maybe this isn't the best time to chat," Evelyn said. Her finger slid beside the mark on Gaia's wrist from where she'd been bound and her smile vanished. "Did the guards hurt you?"

"We're saying they didn't," Gaia said.

Evelyn looked stricken. "Oh, Gaia. I'm so sorry."

"We're here to stay, Evelyn. It isn't going to be easy." Gaia stepped backward down the slope. "Your parents don't know about me and Leon."

"You're kidding. Why didn't you tell?"

"It wasn't the time, believe me," Gaia said. "Can you keep a secret?"

"I can try, but that's news that will travel." Evelyn smiled again slightly. "It will be so amazing to have a sister again. I just wish Fiona could have known you, too."

Gaia could hardly imagine being in the same family with this girl. She seemed so innocent and young, yet she'd been bold enough to go outside the wall to help them, too. "I've never had a sister. You'll have to show me how it's done."

"I'll like that," Evelyn said. She pointed a warning at Gaia.

"Just don't back out on Leon. He seems tough but he's really not. Break his heart and you might as well kill him."

"I know," Gaia said. She looked down the road to where he was waiting. Peter and the others were beckoning her forward, but Leon stood immobile, staring at her, as if seeing her so exposed robbed him of the ability to move.

"Got to run," Evelyn said.

With a wave, she spun and continued up the path toward the Enclave, while Gaia began to run down the last slope of the road. As she reached the edge of safety, Leon lurched forward to meet her and she flew into his arms.

"Hold me. Tight," she said.

He pulled her around the corner and up against the sheltering wall. He held her hard against him, squeezing her nearly breathless, while the Chardo brothers and the other scouts kept watch.

"What did they do to you? Did they hurt you?" Leon asked. Tenderly, quickly, he touched her shoulders, examining her, and then he turned her cheek to see her ear. "What's this?" He took her hands, turning them. The sore marks from the strap still showed clearly on her wrists. His eyes went merciless and hard. "We'll torch the whole place tonight. As soon as it's fully dark."

"You sound just like him," Gaia said.

Leon froze. "Excuse me?"

"I need you to be yourself," she said. "Don't change on me."

A struggle crossed his features. "Gaia," he said, his voice ragged.

She burrowed forward into his embrace again, gripping his shirt in her fists, blind to everything but the relief of being in his arms. He swayed with her, drawing her half off her feet.

"You can't go in there again," he said.

"I know. Not like that."

"Not ever," Leon said, and kissed her.

"Save that for later," Peter said. "We have to move you out of here, Mlass Gaia. We're still too exposed."

A gunshot exploded from the wall as if to prove his point and Gaia flinched. People on the rooftops of Wharfton scrambled for shelter, some jumping off the lower roofs. Peter yelled a command, and armed men and women retreated back from the south gate. Leon took Gaia's hand as they zigzagged downhill through the cottages. Though a few windows offered glimpses of candle-light, most of the cottages nearest the wall were shuttered and dark, as if abandoned or hulking in fear.

When they reached the quad, a crowd of people was gathered outside the Tvaltar, and Gaia slowed.

"We have to keep going," Will said. "To the unlake. It's safest there."

"No, wait," Gaia said, recognizing faces now. People from New Sylum were mixed with her old acquaintances from Wharf-ton. "Did everyone watch the broadcast?"

"Yes," Leon said.

It meant her people already knew she'd promised their DNA to the registry tomorrow, and the people of Wharfton knew it, too.

"Are they mad?" she asked, looking to Will.

"Not everyone's pleased, but we'll work on them," Will said. "It'll be worth it for the water."

"Are you kidding?" Leon said to Gaia. "We just wanted you out. We had no idea what they were doing to you."

"I was all right," she said.

He scoffed out a laugh. "You were not."

"Okay, I wasn't. But your stunt with Evelyn didn't help. You enraged your father. He wanted to come out and exterminate us all. Only Genevieve was able to stop him."

"I don't care," Leon said. "It worked. You're here. If he wants to attack now, let him."

Gaia was about to elucidate the holes in his strategy when a young woman called out to Leon. "You're Derek's boy, aren't you?" she asked.

"Can I help you?" Leon replied.

The woman's rosy cheeks had an invigorated glow, and her eyes were small and bright below a mess of frizzy hair. "You wouldn't know me," she added, as she came nearer, slightly out of breath. "I'm your stepma, Derek's trophy wife. That part about the trophy's a joke. You can call me Ingrid." She pointed a thumb over her shoulder. "Derek sprained his ankle earlier jumping off the roof like a regular dufus. That's what he gets for being a hero. Come by the tavern. All of you." She turned with interest toward Gaia. "You're Gaia Stone, right? Heard a lot about you."

Gaia recognized her now as the woman who had stood behind Derek on the roof earlier. Gaia glanced up at Leon, who was watching Ingrid with a polite, stiff smile. Leon had mentioned to Gaia that he had a stepmother. He hadn't met Ingrid during the first, short time he'd been outside the wall with Derek because Derek had wanted to let his young wife adjust to the idea of an advanced, teenage son showing up in their lives before he introduced them. Or so Derek had said.

Now Gaia was suddenly dying to see Leon interact with his new family. She beckoned to Peter and Will. "Want to come with us to the tavern?" she asked.

"I'm game," Will said. "So's Peter."

Peter deadpanned his brother, then nodded at Gaia.

Dinah came forward to give Gaia a hug. "Are you okay? You had us worried."

"I'm all right," Gaia said. "Who's watching Maya?"

"Norris and Josephine have her down by the campfire. Myrna took Jack and Angie up to your parents' place," Dinah said. Her expression lit up. "Are we going to the tavern?"

"Evidently," Leon said.

"Oh, good," Dinah said, grinning. She pushed back her hair with both hands. "We are long overdue for a little fun."

A bustle of commotion overtook the quad as Peter directed a dozen of Gaia's scouts to keep guard, and the people of New Sylum shifted toward Peg's Tavern. The door was pulled open, and an overabundance of candlelight and stale, hops-flavored air spilled out into the quad, inviting them in. Gaia stepped over the threshold just as the crack of billiard balls broke from the back room.

"Leon!" a voice hailed them from a table by the window. Derek Vlatir had his foot up on an adjacent stool and a cold pack on his ankle. Still, he reached to give Leon a hearty handshake and slapped him on the back. "So good to see you, my boy! Come! Pull up a chair." Derek smiled at Gaia. "I was no use to you today, young woman. No use at all. And now this."

He jerked his chin at his ankle, but when Gaia wanted to see how it was, he shooed her away from it.

"I want to hear about your trip and all these new people." Derek's gaze returned to Leon, and a fatherly hunger warmed his expression. "Have a seat, Leon." He gripped the back of the chair beside him.

"Gaia?" Leon said in a low voice, pulling out the chair on his other side.

"Make yourself useful while you're catching up," Ingrid said to Derek, and she plopped a baby on his lap. A dish of cooked carrots and turnips arrived next, with a small mycoprotein patty and a cup of yogurt. "I've got to help my folks."

The place was rapidly filling up, and after a twitch to the

baby's bib, Ingrid went behind the bar to pull tankards of ale. Gaia saw that Dinah and Peter had been waylaid by a couple of people near the center of the room, and Will had edged over toward a piano, where a young woman was trying to adjust the angle of a candle stand so the light would fall better on the keys.

The low-ceilinged tavern had thick wooden beams crossing overhead, and a dusty collection of hand-blown bottles on a narrow shelf that ran around the upper perimeter of the room. Gaia had been inside Peg's only twice before, when she was much younger, and then only for as long as it took to locate her father and tell him he was wanted at home. It was a strange to be old enough now to be a customer, but no one seemed to question her right to be there.

Gaia felt for Leon's fingers under the table. He tucked her hand into his.

"Meet your little sister," Derek said to Leon, beaming. "Half sister, that is. This here's Sarah."

Leon faced the little girl, a sturdy baby of about eight months, who looked at him with big-eyed interest and then opened her mouth automatically for a spoonful of yogurt from her father.

Gaia couldn't get enough of seeing the three of them together. Even with them both sitting, it was clear Leon was taller than his father. Leon's hair was darker, too, and Derek's mustache and beard made it difficult to know if he had Leon's steady jaw. A kindliness warmed Derek's brown eyes, while even now, smiling, Leon's blue eyes retained a hint of cool reserve. It made Gaia ache for him. Two decades of age separated Leon and his father, and two more decades fell between Leon and the baby, but Gaia could trace elusive similarities in all three faces. She wondered how long it would take to learn what resemblances ran deeper.

"Pleased to meet you," Leon said, and gave the girl's foot a gentle squeeze. He looked up at his father again. "I meant to ask you before. Do I have any other siblings?"

"Not anymore," Derek said. He passed Gaia a basket of dark bread and a plate of cheeses, pointing to her to eat as he kept talking. "Your ma and I had two more little ones after you were born, girls both, but neither of them made it, and then Mary, your ma, died of the fever a few years later, and I moved to Eastern Sector One to start over. You might end up with more siblings if Ingrid has her way." Derek smiled, his gaze going toward the bar, where Ingrid was working. "I know you're thinking she's too young for me. Everybody does. The truth is, I waited as long as I could. I gave her every chance to meet someone else, but she wouldn't hear of it, and I have to say, I never thought I could be this happy again." He turned again to Leon, and his gaze grew warm and gentle. "I loved your ma, Leon. A smarter, nicer, more giving woman you'll never meet. She'd have been proud to see who you've become."

Leon shook his head briefly. "There's no need—"

"No, let me say it. It's a miracle to have you back in my life," Derek said. "Ingrid nearly took my head off when she found out you'd come outside the wall and I didn't tell her. She didn't used to approve of my, shall we say, underwall activities, but she's fully on board now."

"Did you ever realize that Leon was your son?" Gaia asked. "I mean, that your advanced son had been adopted by the Protectorat?"

"Yes. Sure. Mary always knew," Derek said, feeding the baby more yogurt. "She was positive the first time she saw you on one of those Tvaltar specials," he said to Leon. "It took me a little longer to believe it. We were lucky. We were able to follow your progress and see how smart and happy you were. For a while

111

there, at least." He held the spoon over the cup. "Why'd they stop those specials?"

Under the table, Leon released Gaia's hand and he shrugged. "We got busier, I suppose. Teenagers aren't as cute as toddlers."

"We called you 'Liam' when you were a baby," Derek said. "Remember?"

Leon laughed. "No. I was pretty little. Maybe I didn't notice the difference."

Ingrid brought over two fists full of tankards and plunked them down on the table before hurrying back to the bar. Bill and another miner had joined a pool game with some locals. The noise of talking voices was loud in the low-ceilinged tavern, but underneath the buzz, Gaia heard the first notes of the piano. It was a folksy, cheerful tune, not loud, and the volume of the hard voices diminished several notches as if the tavern's patrons subconsciously wanted to listen. Will was leaning near the piano, a relaxed angle to his shoulders, and the musician was talking, smiling up at him while she played. She wore a black ribbon through her dark curls, and her dusky cheeks gleamed in the candlelight.

Wait, Gaia thought. She shifted, searching out others from New Sylum. Dinah had vanished in the crowd, and Peter was surrounded by three young women who were talking and laughing in lively animation. When one of them casually put her hand on his sleeve, he practically jumped. The girl went on talking, clearly unaware of the effect of her gesture, while Peter's cheek turned ruddy with color. *The Chardo brothers are meeting women!* she thought. It was exactly what was supposed to happen, but somehow Gaia felt completely unprepared.

"Gaia, are you all right?" Leon asked, finding her hand again under the table.

112

She blinked back at baby Sarah and Derek, who was also watching Gaia.

"I'm just tired," Gaia said. "I'm sorry. We're you saying something?" She drank from her tankard and licked the foam from her lips.

Leon's smile turned quizzical. "Nothing important. I should take you home."

A solid man in dusty overalls approached their table. "Gaia?" he asked.

She lowered her ale and as she recognized Theo Rupp, Emily's father, she rose eagerly.

"Did you see Emily in there?" Theo asked.

Startled by his lack of welcome, she paused. "I did."

"How was she?"

"She was fine," Gaia said. "I mean, she's mad at me, but she was fine. She's pregnant."

"We know that much."

Gaia came around the table, studying her old neighbor. She glanced behind him, wondering if his wife was with him, too, but he was alone. "How's Amy?" she asked.

"Broken-hearted. How else would she be?"

Gaia took his arm, drawing him aside. In concise, pained words, Theo tallied up the changes in his family since Gaia had left: his son-in-law murdered, his daughter a permanent guest of the Protectorat, his grandsons growing up where he could never see them. Gaia told him the little she could about seeing Emily that afternoon.

"It's wrong," Theo said. "It's just wrong, all of it."

"You blame me," Gaia said. "I can see it."

He shook his head. "No. I can't blame you. Not now that I

113

see you again." He slowly opened his arms, and she leaned near for a hug, inhaling the earthy scent of clay that always clung to the potter.

"I'm so sorry," Gaia said.

"Maybe you'll fix things now that you're back," Theo said softly.

"Have a seat, Theo," Derek said. "Come. Join us. Ingrid's brought you a tankard."

Worried, Gaia watched Theo's sad eyes. Leon hitched over an extra stool. Ingrid poked Theo none too gently in the arm and ordered him to sit. The man lowered himself beside Derek, and settled his gaze on the baby. He quietly accepted a tankard of ale.

"There's one good thing that's come out of all the ruckus with the strike a year ago," Derek said. He glanced over his shoulder and then leaned forward, lowering his voice. "When people heard that Emily got in trouble over the birth record ledgers you stole, that got their attention. Emily had to give back the ledgers, but people here in Wharfton started creating a new record, from memory. We started a clearing house, Ingrid and me. Mothers from every sector have come to tell us the birthdates of their advanced babies, and we've created a new, centralized directory of our own. Now, when any advanced child comes outside the wall, we can tell them who their parents are. And they've been coming out, advanced children as young as ten and some in their early twenties. We've been having reunions all over the place." He nodded at Leon. "A little like this. It's pretty crazy. Emotional."

"Does the Protectorat know about this?" Gaia asked.

"I'm betting he does," Derek said. "But what can he do about it? The Wharfton parents aren't going in. He can't stop Enclave children from coming out."

"But they always had the choice before and they never did,"

Gaia said. "Remember the unadvancement notices? Why is it different now?"

Leon shook his head. "There wasn't a directory before. Those unadvancement notices were a one-shot chance to move outside permanently, but that meant leaving your life and your family in the Enclave behind. None of us wanted to do that. This way, people can get to know each other."

"Exactly," Derek said. "I'm telling you, it makes for a strange situation. There are all these bonds being created across the wall, even while hostilities with the Protectorate are worse than ever."

"What does this mean for us?" Gaia said. "Do you have allies within the wall?"

"It means nothing's predictable," Derek said, shaking his head. "Anything could blow up in your face at any time."

"I'll agree with that," Theo added.

"Can you get inside the wall if you want to?" Leon asked Derek.

"Not at the moment," Derek said. "Our latest tunnels were all discovered and shut down in the crackdown a year ago. We're working on opening up more, but it's no easy feat, getting under that wall. Why? You want to get in?"

Gaia looked at Leon, who took another drink of his ale and left the question to her.

"No," Gaia said. "We're going in through the gate to negotiate legitimately."

The baby on Derek's lap burped up some yogurt, and Derek wiped it with the edge of her bib. "I'm glad to hear it," Derek said. "That's the way to make a lasting difference."

Theo nodded his chin at the baby. "I'll hold her for you, if you want," he offered gruffly.

Derek took the bib off entirely and passed the baby over. When Theo leaned back a little, settling her in his arms, something about Theo's careful, heavy hands showed how much he longed to hold his grandchildren, and Gaia ached for him.

A new song started, a brighter one, and Gaia glanced over to where Will was now turning his slow, thoughtful smile on the piano player. He shoved up his sleeves and crossed his arms.

"Who's that playing the piano?" Gaia asked.

Derek craned his neck. "That's Gillian, Ingrid's friend. She's good, isn't she? She seems to be taking a fancy to your friend there. I've never seen her talk while she plays before."

Gaia glanced at Leon to find him watching her. He lifted his eyebrows and leaned back a bit, smiling at her. There was no reason why Leon's look should confuse her, but she could feel heat rising in her cheeks.

"She plays well," Gaia said to Leon.

"Yes, she does."

She couldn't bear to consider looking around for Peter.

"Ready to go?" she asked.

"Anytime."

She peered out the window. Things seemed to have settled down out in the quad, while inside, the tavern promised to stay rowdy for quite some time. Ingrid came over once more as they were saying good-bye and urged Leon to consider their home his, anytime. "Unless you plan on moving back in with the Protectorate, that is," Ingrid added. "We'd understand if you do. They're your primary family, after all, despite any differences you may have had."

Leon let out a brief laugh. "There is no chance I'll be living in the Bastion again."

"But, I mean, if you and Gaia ever get serious, you know,"

Ingrid said. "Sometimes families work things out and reunite when there's a wedding on the horizon."

Leon took Gaia's hand. "Gaia and I are already engaged," he said. "I hope when we get married, you'll come to the celebration."

"Ah!" Ingrid said. "I thought as much. Congratulations! When's the date?"

Leon turned to Gaia. "That shouldn't be too long now. We're nearly settled, aren't we?"

Gaia laughed and leaned into his arm. He dropped a kiss on her cheek, and they started out.

The night was cooler as they strode through Wharfton, and the streets were quiet again. The swift, nearly silent flight of swallows overhead was welcome in her ears after the bustle of the tavern.

"That was interesting," Leon said.

"I like Ingrid."

"I like Gillian," Leon said.

Gaia wasn't certain what to say. She knew he only meant that he approved of the piano player for Will.

Leon laughed and gave her hand a squeeze. "I'm teasing you."

"I mean, I want Will to be happy, of course."

"I know," Leon said. "Don't worry about it. They're going to be fine, all of them. You'll see. And you'll get used to it, too."

"Poor Theo," Gaia added.

"I know. It's almost like his daughter was advanced as an adult," Leon said.

As they reached the far end of Western Sector Three, Gaia could see the campfires of New Sylum spread out in the unlake below. Already the settlement looked different from any of the temporary sites they'd set up during the exodus. The fires were grouped in a loose pattern of widening rings that dipped

117

organically with the slope of the valley. In the center was the new commons. She could imagine a new matina bell being cast and mounted there eventually. How lovely it would be to have that piece of Sylum's traditions here.

They turned down the path toward clan nineteen. There was a rustling off to the side, and Gaia stopped, instantly alert. "Did you hear that?"

"It's Malachai and some of the excrims," Leon said. "I've asked them to guard you. They won't disturb you."

Her heart was pounding, and she had to make an effort to calm down.

"I'm sorry. I should have told you," Leon said.

"You should have asked me."

"Would you have said yes?"

She hesitated, then began walking again. "Yes. It's not the way I thought it would be here. The minute I think something's familiar, I find it has changed. Nothing feels safe."

"Because it isn't. Not yet. Not for you," Leon said.

"I need to check on Maya. I haven't seen her since I came back out," Gaia said.

As they reached the campfire of clan nineteen, she had a clearer glimpse of Malachai and two of the other excrims, and they nodded to her respectfully.

"We'll stay out of your way, Mlass Gaia," Malachai said. "You'll hardly know we're here."

"Thank you."

Norris stood to give her a warm hug. "You're a sight to see. You're not supposed to worry us like that."

"I'm okay. You missed our first night in the tavern. Where's Josephine?" Gaia asked.

Norris lifted a finger to his lips and pointed. Gaia peeked

under a tarp to see Josephine asleep on a bed of blankets, with little Junie and Maya asleep beside her.

"There's room for one more under there if you want to tuck in," Norris said.

Weary as Gaia was, there was still one more thing she wanted to do. Somehow, seeing Theo had made it all the more necessary. "I have to go home," she said.

"To your old place? Mlady Myrna's up there," Norris said. "With Jack and little Angie."

"I know." Looking at her sister's sweet, sleepy profile, Gaia made a decision. She crouched under the tarp and gently lifted the little girl in her arms.

Josephine stirred and opened her eyes. She shifted up on her elbow. "You okay?" Josephine asked softly.

Gaia nodded.

"Leave her with us," Josphine said, as Gaia's intention to take Maya became obvious. "She's all settled in."

"I want to take her home."

"This is home," Josephine said.

"My old home," Gaia corrected. *I need her with me.* She felt guilty and selfish about it, but it was true. Her experience in the Enclave was still just below the surface, making her restless in a way that only Maya could help.

Josephine blinked sleepily. "Then take an extra blanket," she said, handing one to Gaia. The fabric was already warm with body heat, and Gaia wrapped it around little Maya. She rose again to find Leon waiting for her.

They'd gone only a few paces up the path before he spoke, his low voice carrying easily in the dark stillness. "You're going to tell me what happened to you in the Enclave," he said. "You realize that, don't you?"

CHAPTER 10

on sally row

"JUST LET ME GET home first. Please," Gaia said.

As she breathed in the old, nighttime scents of Wharfton, a mix of sweet grass, chickens, and the dry earth itself, her longing for her parents grew stronger. A quarter moon cast just enough cool, blue light to make the path faintly visible. In her habit, she searched the stars for Orion, and couldn't find it. She patted Maya on her back, cuddling the sleeping toddler along her shoulder and cherishing her limp, heavy weight. Leon's footsteps whispered behind her along the dark path, and she knew, farther out, the excrims were shadowing them.

Candlelight glowed in the window. For an instant, her ordeal in the Enclave and the past year vanished, leaving her just Gaia Stone, the midwife, coming home and hoping to find her parents waiting for her. This was her first time home since they'd died, and she knew, logically, when she stepped up on the porch, that they could not be inside playing chess before the fire, but as she reached for the latch, the feeling of them was so strong, so powerful, that she closed her eyes and heard their voices on the other side of the door.

"Is that you, squirt?" her father asked.

120

"*She must be hungry. Don't move any pieces while my back's turned,*" her mother said. "*I can always tell.*"

Gaia's fingers closed on the cold latch, and she could go no farther.

"What is it?" Leon asked quietly.

She glanced up, peering at him in the dim light, and confusion swarmed around her sorrow. This was the place where she'd last been together with her parents as a family, and it was also where she'd first met Leon. He'd arrested them, and now she was engaged to marry him. How was that possible? With sudden clarity, she realized her parents would have tried to protect her from him, and not just because he was the Protectorat's son. They'd have wanted someone warmer for her, someone more demonstrative and openly loving, like them. They wouldn't have understood Leon.

"It's my parents," she said. *I've grown away from them, choosing you.*

"Sit with me," he said gently. "Stay out here with me, where we can be alone. Just for a little. Want me to hold Maya?"

She shook her head, and sat beside him on the top step of her parents' porch. He braced a hand on the floor behind her, not quite embracing her. She slid Maya to her lap and tucked the blanket carefully around her.

"I can't say the wrong thing if you don't tell me what you're thinking," he said.

She let out a sad little laugh. "This is terrible. I don't think my parents would have liked you."

"Ouch."

"I know."

"You're wrong, though," Leon said. "I'd have won them over. They'd have seen how happy you are with me."

"You arrested them."

"True. But that was a different me, before I met you."

"You wouldn't do it now, would you?" she asked.

"I would bring your mother flowers and help your father with his sewing."

She laughed again, more easily this time. "He never wanted any help with his work."

"I couldn't even hold his pincushion for him?"

She smiled. "No."

"Well, then, maybe you're right. Maybe it would be hopeless."

She slid a little nearer, to where her knee bumped against his leg.

"Any better?" he asked, his voice tender.

She hardly knew what she was feeling anymore. "This day has been insane."

"It can't be worse than what I was imagining," he said. "Evelyn told me they took you straight to the prison."

She nodded, gazing out absently at the dim road and the dark houses across the way. "They took some blood from me," she said. "Several vials. They said I carry the anti-hemophilia gene and my blood is O negative."

"Which doctor did this?"

"His name was was Hickory."

"He used to work with Persephone Frank," Leon asked. "I don't know much about him. Did he do anything else?"

"He injected me with something. I don't know what. And he listened to my heart and lungs."

"This was in a prison office? You cooperated with them?"

Gaia didn't want to answer any more. She didn't understand why she should feel ashamed for being so afraid in V cell, but she was. She dropped her head, focusing on Maya's little fingers curled gently in innocent sleep. "They strapped me down and gagged me to take the blood," she said. "Then they put me in V cell and left me there." She took a tight breath. *I fell apart.*

Leon was very still beside her.

"I can't be afraid," she said. "People need me now. I can't be afraid."

"Iris," he said.

She lifted her gaze. His shadowed face looked like it had turned to stone in the dim moonlight.

"No one even touched me," she went on, "but all I could think about was you and what they did to you. I've never been so afraid. I became completely unglued, from my own imagination. It's some sick, awful game to him, isn't it? Why is he like that?"

"He just is." Leon said. "He just knows. It's like he can empathize completely, but then he uses that knowledge in reverse to hurt people. He did it to me, too. When they were torturing me, back when you first left for the wasteland, he told me that they'd caught you. He said he had you in another room and he could do whatever he wanted to you. I didn't know he was lying."

"You never told me."

"I couldn't stand it," he said. "It was unbearable. And I didn't even know yet that I loved you." He moved then finally, drawing her close so that his arms encircled her and Maya both. "Remember you said we have places where our minds don't meet? I don't want that anymore. Please don't ever close me out," he said. "There's nothing you could ever tell me that would be worse than you *not* telling me what you think."

She understood then. It wasn't just that she could trust him, she realized. He *needed* her to trust him. It was his own craving, to be trustworthy. She felt a new, small opening inside herself. This was what it meant to truly be close to Leon, to let him in. She peered into his eyes, searching the darkness there, and his lips curved slightly as he studied her in return. He touched a warm hand to her cheek.

"It's insane what I feel for you," he said.

She let out a wistful laugh. "I wish we could go somewhere, just you and me and Maya. Leave everything behind."

"It's too late for that, even if you really meant it." He loosened his embrace enough to snuggle her comfortably closer beside him.

A cricket sounded, a thin dry chirp after the lush night noises of Sylum.

"I miss the lightning bugs," she said. "Remember that night? It seems so long ago, but I can still see it so clearly."

"They were unbelievable."

"You wouldn't come out with me," she said, recalling how he'd leaned against a pillar on the porch while she and Maya had circled in the dark meadow grasses, surrounded by thousands of blinking, skimming lights.

"I couldn't," he said.

"Why? Were you still mad at me?"

"Mad. Lonely. Everything. I was still hoping I could get over you."

"What a mistake that would have been," she said.

She felt his arm around her back.

"It's baffling, isn't it? Even then, even when we could hardly talk to each other, I still had to be around you," he said. "I tried to imagine life without you, and nothing made sense. I'm not sure what I would have done if you hadn't finally seen how much we belonged together. Destroyed Sylum in some way, I suppose."

"You wouldn't have," she said.

"I'd have tried," he said. "We'd still be there. Do you realize that? You'd have married Peter and we'd have all stayed in Sylum."

"No."

"Yes," he said. "Or Will. One of those Chardos."

She shook her head.

"Yes," he repeated, like it was a certainty he'd considered at length.

She really didn't want to think about what could have happened with Peter. Or Will. She didn't want to think of them making friends in Peg's Tavern, either.

"Well, you won me over with your pumpkin bread and your smooth moves," she said.

He laughed. "Smooth I was not."

"You were smooth. You were waiting for me that night with no shirt on."

"Maybe a little smooth," he admitted, rubbing his bearded jaw. "I wasn't going to give up without a fight, that's for sure."

She smiled, remembering. "It worked. We're here." She inhaled deeply, trying to keep her tension at bay as she recalled what "here" actually entailed. "Was it good to see Evelyn?"

"Yes. She's incredible. I want more time with her, but I don't see yet how I'll get it." He shifted slightly. "It's hard to believe I have a baby sister now, too. I wonder if I would be more like Derek if I'd grown up with him as a father."

"You turned out fairly decent the way you are," Gaia said. "Besides, if you'd lived outside the wall, you might have died like your sisters and your mother did."

He smiled. "I'd like to think I would have lived and met you sooner. 'Fairly decent,' huh?"

You know what I mean, she thought. "I just wish the Protectorat could see it."

He straightened slowly. "Did he say something about me?"

She tried to find words that wouldn't revive bad memories,

but there was no way around it. "He brought up your sister Fiona," she admitted. "How come he doesn't know what you're really like?"

"Gaia," he said, drawing out her name and sliding his arm away at the same time. "You don't want to go there."

"I'm going to have to deal with him," she said. "I want to understand what's between him and you. You just said I could tell you anything. You can tell me, too."

"It isn't something I can just explain," he said. His voice was different, tighter.

"Just try me."

He pressed his hands between his knees. "I don't know. Maybe this'll give you an idea," he said. "Back when I was about ten, my father's old teacher came to visit for an overnight. He had a little wooden puzzle box that went missing. When the Protectorat found out, he got angry. Embarrassed, I guess he was. We were supposed to be on our best behavior, and it was obvious that one of us kids had stolen it."

"Did you get blamed?"

He shook his head. "I was afraid I would, but they found it in my brother Rafael's things that night. He was about six, but he was old enough to know better, and he'd lied about it, too. That put my father over the edge. I was certain he was going to beat my brother, so I refused to leave the room when my father ordered me out. I thought I could protect him somehow."

His voice tapered off. She waited, picturing the two brothers, the littler one cowering behind the older boy. Leon ran a hand back through his hair, and then leaned forward and pressed his hands slowly, carefully together.

"My father didn't hit him." Leon's voice was dead calm. "He

126

yelled at him and scolded him. He threatened him, but he never hit him. He never even touched him."

She watched his profile. "That's a good thing, isn't it?"

"Of course it is." He angled his profile upward, toward the night sky. "My father never hit Rafael or my sisters. It was only me he hit. You see, until that night, I thought all fathers hit their sons." Old hurt and confusion crept into his voice. "I thought what he did to me was normal."

Gaia hugged Maya more tenderly. "Did he hit you often?" she asked softly.

"No. Two or three months could go by with nothing, and then he might hit me twice in a week," he said. "It wasn't consistent. Once I ruined his favorite watch and he barely mentioned it. Another time, I dribbled milk down my chin when I laughed at the dinner table, and he took a belt to me. That was a bad one."

"I'm so, so sorry," she said. "Didn't Genevieve do anything to protect you?"

"I think she intervened a lot, actually," he said. "I think she's why he went for longer stretches without touching me. But what could she really do? Tell somebody?" He leaned back slightly, bracing a hand behind him again. "I'm not sure why I'm even telling you this. I know plenty of other kids whose parents were hard on them."

"That doesn't make it right," Gaia said.

Leon shrugged. "You get used to it."

But Gaia knew she never could have. Her parents had never been anything but gentle with her, even when they disciplined her. "It's the contempt that would get to me," she said.

" 'Contempt,' " Leon said, as if testing the concept. "I suppose that's what it was."

127

"Did being advanced have something to do with it?" she asked.

"Possibly. Adopting me was his first wife's idea, not his," he said. "He never made any pretence about hiding that, but he went along with it. He used to say I ought to be able to rise above my nature."

"Like you were innately bad? That's awful," Gaia said.

"More *inferior* than bad. And he had a point." Leon seemed to relax slightly. "I was a liar, much worse than Rafael. I liked seeing how much I could get away with. It was always worth it. I was lousy at school and sports, except running, and I never raced when my father could see me. That way I didn't have to care that he never showed up. The one thing I was good at was getting the twins to laugh. I could play with them for hours, and they loved that."

She smiled in the darkness, thinking of how sweet he was with Maya. "I can imagine." The moonlight dimmed, and she looked up to see the crescent glowing through a slow-moving cloud. "Was Fanny your mother's name? Your first adoptive mother?"

"Fanny Grey, yes. Why?"

She recalled how the Protectorat had said it would hurt Fanny to know Leon had taken a different last name. Passing that along to Leon would serve no good. "I just remember you used her name."

"Yes, after I was disowned." His boot made a shifting noise on the step. "I've sometimes wondered if I was his biggest failure," Leon said. "I think he tried to overcome his prejudice against people outside the wall by raising one of us himself. Then it turned out he couldn't stand me, and I was right there, in his family, spoiling everything." He brushed a bug off his knee. "Who was he going to blame for that?"

She took his theory another step. "And then the mess happened with Fiona. I think I see, now." The Protectorat had naturally blamed Leon. He'd been looking for the worst in him for years, and Fiona's death provided the final proof of how evil Leon was.

She suddenly understood a comment the Protectorat had made to Genevieve a few hours earlier: *"He had his hands on her."* The Protectorat had been agonized by the idea that his other daughter Evelyn was still vulnerable to Leon, because the Protectorat didn't believe Leon was innocent. Leon had played on that.

A shiver rippled through Gaia.

Leon turned to her. "There's so much I wish I could undo with Fiona," he said quietly. "I still feel like it's my fault she killed herself. I don't think that'll ever completely go away. But it's better than it was. I can see now that I did the best I could. I was hardly more than a kid myself, and selfish, but I didn't know what she was going to do."

"You are the gentlest person I know," Gaia said.

He let out a laugh. "I wouldn't say that."

"With me, you are." That, she realized, was the kernel of Leon right there. She could trust him about herself completely and knew he'd be loyal to her forever, but she couldn't count on how he might be with anyone who crossed him, or ever tried to hurt the people he loved.

"Gaia, I don't want you to ever underestimate my father," he said. "He is absolutely, completely, irreversibly ruthless. I want you to be ready for that. This isn't Sylum here."

"I know," she said, touching her ear and remembering she still needed to properly clean her cut. "But I have to think of an approach that's going to be right for all of New Sylum. We can't just blow up something. We have to build trust and a long-term alliance with your father. That's much, much harder to do."

129

"You aren't hearing me. You still need to be able to mount a counterattack," Leon said. "What if he tries to arrest you again or assassinate you? You must see that anything's possible. It's your responsibility to be prepared."

He won't assassinate me, she thought. *He needs something from me.* She had an image of Mabrother Iris's piglet in its pen, and had the feeling she was missing something he'd been trying to tell her.

"What sort of thing would you do to prepare?" she asked.

"I'd take a team into the tunnels and sabotage the power grid and the water system."

"Sabotage them how?"

"With explosives on timers."

"And how would you do that?"

He shrugged. "I'd get a couple old friends to help me."

She realized he'd been planning this. "You sound like a terrorist."

He hesitated. "No. I'd just set things up to use for self-defense. I could do it without putting any people at risk. We have to be prepared, Gaia," he said. "The Protectorat wouldn't hesitate to hurt us if he had to."

"This is not how we're going to operate," she said.

"You don't have to authorize an actual offensive, Gaia, but it has to be ready. The Protectorat will respond to pressure if he finds we can nail his resources. It's no different from when he turned off the water for Wharfton," he said. "Don't be naïve. Please. By the time you want to use violence, it'll be too late to set it up if we don't start now."

"You don't understand," she said. "Remember what I said. When you threatened Evelyn, your father was ready to go berserk. I saw him. Threatening him only escalates the problem."

"You have to remember, too. My threats got you out of the Enclave, didn't they?"

He had a point. Gaia ran her fingers into the hair over her forehead. "Tomorrow," she conceded. "We'll work on it tomorrow."

"That could be too late."

"It's just a few hours from now," she said. "It won't make a difference."

"I'll go talk to Peter now and set things up," Leon said.

"Please don't. Please just be with me. Do I have to beg you?"

She swiveled toward the door of her parents' home to listen. All was quiet within, and a faint glow in the window suggested a fire in the fireplace had burned down to embers.

He shifted on the step, and his grave features eased slightly. "That's a change. At least you didn't order me this time." He leaned nearer to kiss her. "Where'd you get berries?"

"I didn't have any berries."

"Let me see." He kissed her again. "You're right. It's more like apple pie. Let me see."

She smiled slowly, kissing him back, and lingering when he took his time. "We have to get to bed," she said. "It's late."

"Fine by me."

"Bed. As in, fall asleep."

He changed his angle to kiss her in a different direction. "But together, right?"

"Um," she began. He really did have a nice mouth. She probably hadn't told him that in so many words, but it was easy to forget her problems while he was—

She backed up. "There won't be any privacy in there," she said.

"Don't you have a romantic little chicken coop out back?"

She laughed. "I am not going in some chicken coop with you."

He gave her a last, light kiss and swiveled to his feet. He held out his hands. "I think rejecting me cheers you up. Give me that girl."

"Be careful. She's asleep. And we should be quiet." She didn't want to disturb Myrna, Jack or Angie. Gaia passed her sister to him. Then she stood and opened the door to her old home.

CHAPTER II

the dna registry

MYRNA SILK TURNED FROM the fireplace with a poker. "I thought I heard voices," she said. Barefoot, she was dressed in a long gown with a shawl around her shoulders. Her white hair fell in a short, silvery braid, grown out since her time in prison. "I'm glad you're safe, Gaia. Are you hungry?"

"I ate at the tavern," Gaia said. "We didn't mean to wake you."

"I sleep light, listening for patients." She hung the poker on the hook by the fireplace, and Gaia did a double-take. It was the same gesture she'd seen her mother do a thousand times, but Myrna wasn't her mother.

That was the first of many changes, obvious and subtle, juxtaposed with the unchanged. In the corner where Gaia's father had kept his sewing machine and fabrics, a pair of bunks had been built into the wall to accommodate Myrna's patients. Jack lay on the lower bed, asleep. Above, Angie was curled in a ball, snoring softly. across the room, a built-in ladder with smoothly worn treads still led up to the loft where Gaia had slept as a girl, and her parents' double bed was still on the right, half hidden behind a damask curtain. Their quilt was gone. In the dim kitchen area to her left, an apron was hooked on the back door.

Gaia's sense of normal began to tip. The table and two straight-backed chairs remained, but the rest of it, her father's sewing things, his banjo, the rocker, the family's games and books and knickknacks, were all gone. Instead, medical supplies were neatly arranged in a new system of shelves and drawers. Translucent tubing was coiled in lengths and hung on hooks beside the window. Gaia looked instinctively along the mantel to the place where her parents had always kept two candles for Jack and Arthur, but the spot was empty.

Yet the place smelled the same, of worn, polished wood and rich, slow cooking and fresh honey butter. It shouldn't have been possible, this aching mix of familiar and alien. She glanced back at Leon, surprised to find her vision misting.

He laid little Maya in the middle of Gaia's parents' bed, and now he pulled Gaia into his arms for another embrace. He felt more familiar to her, more right than anything else. "Get some sleep," he murmured. "You're home."

Gaia awoke at daybreak to the sound of water sloshing on the porch and a tinny, tapping noise that recalled her father shaving. In the middle of the bed, Maya was still sleeping, an arm thrown out in relaxed abandon. Gaia fingered the curtain aside a bit to see Myrna in the kitchen, neatly dressed in blue, her hair in its usual loose bun. Gaia glanced at the bunks to find them empty, and then shifted her gaze upward, toward the loft.

"They're already gone," Myrna said.

"Where to?"

"Jack's out back with Angie. Leon was gone before I woke up."

A soft breeze stirred the white curtain over the sink, and daylight brought a brighter feel to the cottage. Gaia looked toward the open back door, wondering if the water urns were located on the back porch as usual. She was still covered with grit from the trail and longed to wash up. She also needed to get down to the unlake and check on New Sylum.

"You don't have a spare shirt I could borrow, do you?" Gaia asked.

"I suppose I do," Myrna said. "Funny. Last night after you were asleep, Leon asked if he could wash out his shirt."

Gaia smiled. "He doesn't like being dirty. It was unavoidable during the exodus. How long did you stay up talking with him?"

"Not long," Myrna said. "He seems different, though I can't say I ever knew him well."

"What do you mean?" Gaia reached for a hair brush and started on her tangles, being careful around her sore ear.

"He always struck me as an arrogant boy," Myrna said. "And later there were the rumors after his sister's death. I can see he's got character, though, so either I was wrong about him or he's changed."

"You liked him enough to take care of him after he was tortured," Gaia pointed out.

"Yes, well. That was for you, I suppose."

Surprised, Gaia looked at Myrna more closely.

The older woman smiled ironically. "Who'd have guessed the old bat had it in her?" Her gaze shifted and she frowned. "What happened to your ear? Let me see."

Gaia held the brush in her lap and stayed still while Myrna inspected her cut and then fetched a cloth to clean it carefully.

"That's a nasty little gouge," Myrna said, but she didn't ask any more questions.

"Remember Cotty? From Q cell?" Gaia asked. "She once told me I could count on you."

"Cotty's a fool," Myrna said mildly, her voice near to Gaia's ear. "They let her out, finally."

"She said you were married once. Is that true?"

Myrna leaned back. "You gossiped about me. When was this?"

"I just wondered," Gaia said, starting to blush. "I'm sorry. It's none of my business."

"Keep that clean," Myrna said, with a brief pat on Gaia's shoulder. "What Cotty said is hardly a secret. I fell for a younger man. He liked to cook. He fed me well and made me laugh. We married just a few weeks after we met."

Gaia found it hard to imagine Myrna being swept off her feet. "What happened?"

Myrna put away the cloth and sorted through her supplies as she spoke. "It took me only a few days to realize he'd married me for my money. It took me six months to divorce him and another six months to realize he'd had a girlfriend the entire time. He played me good, he did." Myrna rubbed her palms together. "He owns a sauna parlor now on the west side of town and does quite well for himself. A charming story all around."

"I'm sorry," Gaia said.

Myrna's eyebrows lifted ironically. "You can spare me the pity. I was stupid. I've paid for it. Never again." She stepped to the closet where she pulled out a faded brown blouse with dainty stitching down the front. "Try this. And here's some fresh soap. Dab a bit of this on your ear after you're done with your hair." She handed Gaia a small pot of salve, too.

"Thank you," Gaia said.

Gaia fetched a basin, filled it with cool, fresh water, and cleaned up behind the privacy of the curtain. She washed her hair last, relishing the sensation of scrubbing the weeks of grime from her scalp. She toweled the water out of her ears, combed out every last tangle, and dabbed on the salve. When she tried on the borrowed blouse, the fit was a little loose, but she liked the dainty buttons. She adjusted her locket and monocle over the neckline and slid the curtain aside.

"I feel like a new person," she announced.

Myrna eyed her critically without comment, then turned to the tea kettle. "Is it true you're planning to marry Leon?"

"Yes." Gaia slung her damp hair over her shoulder and checked on Maya once more before moving forward to the table.

"He told me you carry the anti-hemophilia gene and your blood is Rh O negative," Myrna continued.

"So?"

"It made me think of your mother," Myrna said. "Tea?"

"I should really wake Maya and bring her down to Josephine and check on things in the unlake before the DNA registration starts."

"Oh, sit down for once. They can manage another ten minutes. You're not that important."

Gaia laughed and reached for a chair. Myrna passed her a mug and set out some fruit, yogurt, and rolls.

"Your mother miscarried quite a few times, didn't she?" Myrna asked.

"Yes, after I was born."

"She must have been Rh negative, too," Myrna said. "I'm guessing your first brother was negative, too, so there was no problem. Then your second brother was positive, and that pregnancy started your mother's antibodies to any other fetuses that were also positive. That's why she miscarried so frequently after her first two babies, but you were okay because your blood and hers were compatible. Both negative."

137

Gaia knew very little about blood types. "Does that mean my father had positive blood?"

"Most likely," Myrna said. "Positive blood types are far more common. They're about ninety percent of the population. Your father was probably positive, with a recessive gene for negative, which you inherited."

"Why are you telling me this?"

"Because you're O negative," Myrna said. "I think you should be aware that if you marry Leon and he's positive, then you're likely to have trouble having children with him. He should know, too. We consider these sorts of things in the Enclave."

We're not in the Enclave, Gaia wanted to say. She was not ready for this news. She and Leon hadn't even talked about having kids really. She couldn't imagine what he'd think. "Did you tell him this?"

"No."

"Don't."

Maya made a stirring noise on the bed, and Gaia glanced back to see the little girl waking up, all frowzy-headed and pink-cheeked. She scooched toward the edge of the bed, and Gaia moved quickly to catch her.

"I have a favor to ask you," Myrna asked.

"What?"

"Since you're O negative, I can use your blood for transfusions to anyone. You're a universal donor. I'd like you to be part of my blood bank."

Gaia looked around the room again, half expecting to see blood stored somewhere, though she couldn't imagine how. "Where do you save it?"

"I'm asking you to be on standby if I need you," Myrna clarified. "I don't have any refrigeration, so it's a living blood bank.

I keep a roster of people I can call on by blood type, on short notice." She gestured toward the bunks. "I hook them up for transfusions when a hemophiliac comes to me, person to person."

"I'm surprised the Protectorat's allowing this," Gaia said. "Isn't it illegal?"

"He doesn't approve. He thinks I'm prolonging suffering and giving false hope. But as long as I keep it outside the wall, it doesn't break any laws," Myrna said. "People come at their own risk."

"This is why you moved outside, isn't it?" Gaia asked.

Myrna shrugged.

"You must have steady traffic," Gaia said, regarding the shelves of tubing, syringes and bandages with new understanding.

"Every single parent of a hemophiliac child has come to see me, just to check things out in case they have an emergency," Myrna said dryly. "Hundreds of them. It should have been done years ago."

"The Protectorat told me he was trying to prevent future cases of hemophilia," Gaia said. "He thinks he's found a way."

"With his Vessel Institute? I promise you, if there's an answer there, it will be only for the elite. You tell me how many people are going to be able to afford hiring a surrogate mother."

Footsteps sounded on the back porch, and Jack entered then with a basket of eggs in one hand. He was steady on his feet again, and with his beard gone, he looked much more like Gaia remembered him: strong, fair, and young.

"You look so much better," Gaia said.

"My antibiotics kicked in, I guess," he said. "Where's Angie?"

"I thought she was with you," Myrna said.

"She's probably out front, then," Jack said. He reached past Myrna to set the egg basket on the counter. "I like what you've done with your hair this morning, Masister Silk. Very flattering."

139

"Don't try that charm on me, boy," Myrna said. She handed him another roll. "Go eat with your sister."

"Which one?" Jack said.

"Both of them. Gaia's hardly had a bite."

Jack leaned back against the counter, tossing the roll in his hand. "Are you one of those girls who don't take care of your-self?" he asked Gaia curiously. "You know, somebody who runs things for the masses but then forgets to eat? I'm just trying to get a clear picture."

"No. I do just fine," Gaia said, smiling.

"I was just going to say, because if you are, that's exactly the sort of girl Leon would go for."

She laughed. "Have you been friends with him long?"

"Since we were kids. Long enough to know how obnoxious he is."

She liked hearing the affection in his voice. "And what about you, Jack?" Gaia asked. "What are you like?"

"I'm a very good brother, it turns out," he said, and pulled out a chair to sit. "I don't know what to say to toddlers, though. How are you, Masister Sis?" he said to Maya.

Maya reached for Jack's roll and he tossed it a couple more times for her.

"Tell me one little thing about our parents, yours and mine," he said.

"Like what?" she asked, surprised.

"Anything."

She glanced up at the mantel. "We had two candles on the mantel, one for you and another for Arthur. We lit them every evening before dinner."

He turned toward the mantel, silent for a moment. Then he spoke lightly. "That's depressing."

"Yes," she said, laughing. "It is. Do you like your family inside the wall?"

"It's just me and my parents. They're basically overprotective and crazy, you know. But great. I've missed them. I have some older cousins, too. Have you met our other brother yet?"

"No. He lives inside the wall. Leon knows him, or at least he did when they were in school. His name's Martin Chiaro."

Jack's eyebrows lifted. "You don't mean Pyrho." He let out a laugh. "Dorky little guy he was back in the day. He set the playground on fire once. That was cool." He scratched at his chin. "It'll be some kind of reunion, getting us all together. Or I guess just a union, without the re-."

"Do your parents know you're back?" Gaia asked. "Your adoptive parents, I mean?"

"I'm going in to see them today," he said.

Myrna turned from the counter. "You were court-martialed *in absentia*. That involves a flogging and jail time if you're caught."

Jack began to cut an apple in white slivers, passing them to Maya's dish.

"I expected no less," he said. He glanced up at Myrna and Gaia. "I can't just hide out in Wharfton. I haven't seen my parents in over a year. They don't even know I'm alive. Besides, sometime or other the authorities will find me. I might as well take my punishment and get the process started so I can start my life again."

"But you're not just an ex-guard anymore. You're my brother."

"Touching, sweetheart," he said, "but I still have to face the Protectorat."

"They might use you for your DNA," Gaia said. "You could carry the anti-hemophilia gene like I do."

"So? That would be a good thing," he said. "Listen, I appreciate your concern. Really. But whatever I face can't be any worse than living with the nomads. That was no picnic. Ask Angie."

"How did you even end up with them?" Gaia asked.

Jack met her gaze briefly, then kept cutting apple slices. "They picked me up in the wasteland when I was practically dead. I was in no condition to refuse their hospitality. I don't care to go into it. It turned out the tribe leader liked my voice and that's what kept me alive."

"You sang for them?" Gaia asked. That was the last thing she would have expected.

"I hope I never sing again," he said. "Angie's mother looked after me. That's why I owe her."

"Do you know why the girl has such trouble talking?" Myrna asked.

Jack nodded. "The tribe leader was paranoid that someone was going to poison him. It probably wasn't paranoia, actually, since half the tribe hated his guts. Angie was his taster. She had to share his plate and take a bite of anything before he did, and drink from his cup. He thought it was funny to make her smoke, too. I'd say she's got some issues."

"How did her parents put up with that?" Gaia asked.

"Her dad was dead. Her mom was sick. As in, dying." He looked around uneasily. "Where is she, anyway?" he asked, rising. "She shouldn't have gone far." He went up a couple of the ladder rungs to peer into the loft.

"I told her to stay with you and Myrna," Gaia said, concerned. "We can ask Malachai what time Angie and Leon left. The excrims were guarding the house last night."

"Do that. I'm heading up to the quad and I'll watch for them there," Myrna said. "The Protectorat wants me to handle the DNA registry. He's having supplies delivered."

"I'm going to find Angie before I look up my parents," Jack said. "Maybe she went to find Norris's cat." He took his hat and was gone.

"Is this a mistake, Myrna?" Gaia asked, rising. "With the registry?"

"I don't see that you have a choice if you want water," Myrna said. "It's not the registry itself that's dangerous. It's what the Protectorat does with the information."

"The last time I helped them, with deciphering my parents' code, he started rounding up girls," Gaia said. "I saw them being marched across the quad."

"He took blood samples and let them go," Myrna said. "There's been nothing else like that. It was an impulsive mistake. He's more careful now."

"But as soon as he starts picking through our data and deciding some genes are valuable, he'll also be deciding what's not valuable," Gaia said.

"I don't see how you can worry about that in the scale of things," Myrna said. "He's already decided that people inside the wall are more valuable than anyone outside. Your people in New Sylum barely merit water. I'd focus on that."

At a table before the Tvaltar, under a brown canopy, Gaia took cheek swabs for the DNA registry side by side with Myrna Silk. She'd seen the insides of more mouths in the past four hours than she had in her whole life, and she was privately appalled at the proportion of unhealthy teeth. A team of doctors and their assistants from the Enclave were set up along a row of other tables and canopies, more than a dozen in all, and they were processing people at the rate of two hundred an hour.

"It's inevitable." That was the message circulating among the people of New Sylum, and while many had balked, the miners in particular, the vast majority trusted Gaia when she explained that the directory was necessary and reasonably harmless.

"Besides, if we don't register, we don't get any water," Gaia finally said bluntly. "Have you found any in the unlake?"

Even Bill could follow that reasoning.

The Enclave provided a pass for each person who registered his or her DNA, which was good for a show in the Tvaltar, a trinket from one of the vendors around the quad, or a refreshment from the Enclave ice man. The people of Wharfton had turned out for the event, and impromptu vendor stalls and carts had popped up in the surrounding streets. The people of New Sylum, who had known ice only in the wintertime marsh, were charmed by the novelty of finding it colored and edible in pointy paper cones.

Even the Enclave guards who had been positioned on the roofs around the quad seemed relaxed, their rifles slung along their backs, and several were eating the extravagant ices as if they, too, were on holiday. Peg's Tavern had opened early to serve egg sandwiches and tea, and business was brisk. Will came out of the doorway, carrying a mug to Norris, then headed back in.

From the bright sunlight, Peter stepped into the shade of the canopy where Gaia was working.

"We've been watching for a delivery of water barrels from the Enclave," he said, "but there's nothing, and no evidence they're starting a pipeline or anything to supply water to New Sylum directly from the wall. Didn't the Protectorat say he was going to make an appearance here?"

She glanced out again at the crowd, noticing the advanced angle of the light. She reached automatically for her locket watch. "Is it past noon?"

"Yes. Nearly one."

"He did say he'd be out this morning," Gaia said. She'd been lied to. She didn't like it. "He's distracted us with colored ice and free passes. Did Jack find Angie yet?"

"No," Peter said. "We've been looking. A man reported seeing a girl her age heading toward the irrigation pipes this morning around dawn, so we're checking around there."

"That makes no sense," Gaia said. The irrigation pipes for the fields were way over on the far side of Wharfton, past Eastern Sector Three. She scanned the quad again. "Has anyone seen Leon?"

When he didn't reply, she looked up impatiently and found Peter regarding her quietly, with focused blue eyes. A tiny shock fizzled through her. She realized that he'd shaved, and the scar on his right cheek, the one she used to think of as an extra smile line, was visible again.

"You want me to look for your fiancé?" he asked, speaking slowly.

Her heart gave an odd lurch. "I'm just worried about him."

"Maybe he isn't interested in staying safe anymore," Peter said.

"Did he talk to you about going into the Enclave and setting up some sort of counterattack?" she asked.

"No, but it's what we need. That'd be good if that's where he is."

She pressed a hand to her forehead. *I don't believe this. He's gone inside.*

"He's gone rogue, hasn't he?" Peter said.

"I'm going to kill him," she said.

What was the good of being Matrarc if she couldn't get her fiancé to stay in line? Out of the corner of her eye, she noticed Malachai. The excrims were stationed unobtrusively around her, still following Leon's orders to guard her. It was totally unfair. She should have made the excrims look after *him*.

Behind Peter, a pretty young woman was hovering, idly drawing the toe of her boot through the dirt, and Gaia's inner radar kicked in. She was one of the women who had been laughing with Peter at Peg's Tavern, and now she kept glancing curiously under her bangs at him, which irritated Gaia.

"What is it?" Peter asked.

Gaia nodded toward the brunette, and when Peter turned, he smiled.

"Hey, Tammy," he said.

"I don't want to interrupt," Tammy said. She smiled shyly, stroking her chin to indicate his missing beard. "I wasn't sure that was you."

"It's me," Peter said.

Gaia wanted to gag. She grabbed Peter's elbow and paced with him in the other direction.

His gaze dropped to her fingers. "You're touching me," he said.

She released him as if scalded. "I don't want you distracted," she said. "We have business."

"Then don't distract me yourself," he said, his voice low.

She crossed her arms tightly over her chest, trying to erase the tingling in her fingers. "We have problems. The Protectorat lied to me about the water. Angie's missing. Leon's inside the wall doing who knows what. If he messes things up with his father, the Protectorat could decide to annihilate us all."

"What do you want me to do about it?"

"*Help me!*" she said, low and fierce.

A muscle tensed visibly in his jaw. "I'll do whatever I can," he said calmly. "I just don't see any solutions yet. You could stop the DNA registration. We could stop cooperating with them."

"Then everyone will know I was wrong to trust the Protectorate in the first place."

"Weren't you?"

"You're not helping," she said, trying to think. She hated feeling powerless, and that was what this was. With a gesture, she beckoned Malachai over.

"What do you know about Leon?" Gaia asked.

"He said he had business to take care of inside the wall," Malachai said. "He said to tell you, if you asked, that he'll be back tonight and you shouldn't worry about him."

"This would have been useful to know. And Angie?" Gaia asked. "What do you know about her?"

Malachai shook his head. "I already told Jack. Angie followed Leon a little later."

"Didn't you think to stop her?" Gaia asked.

"He told me to keep an eye on you, not the girl," Malachai said.

"Do you know where Jack is now?" Peter asked.

"He went looking for the girl," Malachai said.

Gaia looked at Peter and saw the same idea was occurring to him.

"Jack's inside, too," she said, and mentally groaned. "They all went in."

"We don't know that," Peter said. "How could they get past the wall?"

Somehow, they had. Gaia was certain of it. Anxiety was going to drive her mad. She looked back at the lines of her people obediently waiting to register their DNA, and she felt almost sick about them, too. The colored ices were practically mocking her now.

"Here's what I want you to do," she said to Peter. "Gather up some of our people who have already registered their DNA. Tell them to get back in line, but in line for a different station so the doctors won't catch the duplication. Tell them to spread the word and keep going back. Never let any new people get in line. That way it will look like we're still cooperating but we won't be giving the Enclave any new information."

"Cheat, in other words," Peter said.

"Yes, until the Protectorat keeps his side of the bargain. We've been had. And you, Malachai, get Derek and Ingrid to organize storing up as much water as they possibly can, with enough to share with us. Everyone in Wharfton should be stockpiling water like crazy."

"With all due respect, I'm not leaving you, Mlass Matrarc," Malachai said. "Leon told me to guard you and that's what I'm doing."

Gaia turned on him. "You will do what I say, not Leon. You can play bodyguard once you're done, but you will obey me, or I'll have my scouts clap you back in your chains and you'll be the first criminal of New Sylum. Is that what you want?"

"Mlass Gaia," Peter said quietly.

"Is it?" Gaia demanded, ignoring Peter. She stared up at the big, bearded man, her fury building.

"Beg your pardon, Mlass Matrarc," Malachai mumbled. With a quick tip of his hat brim, he was gone.

Gaia's breath rushed out of her. "I need to get a message to the Protectorat," she said. She had to figure out what to do about Leon.

"I'll take it for you," Peter said.

"No. You arrange things here as I requested."

"Ordered, you mean," he said. "And sending Malachai to talk to Derek is a mistake. That should be your job."

148

"Are *you* going to defy me now, too?" she asked, stung.

"You're losing it," Peter said bluntly. "The last Matrarc never raised her voice."

"I'm not her!" Gaia snapped.

A silence fell around her, and Gaia glanced past Peter to see that a loose circle of people had paused to observe their exchange. The young brunette, Tammy, watched with particular interest, as if she couldn't wait to stake out her status as Peter's future girlfriend. Will sidestepped past her and came up beside Gaia. He'd found a chance to shave, too, as if looking sharp were now the top priority of every man from Sylum.

"Everything all right?" Will asked

Gaia said nothing. *What did I expect?* Of course the men would be thinking about themselves. They were vain and useless like everybody else. She frowned at the toes of her boots, unbelievably frustrated.

"She's upset," Peter said.

"I'm *not* upset! Quit saying that!"

What peeved her was Peter questioning her leadership. What infuriated her more was Leon going inside the wall without her permission. And her own stupidity was beyond bearing. She should have known what Leon would do. She should have stopped him.

Will cleared his throat.

Gaia took a deep breath and straightened, looking hard at one brother and then the other. She didn't care if she sounded like a tyrant. "I am not the brilliant Mlady Olivia. I'll admit that. But I am trying my best to find some solutions here. If you could just, please, follow my orders, like normal people, I'd be grateful." She spun and marched off toward the south gate.

a mouse in the pipe

AT THE SOUTH GATE, she borrowed a pen and paper and sent a message up to the Protectorat.

> *Mabrother Protectorat,*
> *We missed you at the registry this morning.*
> *Where's our water?*
> *Gaia Stone*
> *Matrarc of New Sylum*

An hour later, she received a reply:

> *Masister Stone,*
> *These things take time.*
> *Yours,*
> *Miles Quarry*
> *Protectorat*

"He's toying with us," Gaia said, and passed the note to Will. Will, she noticed, did not seem to hold it against her that she'd acted like a high-handed diva. Peter accepted her apology with a brief nod. Neither made a joke about it, which would have been nice. Instead, she was left feeling secretly ashamed of her outburst, and more worried than ever about Leon.

She spent the afternoon forcing herself to work calmly with Wharfton leaders to arrange the stockpiling of water. Before the deception at the DNA registry could be discovered, she asked Myrna, quietly, to find a way to suspend operations for the rest of the day, and Myrna arranged a logistical mix-up with some swab supplies. Slightly more than half of Gaia's people had been registered, and all of them felt cheated when they learned the Protectorat had reneged on the water.

By nightfall, Gaia was gathered around the campfire of clan nineteen with a dozen key people from Wharfton and New Sylum. There was no news about Leon, Angie, or Jack.

"As of now, we have enough water for everyone in Wharfton and New Sylum for two days if the Protectorat cuts us off," Gaia reported. "That means limited baths and washing, but enough for drinking and cooking. We also have teams drawing it off at the wall spigots through the night to bolster our supply."

"Two days is nothing," Derek said, and Gaia agreed.

"We still need the Protectorat to honor his agreement, long-term," she said.

"I don't get where the water's coming from," the miner Bill said. "Do they have springs in there or something?"

"No, they convert steam from the geothermal energy plant," Myrna said. "They also recycle the water from the sewer system and purify that to irrigate the fields out here. The water isn't cheap, but there's enough to share if they want to."

"Just so you know," Bill said, "me and my miners could get you a nice tunnel under that wall in two weeks' time."

Derek laughed.

"What? It's true," Bill said.

"Maybe if you have explosives," Derek said.

"We'd go even faster, then," Bill said. "My point is, we can get inside. We could even pop up inside one of the Enclave houses if we had an ally there. That would be best. Then the guards would never know and we could send in an attack force."

"It won't take care of the problem," Gaia said. She felt like she'd said it a hundred times. "We need the Enclave cooperating with us. They have to trust us and provide us with the water, long-term. Undermining the wall is not the solution. It could even backfire."

"I'm just saying. Don't be so quick to throw out my idea," Bill said. "If we need to move a number of people inside at the same time, we could do it."

"We'd need more than one tunnel for that," Gaia pointed out.

"So we cut more tunnels," Bill said.

"We're not staging some massive attack," she said.

"We need to do something," Bill argued. "We ought to prepare. We can't just sit around out here waiting for the Protectorate to make a move. Vlatir would get this."

"We have a town to build," she pointed out. "You're not exactly idle."

"A town won't do us no good if we don't have water," Bill said.

Everything came back to that. Grumbles moved through the group.

"Possibly Vlatir is working out a solution with his father right now," Will said. The others fell silent again, and Will turned to Gaia. "There's potential there, isn't there?"

"No. I don't think so. He and his father are not on the best terms." Gaia shifted uneasily. "Leon told Malachai he'd be back outside by tonight. He's not."

"Then what's he doing in there?" Bill asked.

She didn't want to say, but as she looked around at her friends, she realized she had to. Their futures were at stake, too. "I believe he's gone in to set up the sabotage of the power and the water system.

The responding murmur sounded like approval to her.

"Don't you know for sure what he's doing?" Bill asked.

Gaia felt color rising in her cheeks. "No."

Bill let out a guffaw. "There's leadership for you."

Gaia stood. She'd had enough. "Anyone else who wants to lead New Sylum can take over with my blessing," she said.

The others quickly objected, and Bill offered a churlish apology. But Gaia really had had it. Her mind was exhausted from trying to reason with people, to come up with plans and backup plans that would satisfy everybody. Even worse, she felt the raw truth of Bill's comment: as one of her citizens, Leon was her responsibility whether he was operating a pivotal stealth mission, or endangering himself and the rest of New Sylum. A better leader would have been able to control him.

A better leader would strive to control him, even now.

She gazed up the dark hillside, beyond the wall to the distant streetlights that shone through the trees. If only the Protectorat would treat them fairly. If only she could find a way to compel him.

If only she knew that Leon was safe.

"I don't see a problem with doing all of it," Peter said. "We'll keep drawing off water around the clock to increase our supply. Bill can start his tunneling. It'll give us more options later. And Mlass Gaia can continue peaceful negotiations with the Protectorat."

"I'll go," Will said. "Mlass Gaia can stay out here to run things."

Gaia shook her head. She knew it would have to be her, one way or another. She fingered the Protectorat's note that she'd saved in her pocket. "I have to go deal with him. It's me the Protectorat wants."

"He doesn't have to get you, though," Will said. "It's your responsibility to stay outside the wall. You're needed here."

Gaia looked around the circle and saw the stubborn determination of her friends. She appreciated their concern, but if they wouldn't let her go inside the wall openly, she'd find another way. She was bad at lying. It was going to be best to keep it short, and not look Will or Peter in the eye.

"All right," she said. "I'll stay out here. Will can be our ambassador."

When Gaia checked on Maya, the girl looked so cozy sleeping beside Josephine and Junie that Gaia couldn't resist slipping under the tarp beside them for a minute. She drew a blanket around herself and as soon as her head was down, heaviness felled her into instant sleep. It was hours before she stirred, and with a jolt of panic, she came awake. The night was still dark. The campfire had burned down so low she couldn't read her locket watch. Quietly, she eased out from under the tarp and started uphill.

Gaia picked her way along the dark path up to her parents' cottage on Sally Row. Malachai, the most conspicuous of her bodyguards, followed discreetly behind her, and Gaia was impressed with his vigilance.

Entering the cottage, she found it crowded with half a dozen people focused toward the bunk beds, where a child lay on the lower level and a teenage boy lay on the one above. They were connected by a translucent tube, and just as Gaia realized it was a blood transfusion, Myrna crimped off the tube and bent over the lower bunk.

Gaia stayed only long enough to collect her satchel. She took a handful of candles from beneath the sink and a box of matches. Then she slipped out the back door and moved silently through the backyard herb garden, past the laundry line, to the chicken coop, which was black and hulking in the night. Soft clucking noises came from within, and she touched a hand to the wooden wall. She crouched over, seeking in the dark behind the coop for the old, rotted wood that had been piled there when her father had dismantled the last outhouse.

There, deep in the angled, rough, decaying boards, a pale light gleamed. She bent even lower, peering inside, and found a dozen glowing stems of honey mushrooms. She'd never liked the taste, but she'd always loved the mysterious way the stems glowed in the dark. The patch was smaller than she remembered, and she was unwilling to clear it out completely, so she took half of the mushrooms, tugging them gently from the boards and slipping them into her satchel.

She turned to look back at the house's windows gleaming with candlelight, and watched for Malachai and the excrims. Though they didn't have the authority to interfere with her, she still wanted to evade them if she could. Moving as silently as possible, she slipped into the neighboring yard. She passed through several more backyards until she reached a narrow track that skirted above Western Sector Three and intersected the path to the water spigot. People were slowly, steadily filling barrels there by the glow of several torches. She dipped lower again, and wound her way through the narrow, dusty roads of Wharfton.

It had been ages since she'd last been out alone in Wharfton at night, but she knew every path and corner. So many times in the past, she'd delivered babies to the south gate at all times of the day or night, and as she passed between the dark, wood and stone buildings, she was home again in yet another way. It was like playing hide and seek in the dark, but alone and with a destination.

If Leon, Angie, and Jack could get into the Enclave, so could she.

She passed below the quad to avoid the activity there, and heard the distant piano from Peg's Tavern. She passed down the street where Emily had lived with Kyle in Eastern Sector Two, back when they'd sheltered her before her escape to the wasteland, and then she headed farther east toward the fields. The moon came out from a high, thin cloud and dropped enough pale light over the crops to give them a colorless, alien quality.

She looked back to see if anyone was following her and saw figures down the road. Picking up her pace, she hurried along the contour of the hill in parallel with the wall. Faint reflections of moonlight along the upper edges of the irrigation troughs made a great web in the fields. The troughs rose gradually to converge at a series of junctures, and finally met up with a big pipe in the slope below the wall.

Now she had to hope for a clue to how the others had gone in. Angie had been seen near here.

The ground pitched more steeply beneath her feet as she hurried toward where the main pipe met the hillside. She wasn't exactly sure what she'd been hoping for, but even with a lit candle, she found no gap, no narrow channel she might crawl up.

She set a hand on the cool metal of the pipe, blew out her candle, and headed down the slope several meters to where the pipe opened into the main trough. She crouched down, peering around the edge into the pipe's interior. The darkness was impenetrable. She lit her candle again and held it forward. The inner surface shone with moisture from where water had run earlier, but what struck her most was how narrow the pipe was, not even a meter across.

They couldn't have gone inside, she thought. There would hardly be room to crawl.

But what if they did?

Water could come pouring down at any time. Her heart began to pound. She could get trapped in there. She had no way to know exactly where the other end led. She didn't even know for certain if Leon, Angie, and Jack had gone up the pipe. It seemed impossible.

Her eye caught on something near her foot, just beside the edge of the trough. She leaned to pick it up, and the instant her fingers touched it, she knew what she'd found: Angie's goggles.

You know you're going to do it, she thought, and let out a squeak. Just because she was going to go in didn't mean she wasn't terrified.

A noise behind her made her turn. Malachai was advancing rapidly along the hillside with three other men. He had the sense not to call out anything that might alert the guards on the wall, but she knew he would never let her disappear into the pipe if he caught her. She had no time to waffle.

She scrambled into the pipe, thrusting the lit candle before her. Pausing only to settle her satchel high on her back by its strap, she crawled deeper into the sloping concrete cylinder.

"Mlass Gaia, come back!" came Malachai's voice from behind her. Then a grunt.

"I won't be long," she called back. "I have to get Leon. Chardo Will is in charge."

"You'll never find Leon! Don't be a fool! You could die in there!"

"I have to try."

There was another grunting noise behind her.

She kept going faster, finding her rhythm, crawling on her two knees and one free hand. The inner surface of the pipe was a slick beige interrupted only by occasional seams in the concrete where threadlike veins of water gleamed in her candlelight. The air was thin and motionless, so that the wavering heat and smoke of the candle clung around her.

She heard one more bumping noise behind her, distant now, and hurried onward, meter by meter. The narrow space must have been even tighter for Leon and Jack, she realized. She had to go fast. The longer she was in the pipe, the greater were the chances that water would start down the chute toward her, and there'd be no escape.

A faint clicking sounded ahead and she stopped, listening intently. The candle flame burned upright in an unwavering, vibrant yellow. She could hear her breathing, quick and anxious, but nothing more in the close silence. Then another click. Something was happening up ahead. She began scrambling faster, and then she heard the gurgling sound of water. A pocket of cool air moved against her face.

"Wait!" she called. She dropped her candle to use both her hands, crawling in a race, in a blind nightmare of nothingness, terror in her throat. Her satchel slid down, ensnaring her arm, and she stripped it off in alarm. The air grew cooler, and suddenly the pipe began rising more steeply.

She plunged and crawled madly up the pipe, terrified, and a circle of gray appeared far, far ahead.

"Wait!" she called again, screaming.

The trickling noise grew closer. She kept her eyes glued to the gray circle and then she saw something small and black scurrying toward her down the pipe. She raced toward it, hearing a faint rumble of laughter. The mouse ran silently beneath her, a stream of water in its wake, and then Gaia was crawling in cold water.

old friends

"WAIT!" SHE SCREAMED AGAIN. "Stop the water!"

She scrambled onward through the increasing water flow, panicking. Did nobody hear her? She screamed again. The gray circle before her expanded, grew brighter, and then, as an on-slaught of water deluged down the pipe, an opening suddenly burst wide above her and she stood up into a shower of pouring cold water.

She lunged over and clung precariously to the slippery side of the big funnel that contained her. Blinking back water and open-ing her mouth wide to gulp in a lungful of air, she looked up des-perately. Water was rushing loudly out of another pipe above her, into the funnel, and spiraling down into a whirlpool that emptied into the pipe where she'd just been.

She leapt upward to get a finger hold on the top of the funnel and scrabbled her feet against the side. She slung an elbow over the upper edge and hauled herself out. She toppled in a heap to the floor of a waterworks facility, shivering from residual horror. If Malachai had followed her into the pipeline, he would be en-gulfed in rushing water by now, as doomed as the mouse. If she had been sixty seconds farther back, she would be dead.

She sat upward. The loud room was hung with pipes that could be swiveled into big vats and funnels like the one she'd crawled out of. The area was deserted, but an open doorway shone with light, and she knew whoever had started the water could return at any moment. Above her, a hatchway was open to the night sky. On instinct, she grabbed the rungs bolted into the wall and quickly climbed up through the hatchway to the roof, leaving the crashing noise of the water behind her.

She hugged her arms around herself, struggling to catch her breath and get her bearings. Dark water gurgled in a series of huge, deep holding tanks to her left, and a pump was chugging a spout of splashing water. She could see downhill to the dark fields she had left below the wall. To the right, below the south gate, spread the dark buildings of Wharfton, and even farther, pinpoints of light shone from campfires in New Sylum.

Gaia circled around. The gleaming obelisk rose from the Square of the Bastion, and the towers of the prison and the Bastion stood behind.

And then she looked up. Half the sky was black, but in the cloudless half, the crescent moon hung serenely, its cusps sharp, and brilliant stars shone as close and clear as she'd ever seen them. She searched for Orion, finding low in the southeastern sky the three distinctive stars of his belt, newly risen. Gaia cherished the memory of her parents in those stars, and at the sight of the constellation, gratitude for their love swelled with her joy in being alive.

She brushed the wet hair back from her face and straightened her soaked shirt.

Hey, Mom and Dad, she thought, sending her silent voice out into the night.

She missed them, but they were with her, too. And this felt right.

For the first time in ages, the first time since she'd been elected Matrarc, she was consulting no one and acting independently, as herself. The freedom was unbelievably sweet.

Then a startling thought hit her: the freedom must have felt good to Leon, too. Every time he'd tried to take initiative, whether to go after her missing scouts or to protect her coming into Wharfton, she'd told him no. Even the night before, when he'd argued that it was time to prepare counter-offensives for New Sylum, she'd put him off.

No wonder he went rogue, she thought.

Leon knew the Enclave better than anyone, yet she had dismissed his urgency. That was another mistake she'd made.

Soft, aromatic air stirred in the night, drawing out the moisture from her wet clothes and chilling her skin. She still had to find him. If Angie and Jack weren't with him, she would deal with locating them next.

She would start with the Jacksons and wing it from there.

Traveling at roof level, Gaia picked her way along the water mains that connected the buildings. The trick was to walk slowly and watch her feet on the tread boards alongside the pipes. At one crossing, a girl in red passed below Gaia, triggering a motion-detector on a streetlamp, and Gaia froze until she was gone. A bat whipped into the light and careened away.

As she neared the street to the bakery, Gaia could see the top of the obelisk illuminated in the Square of the Bastion a few blocks farther uphill. Stealthily, she ducked under a roof laundry line and lowered herself down a ladder to ground level. If anyone saw her and recognized her face, she'd be doomed. Shivering in the darkness, she watched the quiet street. The shop windows of Jacksons' bakery were lightless, but around the side, a crack of illumination outlined the drawn shutters. Someone must already be up, working. She tapped lightly on the door. An instant later, the crack of light went out. Gaia waited, hearing nothing, and then she tapped again. A click came from the door, and a dark gap opened.

"Who's there?" came a soft, low voice.

"It's me, Gaia Stone. Is Mace home?"

She was swiftly drawn within and the door closed firmly behind her. Warm air enveloped her, surrounding her with the rich smell of baking bread, and with a pulling noise, the light over the table came on. Mace and his wife Pearl beamed at Gaia in joyful welcome. They reached simultaneously to envelope her a hug.

"Thank goodness!" Pearl said. "I've been dying to see you ever since Mace told me you were back. Are you all right? You're all wet!"

"I'm fine," Gaia said, grinning. "I can't believe how good it is to be here. How are Yvonne and Oliver?"

"Good. Sleeping," Mace said.

She couldn't see enough of her friends. Mace's apron stretched across his robust belly, and his strong hands were flecked with dough. Pearl was thinner than Gaia remembered, with new streaks of gray at her temples.

"You're taller," Pearl said. "And tan. And not a girl at all anymore, I see."

"What did I tell you?" Mace said. He smiled at Gaia. "Turn around for her."

"Come on," Gaia said, laughing.

"No. Let's see you," he said, taking her hand to twirl her. "I hardly recognized you the other day. What a surprise! Leon didn't tell us you were coming."

"He's here?" Gaia asked.

A shuffling noise drew Gaia's eager gaze upward. Angie was

hunched at the top of the narrow staircase, swamped in an over-large nightgown.

"You're here!" Gaia said, her heart swelling with relief. She looked back, questioning, to Pearl.

"He's gone. He left her with us," Pearl said

Gaia reached up a hand to Angie. "We were so worried about you, Angie."

"Leon's mad at me," Angie said.

Gaia smiled. "I can't say I blame him. Did you follow him in, through the irrigation pipe?"

The girl nodded. "I tried to be quiet, but he heard me."

"Come down," Gaia said.

"Are you mad, too?" Angie asked, descending cautiously.

"Mostly I'm relieved. What you did was incredibly dangerous," Gaia said. She turned to Mace. "Where's Leon now?"

"He went into the tunnels," Mace said.

"And Jack Bartlett? Has he been here?" Gaia asked.

When Mace and Pearl only looked puzzled, Gaia glanced up and saw Angie's eyes had grown larger.

The girl's voice dropped to a hush. "No. Did he come in, too?"

"He was looking for you," Gaia said.

Angie looked stricken. Gaia drew her down the last steps and cuddled her into her arms, tipping her cheek on top of the girl's soft hair. "You left your goggles so we could find you, didn't you?" Gaia asked.

The girl nodded. "Just in case. But I didn't think you'd really come. Where's Jack?"

"Nobody knows." Gaia glanced at Mace and Pearl again. "When did Leon bring her?"

"Early yesterday morning, just before dawn," Mace said. "He asked us to take care of her until he came back."

164

And that obviously had not occurred.

"Where did he enter the tunnels?" Gaia asked.

"Don't get any ideas, now. Smugglers have died down there," Mace said. "Best to wait here for when he comes back."

"Could he have been arrested?" Gaia asked.

"No. There was some fuss around the Bastion today, but I didn't hear of any arrests, and I would know," Mace said.

"How?" Gaia insisted.

Mace glanced at Pearl.

"We have a kind of network now," Pearl said. "It's complicated. The point is, you should stay here with us. Mace is right about that."

Gaia felt the absence of her satchel and glanced around the room. "I'll need some candles or a lamp."

"You're not going. You'll get lost down there," Mace said.

"I'll be careful. I'll mark my route," she said.

He looked more skeptical than ever. "With what?"

Her glowing mushrooms were gone with her satchel. "Do you have any honey mushrooms?" she asked.

Mace laughed. "You've got to be kidding."

Pearl put a hand on her shoulder and gave her a squeeze. "Let's get you in something dry. What are these trousers you're in? Is this what the new women are wearing? They look very practical."

Gaia ran a hand through her damp hair. "You can't distract me. Leon might be hurt down there," she said. "If you won't help me get into the tunnels, I'll get in by the honey farm. I know there's an entrance there."

Mace and Pearl exchanged a wordless glance, and then Pearl cleared her throat. "I'm getting you some dry things. Mace, keep it simple." She stepped out of the kitchen.

"Angie, you run on up to bed," Mace said.

"I'm going with Mlass Gaia," the girl said.

Gaia turned, regarding the girl with a lifted eyebrow. "I'll come back for you before I leave the Enclave. You'll be safe here. Go on up."

Angie stubbornly shook her head and sat down firmly on the bottom step.

Gaia let a beat of silence pass, and then moved in front of her. "You know I'm the Matrarc, right?"

Angie nodded, watchful.

"And you want to help me, don't you?" Gaia went on.

The girl put a hand to her throat, spreading her fingers along her voice box.

"Then you'll listen to me," Gaia said. "I don't put up with people who can't follow orders. You will stay here and obey Mace and Pearl in my absence. You'll be respectful and work hard. I told you to go to bed. Now, go." She pointed up the stairs.

Angie's eyes watered up. Her chin wobbled. Gaia did not yield. The girl spun to her feet and clambered up the stairs, and a second later, a door closed.

Gaia turned to find Mace considering her, his lips pursed. "Like I said. You've grown up," he said.

"I don't always like it," Gaia said. She knew Angie was fragile enough as it was without turning on her, but she couldn't have the girl following her.

He pulled a mound of dough toward him and started kneading. "You've heard about Myrna Silk's blood bank?"

"Yes."

"Some of the parents who have lost children to hemophilia have organized here inside the wall," he said. "We donate resources to Masister Silk when we can, and there's a movement of reformers who want to overhaul the Enclave's health system. We haven't gotten too far yet, but we meet up once a month. We're talking."

It made her think of Derek and Ingrid working with people outside the wall to create a clearing house for advanced children who wanted to find their birth parents, and the relationships that formed from that. All sorts of new alliances were happening now. "This wouldn't be connected to Derek, would it?"

Mace looked at her shrewdly. "There's some overlap. The issues are different, but the point is, people are finding each other. We're using our connections."

"Does the Protectorat know?" she asked.

"No. And I'd rather he didn't," he said. "I'm just telling you because if you need anything, I think I could find people to help you."

"What we need is water for New Sylum," she said. "Not just deliveries of barrels, either. We need a reliable pipeline, or better yet, our own waterworks system tapping directly into the geothermal plant."

"That's going to be expensive," he said. "I'm not sure what we can do, but my friends would be sympathetic, at least. We've heard some of the wealthier people want a change to the health care, too. Some of the people behind the Vessel Institute. We're not sure how to approach them, or if it's safe to."

"Leon might be able to help with that. He knows the wealthy families. He grew up with them. Did you tell him?"

"It didn't come up." Mace kneaded the dough a couple more turns, set it aside, and reached for another mound.

Understanding gradually came to her. "You still don't trust him, do you?" Gaia asked. "That's why you don't want me going after him, either."

Mace rubbed at his eyebrow with the knuckle of his thumb. "We took in Angie when he brought her," he said.

"That's not an answer."

Mace shrugged. "Derek vouches for Leon. I know that. And I gather he's important to you. I don't suppose anything as boring as my own concern for his reputation would make you reconsider your feelings for him."

"We're engaged," Gaia said.

Mace stopped kneading and looked up with sharp eyes. "Are you, then."

Gaia gathered he wasn't exactly thrilled. A slow burn began in her gut, as if he disrespected her, too.

"Is there anything else I should know? Are you expecting?" Mace asked.

Ouch, she thought. "No. Not that it's any of your business."

Pearl reappeared in the doorway, a pile of clean clothing in her hands. "I was trying to find a red cloak," she began, then stopped, looking back and forth between them.

"Gaia tells me she's engaged to Leon Grey," Mace said.

Pearl eyebrows pinched in confusion. "Are you *sure*, Gaia?"

"Of course I am," she said stiffly. "And he's Leon Vlatir now."

"I know who he is," Pearl said. She put up a hand. "It's just such a big decision and you're so young."

Gaia's heart sank a notch lower. She'd thought of Mace and Pearl as family, but apparently they weren't. Or worse, maybe they were. This was the disapproval she'd expected from her own parents.

"Thanks. You know what? I'm just going to leave," Gaia said.

"Nonsense. You just caught us by surprise." Pearl gave a be-lated smile. "We wish you all happiness, of course. Let's get you changed. Mace, turn your back. Did he tell you that Leon went in through the library?"

"We didn't get that far," Mace said, facing away.

"We were busy discussing if I was pregnant," Gaia said.

"Mace!" Pearl said.

"She's not," Mace said.

"Well, thank goodness for that," Pearl said. "I should hope not. You, pregnant, and hardly more than a child yourself. The idea. Now here, hand me those wet things before you die of chill."

Gaia stripped off her wet trousers and her blouse, and stepped into the dry, blue skirt Pearl handed her, then a clean blouse. The clothes were roomy, but she tucked in the blouse and rolled the waistline of the skirt neatly once to cinch it tighter. She took a moment to inspect her knees, which were bruising from her desperate crawl through the pipe. She touched the skin tenderly, then let the fabric drop to hide them.

"She's good now," Pearl said. "You can turn around."

Mace flicked his gaze toward Gaia, and then started kneading again.

"There's a library on the Square of the Bastion," Pearl said. "Leon said there's an entrance to the tunnels in the basement. I had no idea, but it's supposed to connect to a tunnel that runs right under the square and straight toward the Bastion." She explained directions to the library's back entrance.

"Will they let me in?" Gaia said.

"I don't know. Leon said he knew the librarian," Pearl said. "Maybe you can explain that you're a friend. Let's see what I can find for candles. And your honey mushrooms gave me an idea."

Pearl pulled up a wooden box from a low cupboard and began rummaging around. "Ah," she said, producing what looked like a

169

wide gray bar of soap. She stepped to the table and held it up to the light bulb, turning it slightly, and to Gaia's surprise, it began to glow a soft green color.

"Oliver made this for a school project," Pearl said. "It's glow-in-the-dark chalk. It doesn't last long by itself, only a few minutes, but if candlelight hits it, you'll see it easily. You can draw arrows or marks on the tunnel walls as you go."

Gaia took the stick, feeling the powderiness of the chalk. "What's it made of?"

"Zinc sulfide mostly," Pearl said.

Gaia felt more hopeful as she took the chalk in her hand, giving it an experimental turn under the light to see the pale phosphorescence. A hint of outside gray light showed in the crack of the shutters, and Gaia didn't dare wait any longer. Pearl rapidly put the chalk together with some candles and matches in a bag, and Mace wrapped a couple of warm rolls in a paper before dropping them in.

Pearl pulled Gaia close in another hug.

"Get over here and try to say something nice," Pearl said to Mace.

"Next time, plan on visiting longer," he said to Gaia. He set a warm, heavy hand on her shoulder and looked frankly into her eyes. "Bring your fiancé by so we can have a chance to get to know him."

"I will," she said, feeling marginally better. "Take care of Angie," she added, and slipped back outside.

Gaia walked quickly through the dim quiet streets, letting her hair fall forward to cover her left cheek. A couple of the coffee shops were opening, plus a small corner store that sold milk and eggs, but the rest of the merchants had yet to open their doors. It wasn't long before Gaia turned down the alley that backed up along the buildings on the Square of the Bastion, and followed Pearl's directions to a narrow green door. Old copper numbers bled green into the stone lintel: 49. She rapped. Then she curled her hands around her face and peered in the little window in the door.

A sconce light came on down a hallway, and a slender figure came progressively nearer. The door opened a crack and a young woman peeked out.

"Yes?" she asked.

Recognition took only an instant on both sides. Rita opened the door farther. "Come in. Quickly," Rita said, guiding Gaia into a narrow hallway and bolting the door behind her.

Rita was no longer dressed in the distinctive red of the young female students who served in the Bastion, but in beige and cream. Her blonde hair was pulled back in a tidy ponytail, changing her appearance considerably, but her eyebrows arched over the same almond-shaped eyes, and her face was as delicately expressive as Gaia recalled.

"Leon didn't tell me you'd be coming," Rita said, keeping her voice low.

"He didn't know," Gaia said.

"Great," Rita said. "Am I going to get filled in at some point?"

"What did he tell you?" Gaia asked.

"He didn't want me to know anything, for my own safety, like he's some big master spy now," Rita said.

"I'm worried he's gotten hurt," Gaia said.

"You don't know our boy very well if you can say that," Rita said. "Have a little faith. He thinks fast on his feet."

"Unless he's unconscious."

Rita glanced briefly over her shoulder. "All right, I'm worried, too, but what's there to do? My aunt will be coming down any second. You can't stay here."

"I'm going after him," Gaia said.

Rita regarded her skeptically, and then apparently made a decision. Following Rita, Gaia bypassed the library's main reading room and took a staircase down to the archives. The close, dry smell of ink and old paper made Gaia sneeze. Dozens of shelves were packed so closely together that Gaia's shoulders would have touched both sides if she were passing through the aisles straight.

"Watch your step there," Rita said, as they descended into a second room that was even more tightly packed.

Little wisps of colored paper poked out between the books like flags, and Gaia inadvertently brushed her cheek against one.

"Have you been friends with Leon a long time?" Gaia asked.

"We were in the same class as kids," Rita said. "He and Jack Bartlett and I ran together. Didn't he ever say anything about me?"

"He mentioned Jack."

Rita laughed. "Perfect. He is so clueless. I only had a crush on him for four years in a row." She glanced back, her eyes bright. "Don't worry. I'm over it. Sort of. Here we are." They reached the end where an old, narrow door was fitted with clamps for a heavy beam. The beam was leaning against the wall. "Normally, we don't want any surprise intruders, but I've been leaving it open in case Leon comes back. Do you have any idea where you're going?"

Gaia replayed their progress through the house, remembering the turns, and pointed to her left. "I go that way toward the Bastion."

"Correct," Rita said.

"Thank you," Gaia said. "I mean it."

"I'll feel really stupid if you don't come back. So come back."

"I will."

Gaia lit a candle and then, with a last nod to Rita, she stepped through the door. She followed the dusty tunnel downward into air that had a different, fetid staleness. She held her candle high to illuminate the tunnel. To her right was darkness. To her left, far ahead, she could see daylight filtering down. A shallow gully cut down the center of the passage, with bits of rotting detritus that she surmised had been washed there by the last rain. She left her first glowing chalk mark at the base of the ramp: an arrow that pointed the way she was going.

Silence settled into her ears, nudged only by her own soft footfalls. The passage was nothing like the old mine routes she'd traveled with Leon, but she hoped those were ahead. As she came to the patch of daylight, she looked up several meters through a storm grid to a square of early morning sky. Faint voices and a rumbling of cartwheels sifted down.

Another patch of light shone farther along the tunnel, and when she looked up through that opening, the top of the obelisk was just visible. A pile of incongruously fresh-looking wooden boxes blocked much of the passage, as if someone had recently stored something there, but she was able to squeeze past to where the darkness was complete again. She lifted her candle to see glimmering spiderwebs, and pushed on.

When a scurrying passed over her shoe, she jumped. The hairless tale of a rat disappeared before her. The tunnel branched, and Gaia made another arrow mark at eye level on a stone that bulged out into the tunnel. She went only a little farther before she realized that finding Leon was going to be nearly impossible.

She didn't know which way he'd gone.

Or the tunnels themselves.

She should go back.

Gaia knew this, but when she thought of returning to the Jacksons' and doing nothing while he could be down here somewhere, hurt and needing her, she couldn't give up.

"Leon?" she said. Her voice sounded muffled and foreign.

A new passage on her right narrowed and descended into black granite, but the walls ahead were cut into a creamier stone, more like sandstone, so on instinct she went straight, hoping to find the tunnels she'd once traveled with Leon. Every time she came to a turn, she marked an arrow at eye level, and lifted the candle toward it to check that it glowed. She lost her inner sense of direction, and she couldn't help thinking again that this might be a mistake. But the tunnels had to lead somewhere, and she kept hoping she'd recognize some landmark from her earlier time there, like the fort area where Leon and his sisters had played as children.

She stopped often to call Leon's name and listen. A mine shaft opened up, wide and low-ceilinged, with cooler air, and she followed that. When she came to another fork and began to write her arrow, she saw a glimmering of pale green light on the adjacent wall.

She stepped nearer, staring.

It was one of her own marks.

It could mean only one thing: she'd gone in a circle.

CHAPTER 14

circles

SHE STOPPED, FEELING THE sweat along her neck, while her mind rapidly grappled with the significance of the circling.

"Stupid," she said.

Before she could get confused, she deliberately made another mark with a 2 under it in the place where she'd just discovered the doubling.

Her heart kicked in hard. Just how much danger she truly was in became suddenly, painfully obvious. This was no longer about Leon. If she lost track of her back trail, if she became lost, there'd be no way to get out. She needed to head back directly.

She realized suddenly how thirsty she was, but because she'd arrogantly assumed she would only be down for an hour or so, she hadn't thought to bring anything to drink. *Unbelievable*, she thought. How stupid could she get? Had she learned nothing about preparation or caution being Matrarc?

She struck back along the path she'd taken, crossing off each mark as she retraced her steps. She went carefully, deliberately taking the time at each intersection to check each tunnel for faint green marks to be certain she wasn't missing any

When the 2 appeared before her again, she became seriously scared. She did not understand, logically, how she could be making loops back to the same mark. She had to be missing some faint trace that was supposed to guide her to the original path, but she'd checked carefully at each branching of tunnels and didn't understand how she could have missed it.

"How am I supposed to get out?" she said.

She forced herself to stop and rest, trying to clear her mind of panic. She listened to the complete stillness until it became an oppressive presence in her ears, and she had to rub her fingers together just to hear anything and know she hadn't gone deaf. She lifted the candle, her second of five, to watch the flame. If the flame would waver even the least bit, she would know some movement of the air existed, promising an exit.

It did not flicker. The steady yellow flame cast echoing images of blindness on the walls when she blinked away from it.

She checked her locket watch, dismayed to find that more than four hours had passed. It must be close to noon outside. Leon could have traveled back through the tunnels and left by now.

Smugglers have died down there, Mace had said.

It could happen to her. She was seriously lost now. She closed her eyes and touched a hand to her cheek, finding tear tracks.

The prospect of death brought biting clarity: she wanted to marry Leon, raise little Maya, have kids of her own someday, and deliver babies. Period. The rest of it, all the managing and diplomacy and frustration of being Matrarc was completely secondary. Her secret pride and her power meant nothing. And yet she needed a just, fair society in order to have her ideal life with Leon, which brought her back to her responsibilities.

Gaia gazed wearily at the candle flame again. Like it or not, she was Matrarc. She had to get herself out of here and do her job as long as it was hers. Despair was a luxury she could not afford. She set her hand on her knee and hauled herself up again. If she couldn't find her old way out, she would find a new one.

Many hours later, Gaia stopped at of the opening of another passage, checking the flame of her fourth and last candle to see it flicker slightly. She turned her face, concentrating, and thought she felt the faintest hint of moving air trace the scar on her left cheek.

The passage aimed downward, defying her instinct to go upward, but she tried it anyway and eventually the tunnel leveled out and began to rise, lifting her hopes with it. *Please*, she thought. *Let this be a way out.* In the silence, she heard a distant cough, then nothing. She headed onward, her ears aching for another sign of life, until the tunnel turned a sharp bend.

Diffused sunlight dropped down a deep shaft from high above. Gaia gave a whoop of happiness, and then a sob of gratitude.

A naturally hollow, open space, five meters high and twice as long, had been outfitted as a shelter. A basket of knitting rested beside a rocker, and an unlit globe lamp was centered on a small table. Blankets were heaped on a cot, and Gaia was wondering how anyone could have brought a bed this far through the tunnels when the blankets moved. A teenage girl gave a snuffly snore and opened sleepy eyes.

"Hey," she said, perching herself up on an elbow. "Wait. I know you." She frowned, crinkling her nose. "Aren't you supposed to be rotting somewhere in the wasteland by now?"

Gaia was so happy to see another human all she could do was laugh. "I'm alive. Go figure."

She took a step nearer, taking in the deep circles that underscored the girl's eyes, her spindly, pale wrists, and her swollen belly. Blonde braids fell around the petite, pert face, and Gaia finally put the details all together.

"Sasha?" Gaia asked.

The girl sat up completely and rubbed her nose with the heel of her hand. "Who else?"

Gaia was speechless with amazement. Sasha, Emily, and Gaia had been inseparable as little girls in Wharfton, but due to a falling out, years had passed since Gaia and Sasha had been close. Meeting her anywhere would have been awkward, but this was bizarre. "What are you doing here?"

"I left. I quit the Vessel Institute," Sasha said.

"So I heard, but why are you here? Where are we?" Gaia asked, looking up the long shaft toward the natural light. They had to be a dozen meters underground.

"We're under Summit Park," Sasha said. "Didn't Mabrother Cho send you?"

Gaia didn't recognize the name. "I found you by chance. I've been lost down here for hours. I was looking for Leon Vlatir, the Protectorat's son. You haven't seen him, have you?"

"I think I'd have noticed him. The answer's 'no.' "

Gaia swallowed thickly. "Could I have some of your water, please?" She'd eaten Mace's two rolls but nothing else all day.

"Sure," Sasha said, pointing to a jug on the shelf. "Help yourself. Have you seen my grandpa? How long have you been back?"

"Just a few days," she said, and drank a long swallow of the cool water. "I haven't seen your grandfather. Why haven't you gone out to Wharfton?"

Sasha snorted. "Because I'm not stupid. They said we could leave whenever we wanted, but that was a crock. Rhodeski doesn't want any failures, not with his precious pilot program."

Gaia focused on Sasha's wrist, which bore no bracelet. She pulled a stool over nearer to the bed. "I don't understand. Emily said anyone could leave," Gaia asked.

"Yeah, well, she lied," Sasha said. "When I told Emily I wanted to quit, she got all upset. She told me, as a friend, I had to reconsider. And I was like, what? They can't make me stay, and she said there's a room in one of the towers where they'll put anyone who tries to quit. She said I'd be stealing the promised baby, so they'd have the right to imprison me."

"Then how did you leave?"

"I snuck out." Sasha shifted around on the cot so her feet came over the edge, and Gaia could see the worn soles of her droopy socks. Her ankles looked swollen with edema. "I couldn't stand it anymore. I don't want to give up my baby. So what if it's not mine, biologically? It could be half mine. And even if it isn't, it *feels* like it's mine. *All* mine." She spoke as if she'd been just waiting for a chance to explain her reasoning. "It wouldn't be alive without me. I'm not just some vessel. It knows my voice and it travels with me everywhere. I even know when it hiccups. It's the sweetest thing, Gaia. It's changed me into a mother. I'm not going to let that go."

Gaia's heart went out to her. What Sasha was saying matched what Gaia believed, and she'd vicariously felt the same conviction countless times while she'd attended childbirths. But she'd only ever known mothers carrying their own children. Now she couldn't help trying to see it from the other side, imagining the dreams of the biological parents.

"Have you thought about the other parents, though?" Gaia asked. "They might be ready to love the baby just as much as you do."

Sasha leaned forward and her sharp eyes glittered. "I don't care if this baby was promised a hundred times over. This baby is part of me. It is *mine*. Forever."

Gaia brushed some of the cobwebs off her skirt. "I understand. But you can't stay down here."

"I can for another month," Sasha said. "Then I'll have the baby and I'll sneak it outside the wall somehow."

"It's not safe. You can't deliver down here alone."

"I'll get some help. I have a friend who brings me food. He can help. Besides, it's a natural thing, right? My body will know what to do." Sasha poked a pillow behind her back. "You probably don't want to hear this, but there were plenty of mothers outside the wall who had babies on their own when they were afraid you midwives would take them away."

Gaia could hardly think how to reply. "Plenty of those babies and mothers died, too," Gaia said. "Childbirth is not something you play around with."

"Okay, listen. If you're just going to bug me, why don't you leave?" Sasha said. "You never liked me anyway, so don't pretend you want to help."

"Excuse me?" Gaia said.

"Ever since we were kids," Sasha continued. "Remember? One minute you and me and Emily were best friends, going to the Tvaltar and whatnot. I used to laugh so hard I peed my pants. The next minute you wouldn't even talk to me. You were off playing your little fancy word games with Emily."

Gaia was shocked. Hurtful memories raced back. "*You* were the one. You didn't go to Emily's birthday party because I was there. You said I was too weird and ugly."

Sasha scrunched up her nose. "So? I'm sorry. I was stupid.

You didn't have to hold it against me forever. Emily finally was nice to me again, but you never gave me another chance."

Gaia looked at the petite, pregnant girl with her droopy socks and felt the old sting dissolving. At this moment, there wasn't one thing about Sasha's situation that Gaia envied.

Sasha leaned back and shook a finger at her. "You're still weird looking, come to think of it."

Gaia let out a laugh. "I don't know what we're going to do for you."

"There's nothing to do. I have to stay hidden. If they find me, they'll keep me until I deliver, and then they'll take the baby and say I died in childbirth."

"They wouldn't."

"Want to bet? They can't leave me alive," Sasha said. "A sorry dead girl is better than a rebel in the Vessel Institute, isn't it?" She picked up a hand mirror and turned it in the soft glow of dropping sunlight, sending an oval of reflected light around the stone walls.

"Are there other women in the program who feel the way you do?" Gaia asked.

"What do you think?"

"How many?"

"Six that I've spoken to," Sasha said. "They're all terrified. They don't see any solution except to play along."

"They should all speak up," Gaia said. "The pilot program should be stopped."

"Clue in, Gaia," Sasha said. "Rich Enclave couples are paying huge amounts for our babies, a hundred times what we earn for our stipends. When the Vessel Institute reports one hundred percent success, they can expand like crazy. They've already picked

181

out the next girls to invite in. Soon they'll have dozens of us in their baby factory."

"How do you know this?"

"Because I've got ears," Sasha said, sarcastic. "I'm not smart the way you and Emily are. I'm not educated, but I listened enough to know what was really going on before I cut off my bracelet and came underground."

Gaia didn't want to believe it, but she knew in her heart that it was possible. People desperate for babies could easily be indifferent to the women who bore them, especially if the eager parents were paying a steep price and the breeders were removed out of sight.

"I can't believe Emily is part of this," Gaia said.

"She doesn't care jack about anything since Kyle died, except her boys."

Gaia thought back. "She blames me for Kyle's death."

"Well, yeah," Sasha said broadly. "That was easy to do when you weren't even here. Easier than blaming herself or Kyle for choosing to do stuff that got him killed, that's for sure." Sasha brought the mirror before her face.

Gaia noted the circles under her eyes again. "When's the last time you had a checkup?"

"Don't get any ideas."

Gaia smiled. "Come on, Sasha. You know I do this all the time."

"Nuh uh. Not happening."

"At least come out with me," Gaia said. "I have friends you could hide with in the Enclave. The Jacksons. I know they'd help you. Don't be stubborn about this."

"I'm not stubborn. I just don't trust anybody."

Gaia wished she could simply tell Sasha what to do, but she

wasn't one of the people of Sylum. "I have to get back to the tunnel under the library, by the Square of the Bastion. Do you know the way?"

Sasha's eyebrows lifted, and then she pushed to her feet. "That's far from here. I'll walk you back. You'd never find it."

Sasha carried a lantern and with unerring footsteps, led Gaia back to the tunnel below the square. Sasha refused Gaia's repeated offers of help, and stopped at the bottom of the ramp to the library. "I'll be fine," Sasha said.

"I don't even know how to find you again," Gaia said.

"Mabrother Cho does. He cooks for the Bastion. If you really need to find me, he can lead you."

"Promise me you'll get help when you go into labor," Gaia said.

Sasha gave a wry smile. "I'll try. If you could get word to my grandpa to tell him I'm okay, I'd appreciate that."

Gaia didn't think Sasha was okay at all. She reached gently around her to give her a hug. Then, with a last good-bye, she headed up to the library and pushed the door open.

Gaia brushed silently through the shelves, and climbed the basement steps. She avoided the front of the library where people were softly talking, and tiptoed down the hall to the back entrance. Gaia cracked open the door and peeked through the crevice. After her hours in the tunnels, her first breath of outside air was unbelievably sweet and fresh, but she was also frustrated by how much time she'd lost: practically an entire day.

She wished she could return to Mace's to see if he had any news of Leon, but she didn't see how she could walk openly in the streets, or even over the roofs in the daylight. Her scar would never go unnoticed.

"Gaia, wait," Rita called softly, coming down the hall. "What happened? You were gone for hours."

Gaia glanced down at her clothes to see that she was covered with stringy spider webs and dust. She touched her hair and more dust came free in her fingers. "I got lost. I'm fine, though. Did Leon come back?"

Rita drew her aside into the kitchen. "No. I was worried about you. I went to the Jacksons to see if they knew anything about you, but they've disappeared."

"Are you sure? Were they arrested?"

"I don't know, but their place was clearly deserted. I couldn't stay around to ask questions. The water was shut off for part of the city this morning. It's only just come back on, and there are rumors of terrorists. Guards are patrolling everywhere, looking for any intruders from outside the wall. Is it true? Are you terrorists?"

"Of course not," Gaia said.

"If they're trying to make us scared of you all, it's working. And another thing. One of the vessel mothers had her baby. It's the first one. There's going to be a party at the Bastion tonight."

"Will you be there?"

Rita gave her an odd look. "You know I was fired from the Bastion, right? They never proved I helped you and your mother, but they never proved I didn't, either."

"I'm so sorry," Gaia said.

Rita shrugged. "Things change. This job's okay. I'm glad you made it out. And back, I guess. What now?"

"I need to get outside the wall again," Gaia said.

Rita gave her a once-over. "I still have one of my old red dresses and a cloak. You could impersonate one of the Bastion servants. Nobody bothers them."

Gaia was reminded of the first time she'd entered the Enclave, way back before she knew anything. Rita fetched her things, and Gaia changed quickly in a small bathroom off the kitchen. A fleck of dirt was under her right eye, and she leaned near to the mirror wipe it free. The wasteland sun had deepened her complexion, and it was different to see the neckline of the bright red dress framing her collarbones and dipping lower over her chest. Gaia commonly wore natural tones, and the red dyes in Sylum had been a different hue, not nearly this vivid. Rita's dress was the boldest garment she'd ever worn.

"I miss wearing the red," Rita said, as Gaia stepped out. She eyed her critically. "That's good on you. Leon will like it."

Gaia's cheeks grew warm. "That hardly matters."

"Oh, it always matters," Rita drawled. "Don't pretend otherwise."

"Leon doesn't like me for my looks."

Rita let out a laugh. "He will in that dress. Try to look bored and a little haughty," Rita advised her. "People will notice you less than if you skulk, and it intimidates the guards."

"I don't skulk."

"I'm just saying. They won't look under your hood so closely, either." Rita passed Gaia a basket like the kind Bastion servants carried.

Gaia twitched the hood closer around her face. "All right?"

Rita nodded and held the door for her, an oddly wistful expression softening her features. "Good luck."

"Thanks, Rita." With a last wave, Gaia slipped out.

Gaia passed down the alley and at the first corner turned onto the main street, staying on the left side so other pedestrians would pass to her right where they'd be less likely to see her scarred left cheek.

She hadn't gone more than twenty paces when she noticed a man on the other side of the street carrying a large ceramic urn. He kept even with her as she walked, like a parallel shadow. It could not be a coincidence. She feared at first that he was some sort of guard, but he was dressed in brown trousers and a pale blue shirt, like a workingman, and as she proceeded down another block, his stride remained relaxed and easy. Once he looked across at her and nodded.

She didn't know what to think. He was a complete stranger to her, a slender man in his early twenties, with brown hair under his gray hat. Occasionally, he switched the urn from one hand to the other, carrying it lightly despite its size. People passed between them, and once she lost sight of him entirely, but as she reached the last, long descent of the main road that led toward the south gate, he crossed the street and fell into step beside her.

"Keep walking," he said.

"Who are you?"

He ducked his head and gave a lopsided smile. "Take a guess."

She stopped, staring at how his long bangs hid his eyebrows. His lively eyes regarded her with frank pleasure, as if he delighted in secrets, just the way her father always had.

Arthur? she wondered, speechless.

"Right," he said, nodding. "Your brother. Keep walking."

invitation

"CALL ME PYRHO," HE said, touching her elbow to turn her along the road again. "Mace sent me to look out for you. I've been watching that alley for hours. He thought you might need a little help getting out of the Enclave."

"He was right. Do you know where Leon is?"

"More or less. Keep moving."

"But where is he?" she demanded. "Is he still in here?"

"Yep."

"Is he okay? How can I find him?"

"I'd rather not get arrested with you right now," Pyrho said. "How about we get outside the wall and we'll discuss it all then?"

"Why do you have an urn?"

"It's an excuse. There's a guy outside the wall who repairs them. Coming?"

He kept up a steady pace, and she lengthened her stride to match his. The wall was getting closer now, casting a sharp shadow under the arch where several doctors were entering the Enclave, followed by men with boxes of supplies. The DNA registration must have continued in her absence, which either meant more of her people had been swabbed, or they'd contin-ued the charade they'd started the day before.

"Keep steady," Pyrho said. "Follow my lead."

As they reached the open area before the gate, one of the guards lifted a hand. "Hey, Pyrho," he said. "What's up? Will there be fireworks tonight with the party?"

"Not this time," Pyrho replied easily. "How's Lou? He's not still upset about losing his queen, is he?"

"No, he's good. You coming by for the tournament next week?" the guard asked. He eyed the urn.

"Sure enough. See you then."

"Who's this with you?" the guard said, coming nearer.

Gaia instinctively kept her face turned so her scar wouldn't be visible.

Pyrho spoke in his same unhurried, relaxed manner. "Show him your face, Stella. That's the point isn't it?"

With her heart thumping, Gaia turned to face the guard.

"Aren't you that midwife?" he asked, startled.

Pyrho laughed. "Perfect. It's for her psych assignment. She's supposed to see how people react to disfigurement. It's makeup."

The guard frowned, stepping nearer. "I think you overdid the ugliness," he said. "But otherwise it's pretty convincing."

"It should be. She worked on it long enough," Pyrho said. "Come on, Stella. We have to get going."

Gaia remembered Rita's advice and slightly lifted her chin, trying to look haughty. "I'm happy to serve the Enclave."

"As am I," said the guard. He tipped his hat and stepped back to let them pass.

The next moment, Gaia and her brother were under the arch and heading down the slope into Wharfton.

"That's the first time I've been disguised as myself," Gaia said.
"It worked, didn't it?" Pyrho said, smiling.

They turned in to Peg's Tavern, where friends from Wharfton and New Sylum alike squeezed into the room and called for ale. Gaia was welcomed back with hugs and scoldings, and news flew.

Gaia pulled Pyrho over to where sunlight fell cheerily through small, circular panes of window glass onto a scuffed table.

"Tell me about Leon? Do you know when he's coming back out?" she asked.

"He should be out soon. He was going to take Jack to his parents' place and tie up a couple loose ends. I checked in with Mace and then I was supposed to meet Leon out here," Pyrho said.

Gaia was not exactly reassured. "Was Leon behind the water shortage this morning?" she asked.

"He sure was," Pyhro said, smiling. "He wanted to play a trick on his father and mess with his head a little. He put a couple of his old comic books in his dad's bathroom sink, and then we rigged the water so it wouldn't come on. Anywhere."

Gaia could imagine how that would infuriate the Protectorat. Beyond the annoyance and disruption, it would also make him aware that Leon could get anywhere in the Bastion, even within the family's private quarters, so it would serve as a nasty threat.

"Did you say Jack was with you, too?" Dinah asked.

She and Peter joined their table. Norris swung open the nearest two windows to let in more air and light, and leaned against the sill. Myrna moved beside him, crossing her arms over her chest.

"Yep." Pyrho said. "Jack's not a hundred percent, but he

189

insisted on tagging along, just like a little brother. And you're our kid sister." He patted his hand on hers. "How very nice this is."

Pyrho had a way of smiling with closed lips that Gaia found reminiscent of their mother, and very dear.

"How long have you known?" she asked.

"The Protectorat sent for me to have some blood work done shortly after you left for the wasteland," Pyrho said. "When I snuck a peek at my file, I saw you listed as my sister. I thought that was cool. You're famous, you know."

"What about you, Gaia?" Will said. He passed her a steaming plate and hitched up a stool beside her. "What did you do in the Enclave?"

Gaia was famished, and the cheese omelet was unbelievably rich and buttery. She told about finding Angie at the Jacksons', and about getting lost in the tunnels. She glanced around the room for her old neighbors from Western Sector Three. "We have to get a message to Sasha's grandfather," she said, and explained about finding Sasha living in the tunnels.

Outrage swelled as more of the wharfton families realized their daughters might, like Sasha, be miserable with the Vessel Institute.

"There was a baby born today." Gaia added. "We can get another perspective from that mother, too, when she comes out soon."

"If half of the vessel mothers feel the way Sasha does, it will totally undermine the pilot program," Will said. "The institute won't be able to expand." He passed Gaia a napkin, smiling as he mimicked where she should dab at her chin. "You sure you're all right?" he asked.

She nodded, her mouth full. She swallowed and licked her

lips. "I'm exhausted. But mostly, I feel stupid for getting lost in the tunnels for so long. Tell me what I missed out here."

Around the table, people shared their news. Peter reported that the combined communities of Wharfton and New Sylum had held their water supply to a two-day cushion by curtailing washing and constantly drawing from the wall spigots. The Protectorat had not sent any other water supply out, even though the DNA registry, on paper, now looked complete. He hadn't sent out any correspondence, either, so negotiations were at a standstill. The Jackson family, tipped off that they were likely to be taken in for questioning, had walked out of the Enclave empty-handed and were staying with Derek's family. They'd brought Angie out with them, so she was safe, too. The miners had chosen a place to start their tunnel.

Gaia slumped back on her bench and moved her fork tines over her empty plate. "It sounds like you didn't need me out here at all," she said truthfully.

Will's hands were on the table beside her, where he'd been absently twisting a strand of twine between his fingers. At her words, his fingers went still. He turned to face her, his eyebrows lifting slightly. "You're quite wrong. You've been missed."

His quiet, serious expression held her for a moment, until she had to look away.

The barkeep arrived with a tray of pints, smaller than the normal tankards. "We're rationing," he said, before heading back to the bar.

Gaia turned again to her brother. "Does Leon know I was in the Enclave?" she asked.

"I don't see how he could," Pyrho said. "I had no idea myself until I found Mace and he told me."

Mace was involved now more than ever, Gaia thought. She recalled how he'd lost his older daughter to hemophilia, and wondered if he'd ever guessed how far that loss would ripple forward into his life.

"I wonder if you carry the anti-hemophilia gene," Gaia said to her brother.

"I don't," Pryho said. "They only found a handful of people who have it, from what I hear. Do you know if you do?"

Gaia nodded. "The Protectorat told me the other day."

Pyrho made a whistling noise. "He probably wants you to start having babies pronto. Has he invited you to come live inside the wall?"

Gaia felt many eyes focusing on her. What would her friends think if they knew the answer was *yes?* "I have no intention of moving inside the Enclave," she said.

"I was only going to say, if you and Leon ever need a place to stay inside, my parents and I would be happy to have you," Pyrho said. "That's if you don't want to stay at the Bastion. Our place isn't as fancy, obviously, but still."

Her gaze flew to his. "You are so nice," she said, touched by his generous offer. "My home's out here, though. With the people of New Sylum."

Peter straightened, catching her eye. "I'm glad you remembered us," he said. "You are not to go back into the Enclave without an escort. For any reason. That was a serious mistake."

He hadn't spoken loudly, but the chatter around the table fell silent.

"I know," she said. Under the table, she gripped her hands together hard. "I'm sorry. I shouldn't have left like that."

"You lied, Mlass Gaia," Peter said.

"I know," she said, ashamed. "I'm sorry."

The hum of voices gradually picked up again, but Gaia could barely bring herself to lift her gaze from her plate. When she did, Will was watching her with kind concern.

"You meant well," he said gently.

She let out a soft, pained laugh. "No. I messed up," she said.

He watched her steadily. "Then make it up to us," he said.

She would have to, somehow, she thought.

"What do you do for a living, Pyrho?" Peter asked.

"Fireworks," Pyrho said. "My family's had an exclusive contract with the Bastion for generations."

"So you know how to use explosives," Peter said.

Bill and several miners turned in Pyrho's direction.

Pyrho was nodding. "I've always liked blowing things up."

There was movement by the tavern door, and a pair of Enclave guards entered. Peter stood and drew his sword in one fluid movement, and half of the company reached for their arms. Gaia rose.

The Enclave guards slowly put their hands up.

"Take it easy," said Marquez, the man from the Protectorat's headquarters. "I just have a message for Masister Stone. That's all."

He gingerly lifted an envelope into the air. Peter took it and passed it over to Gaia.

"Thank you, Mabrother," she said. "You'd better go."

Marquez bowed briefly and took his companion out with him. Gaia fingered open the flap and slid out an invitation on heavy, cream-colored cardstock.

THE PROTECTORAT
AND
THE VESSEL INSTITUTE

KINDLY REQUEST YOUR ATTENDANCE AT THE
BIRTH CEREMONY
OF
THERESA SANNI GOADE
3.6 KILOS, 51.5 CM
AS SHE IS PRESENTED TO HER FATHER
MATTHEW ALOYSIUS GOADE
7:00 P.M.
THIS SECOND DAY OF OCTOBER
TWO-THOUSAND, FOUR HUNDRED AND TEN
BASTION OF THE ENCLAVE

In the corner, a handwritten note was scrawled:

*So looking forward to continuing our conversation.
Your fiancé sends his regards.
Yours,
Miles*

birth ceremony

"**T**HEY HAVE LEON," SHE said. It shouldn't have surprised her, but she felt stunned nevertheless.

She stared up at Peter, and then around, at the rest of her friends. They regarded her with obvious concern, and a sobering dose of caution.

Her resolve hardened. "We're going in for him."

"It's a trap, obviously," Peter said.

"I don't care."

"Mlass Gaia," Will said. "You just agreed it was a mistake for you to go in before. You can't go in again now."

"We're going in through the gate, on our own terms. You can come with me. I'll take as many scouts as you like. But we're going to be there at seven o'clock." She tossed the invitation onto the table. "The Protectorat has a hostage now. We're not leaving Leon in there."

The rest of the table erupted into plans and discussion.

"You're not going like that, are you?" Myrna asked, stepping around the table.

"What?" Gaia asked, looking down at her red dress.

"It's a formal invitation. They'll be dressed up," Myrna said.

Gaia laughed for the first time in ages. "I'm not going to socialize," she said.

"You're not going to serve them either, which is how it will look if you go to the Bastion dressed like that," Myrna stressed. "And you don't arrive at seven. You go at seven thirty or later if you're important."

These were niceties that wouldn't have occurred to Gaia. "You should come with me."

Myrna lifted her eyebrows. "I wasn't invited."

"So crash. You have influence with people, Myrna," Gaia said. "It's time to speak up. You should be at the Bastion."

"I need to still be here after the dust settles," Myrna said. "I'll stay out of it until the wounded need me. I assure you, the time will come."

"I'm not leading us towards violence." Gaia said.

"No? Don't deceive yourself," Myrna said. "And get yourself out of that red. You're no servant."

Gaia entered the Enclave for the third time since returning from the wasteland, this time by invitation, and escorted by Peter and a dozen scouts. The guards at the south gate stepped back respectfully.

"We've been expecting you, Masister Stone," one of them said, tipping his hat.

Behind him, Sergeant Burke was talking into a device, regarding Gaia with watchful eyes.

"It's still a trap," Peter said.

It didn't matter if was a trap. She had to go.

"You look very nice," Peter added.

She let out a laugh. She'd conceded to Myrna's advice by taking off Rita's red dress and donning clean clothes she'd worn as

Matrarc in Sylum: brown trousers and a white blouse. Josephine had insisted on loaning her a lightweight jacket of very soft leather, which hugged her slender arms and figure. What Gaia appreciated most, however, was a spare dagger Norris had given her for her boot. She knew she didn't look particularly dainty or nice, but with her clean face and freshly brushed hair, her necklace and Leon's bracelet, she felt like herself.

"Thanks," she said to Peter.

"No return compliment for me?" he asked.

She didn't bother to look at him. Peter looked good no matter what he did. It was a freakish fact of nature.

"No. Don't be annoying."

The rest of the escort was a couple paces behind, and Gaia glanced back to see they were looking around the city with interest.

"I can't help wondering," Peter said. "Do you enjoy having backups?"

"What do you mean?"

"If anything ever happened to your fiancé, do you think you'd pine away for him forever, or do you think you'd call up one of your spares?"

"Don't even *think* that," she said. "What an awful thing to say. That's sick."

"It's just honest."

"It's just sick."

"I guess that's an answer," he said.

She turned. "Malachai. Come up here with me," she said, and waited for the big man to step forward and walk between her and Peter.

"I get the point," Peter said dryly. "I apologize. Most sincerely."

You're supposed to be over me by now, she thought. He was

197

finally making it easier for her to dislike him, especially considering how worried she already was about Leon. She had to get him free from his father, and she had no idea where he even was. She refused to think he could be back in V cell.

Peter leaned around Malachai. "I said I'm sorry," he said once more.

"Fine."

They progressed steadily through the Enclave, up the main road, until they reached the terrace of the Bastion. Light streamed through the windows, and white-clad guests were passing in, bringing brightly wrapped gifts. Gaia could hear laughter and distant music.

When she moved toward the door, the butler Wilson greeted her and ushered her in with Peter and Malachai. The rest of her scouts filed in behind.

Ahead, guests were mingling in the great hall between the sweeping, curved double staircases. More were visible in the solarium beyond, and the music, nearer now, was a lively swing melody. Gaia spotted one of the pregnant women of the Vessel Institute in a white gown, her glimmering bracelet distinguishing her like a badge of honor among the other elegant, white-clad guests. Children in white party clothes and polished shoes were playing with a kitten at the base of the stairs. Two young women dressed in red cradled babies in their arms, and waiters in black were circulating with trays of drinks.

Wilson extended his arm toward a pair of footman. "Your guards might be more comfortable in the billiard parlor," he said.

Gaia's scouts were staring in open amazement. Nothing in their lives in Sylum had prepared them for the majestic scale and bright lights of the Bastion, and they were clearly dazzled. She'd felt something similar once.

"Peter and Malachai, stay with me," Gaia said. She spoke in a low voice to Peter. "They're not going to physically attack us among all their friends."

"You can go," Peter said, quietly gesturing the other scouts towards the footmen. They headed for an arched opening on the right,

"Gaia, you've arrived!" Genevieve said, coming forward with a broad smile. She passed her glass to Wilson and took both of Gaia's hands in her own. "Do come in. We have so many people who are anxious to meet you."

"Where's Leon?" Gaia asked.

"He's here somewhere," Genevieve said airily. Her golden curls were toppled on her head in an artful hairdo, and her white dress shimmered with a delicate design of gold. "You should have told us you were engaged! What a wonderful surprise."

"Did Evelyn tell you?" Gaia asked.

"No, Leon did himself. We wanted to wait until you were here with him so you could announce it together, but I'm afraid some little bird let it out of the bag and the gossip's already circulating," Genevieve said. "You've brought your friends?" she smiled pleasantly, turning to Peter and Malachai.

Gaia introduced them, and was impressed by Genevieve's cordial welcome.

"So handsome, my goodness," Genevieve said as she released Peter's hand. "Would you care for some punch or wine? Our chef makes a wonderfully festive punch with sorbet in it. You'd like it."

"I just want to see Leon," Gaia said.

"He was just here. Let me introduce you to some of our friends while we look for him." Genevieve drew Gaia toward the solarium, leaving Peter and Malachai to trail behind. "The Goades and the Rhodeskis are becoming grandparents tonight and they are thrilled. Such generous people, too. All the donors to the Vessel Institute are. They're wealthy beyond anything you can imagine and they've given countless sums to our latest new civic projects. As a matter of fact, they've taken a great interest in providing a pipeline for New Sylum. Here we are!"

Genevieve led them to the solarium, where Gaia paused on the threshold. On all four sides, every French door was open now, affording glimpses of more rooms beyond, and Gaia could see the farthest doors led into a larger room where the music originated. Ferns grew in lush fans around her, and palms reached high toward the glass panels of the ceiling above. Lovely as the interior garden was, Gaia was struck by how pitifully tame it was compared to the wild, teaming expanse of the Dead Forest and the marsh she'd left behind in Sylum.

Guests strolled through the verdant, inviting space in an ever-changing array of faces, including Masister Kohl, Tom and Dora Maulhardt, and others she recalled from before.

A strange thought hit her. Leon had grown up in this wealthy milieu, among these people. When he was disowned at sixteen, he'd left his family bitter and angry, but this was still his heritage. Civilized, elegant parties like this one had to be a formative part of his childhood, yet he almost never mentioned this part of his life. She could easily picture him here, but she couldn't find him.

A waiter offered her a small cup of a frothy, amber-colored drink. She took one from the tray, and Peter and Malachai followed her example. Her first cold sip was of tang and foam, and it slid down her throat like pure luxury.

"Do come," Genevieve said, drawing Gaia forward. "There's someone I want you to meet."

Gaia glanced back. A middle-aged, short man had paused to

talk to Peter, and Malachai lingered with him, looking rather awkward. He looked questioningly at Gaia, but she nodded for him to stay there.

Genevieve guided Gaia to an elderly man in a white jacket who was passing out lollipops to a couple of children. More of the candies bulged in his jacket pocket.

"Mabrother Rhodeski's about to become a grandfather," Genevieve said. "Isn't that marvelous?"

Mabrother Rhodeski straightened from the children and held out a hand to Gaia. His gaze flicked briefly over her scar, and when he smiled, his deeply set eyes gave the impression of both pleasure and ages of sadness. "I can't tell you how excited I am to meet you, Masister Stone," he said in a smooth bass voice.

"Mabrother Rhodeski's the heart and soul of the Vessel Institute," Genevieve added. "This is a very big day for him and his family. Congratulations again, Mabrother."

Gaia found it hard to believe this soft-spoken, kind-eyed man was the mastermind behind a heartless system, but then, she knew appearances could deceive. She wondered if he had any idea Sasha had defected and was living alone in a tunnel.

"Give us a few minutes," Mabrother Rhodeski said, his gaze never leaving Gaia.

"Of course! Take all the time you need," Genevieve said. "Where's your son?"

"Matt's with Vicki. Try in the ballroom," he said.

Gaia looked around again for Leon, wondering where he could be. Peter and Malachai were still in conversation near the door, and a waiter was passing them more punch.

"Please tell Leon I'm here," Gaia said to Genevieve.

"Of course," Genevieve said, heading in the direction of the music.

"I don't supposed you'd care for a lollipop," Mabrother Rhodeski asked Gaia, offering.

"How can you support the Vessel Institute?" Gaia asked in a low, urgent voice. "Are you aware of what it's doing to some of the pregnant girls? Do you realize where Sasha is at this very moment?"

"This is a bit awkward, actually," Mabrother Rhodeski said. The elusive sadness in his eyes deepened further. "I'd hoped to have time to explain things for you very carefully and give you all sorts of back story, but as things have developed, with the baby being born today, we'll need to capitalize on the publicity."

"Is that right? Does Sasha's scandal merit some publicity?"

"Please," he said simply.

The man took her elbow, turning her toward a trickling fountain. Votive candles had been spaced along the stone path, and a dense patch of irises grew in a raised bed, their delicate blossoms deeply purple. She glanced back to see Peter and Malachai were still clearly in sight and atuned to her movement.

"You look like you're about the same age my daughter Nicole was when she died," Mabrother Rhodeski said. "She had hemophilia. Are you seventeen?"

"Yes. I'm sorry about your daughter," Gaia said.

"She was a gift, every single minute of her life." He tilted his face slightly. "My daughter died ten months ago. I often wonder what she would think of all the changes that have happened since then."

Even as she was wary of being manipulated, Gaia couldn't help but be sorry for him. She guessed, from his age, that he must have had his daughter quite late in life. "Did you try Myrna's blood bank for her?"

He nodded. "We did. We're very grateful to Myrna. But

something went wrong with bleeding during Nicole's menstrual cycle. We could do very little besides keep her from feeling too much pain near the end." He smiled briefly, shaking his head. "She was such a forward-looking person. She would be so happy about this day."

"When you become grandparents," Gaia said.

"Yes, you see, Nicole married her childhood sweetheart," Mabrother Rhodeski said. "Matt's like a son to us now. He was the one who first came up with the idea of keeping part of her alive. After Nicole died, we had her eggs harvested."

Gaia couldn't hide her surprise, and then she started putting together his information with what Emily had told her. "That's how you had eggs to implant in the surrogate mothers," she said. She hadn't considered that aspect before.

Mabrother Rhodeski nodded. "They're Nicole's eggs. We were able to save only a dozen. We'd never done anything like it before, but we fertilized them with Matt's sperm. Tonight, we're getting Nicole and Matt's biological child, our very own granddaughter. Can you imagine what this means to us?"

It was no less than getting a baby out of a grave. "It must change your lives," she said.

His smile was radiant with pleasure. "It's like getting a piece of Nicole back, but new. A new life. I can't describe it. It's unbelievable."

Gaia looked down at the lollipops the man still held in his fingers. He'd had to invent the Vessel Institute to make it possible. "Was it worth it?" she asked.

"The cost? Of course it was, but please don't misunderstand," he said. "The Vessel Institute isn't only for my family. There are hundreds of parents all over the Enclave who long desperately to have their own children. Infertility is a problem that breaks hearts here, month after month, every time a couple tries to conceive and can't. We've finally found a way to do something about it." He paused. "You don't look very happy."

"It's wrong," Gaia said, thinking of Sasha. "The pilot program is nothing more than a whitewashed prison full of brainwashed prisoners."

"It's life," Mabrother Rhodeski said. "We're paying for life."

"You're buying life. It's different. And what about Sasha?"

Mabrother's eyes deepened once more with sadness. "I'm sorry for Sasha. If you know where she is, I hope you'll urge her to come into the open. She needs care. She's very confused."

Gaia let out a short laugh. "She doesn't want to give up her baby. She's very clear about that."

"You know this? You've actually spoken to her?"

"Yes."

"Then tell her the parents of her promised baby will do anything to have her safely deliver their child," Mabrother Rhodeski said. "They'll give up custody, they'll pay for the child's upkeep and education. They'll do anything if only their child can live."

Gaia stared at him, amazed. "She thinks she'll be killed if she's found," she said.

Mabrother Rhodeski shook his head. "We're about life, Masister Stone. Not killing."

Gaia glanced around to see much of the solarium had emptied out and the music had stopped. She looked past Mabrother Rhodeski's shoulder for Peter, who was still talking to another guest by the doorway. She couldn't see Malachai.

"It's time for the ceremony!" a young boy called, running past the fountain with two little girls in tow.

"We're coming," Mabrother Rhodeski said.

Gaia was unable to reconcile Mabrother Rhodeski's version of the truth with Sasha's. "Someone's lying," she said.

"Or someone's mistaken and confused," Mabrother Rhodeski said. "It's understandable, but we can find solutions if we talk to each other."

"Talking is what I've been trying to do. It hasn't worked so far," she said.

Mabrother Rhodeski looked concerned. "I understand that the Protectorat has not treated your people the way he should. I'd like to change that for you. I'd prefer to avoid problems like this morning's disruption of the city's water, too. I can arrange a pipeline for New Sylum, but more than that, I'd like to build you a waterworks system of your own outside the wall. Then you won't be dependent on the Enclave for water."

Gaia's was surprised. The cost of such a project would be astronomical. "I already told the Protectorat I'm not interested in being a vessel mother," she said. "I don't want any part of the Vessel Institute."

"I'm not asking you to be a vessel mother," Mabrother Rhodeski said. "That's not what this is about."

A voice called to him from the ballroom.

"Then what?" Gaia asked.

Mabrother Rhodeski held up a hand apologetically. "I won't rush this. I'm terribly sorry. I need to join my family now. But I'm delighted to know you're open to talking. Shall we?" He gestured toward the ballroom.

Gaia looked back over her shoulder uneasily. Peter nodded as she caught his eye. "Go ahead," she said to Mabrother Rhodeski. "Please."

Mabrother Rhodeski smiled again, leaving as Peter came forward to join her.

"Malachai's looking for Leon and checking on the others," Peter said.

"I don't think Leon's here," Gaia said.

All the guests were moving to the next room, and with a last hope of finding Leon in the crowd, she followed along.

The center of the ballroom had been cleared, and people stood in a loosely formed circle. In the middle, a young woman sat in a wheelchair, holding a baby. Her cheeks were delicately pink, her hair was neatly parted, and she was dressed in a soft white gown. When she reached nervously to tuck a lock of her dark hair behind her ear, the gesture highlighted her bracelet, which glowed blue and glittered with hints of gold.

The other vessel mothers were gathered around, conspicuous with their rotund bellies and matching bracelets. They were smiling with different degrees of serenity and pleasure, beautifully dressed, radiating health. Emily stood among them, an infant in her arms and a toddler at her feet. If Gaia hadn't seen Sasha with her own eyes and spoken to her, she would never guess that at least half of the vessel mothers secretly regretted joining the Vessel Institute.

Behind the wheelchair stood a calm, smiling woman in pale blue, and Gaia took a moment to recognize Sephie Frank, one of the doctors she'd first met in Q cell. To Sephie's left, Mabrother Rhodeski held hands with a woman about his own age, and beside them, the Protectorat was making a speech. It struck Gaia that he never mentioned the vessel mother's name, calling her instead "Our little vessel mother" with great warmth. A young man, apparently Mabrother Rhodeski's son-in-law Matt, leaned over the mother's wrist, and with a golden scissors, he clipped her bracelet free and lifted it high. The crowd applauded.

Matt passed the bracelet to Mabrother Rhodeski, and next he held out his hands towards the baby.

Under her rouge, the vessel mother's cheeks turned bloodlessly pale. Her profile was aimed down toward the child on her lap so that her dark hair partly obscured her face. Though Matt was clearly speaking to her, she remained still as if she had gone suddenly strengthless. The Protectorat said something and the crowd laughed uneasily. Matt leaned nearer, which let his tie fall forward above her knee. Then the mother lifted the newborn off her lap. It was hardly more than a centimeter, not even enough to clear the baby's blanket from her knees. Matt slid his hands around the child then, and lifted her close against his own chest. He took a half step backward and dipped his head over the baby, cradling her close. The crowd waited, patently expecting something more, but when Matt simply stood there, holding his infant daughter, the hushed moment expanded into something raw and painfully private.

A faint breeze stirred through the still room.

More than one person quietly looked away. Mabrother Rhodeski stepped nearer to put a hand on his son's back, and Matt turned mutely into his father's embrace. Others circled around them then, and with a great release of collective breath, the audience tentatively applauded a second time.

Waiters began passing out glasses in preparation for a toast. The vessel mother's head sagged forward and her hands went limp on her lap. Sephie quietly wheeled her out of the room.

Gaia took a step back, wanting Peter, and bumped into Mabrother Iris instead.

"Quite a touching scene, wasn't it?" he asked. He lifted a cup of punch in a jaunty little motion.

"Where's Peter?" she asked, scanning the doorways in alarm. There were guests everywhere, but none of her people.

"He ducked out, I'm afraid."

She backed away from him. "I have to find Leon."

"Don't you want to know what Mabrother Rhodeski wants from you?" Mabrother Iris asked.

"It doesn't matter," she said, shaking her head.

"Not even in exchange for water for New Sylum? It would have to be something incredibly valuable to be worth such a price."

"You don't know what you're talking about," she said, backing away.

"I think you know, anyway," Mabrother Iris said. "You heard the story of Nicole. Remember my pig?"

Gaia's feet froze to the floor. Mabrother Iris started nodding.

"We want your eggs," Mabrother Iris said. "Your ovaries, to be exact. Of course, Nicole had to die before we could take hers, but maybe we'll get lucky with you."

It was such a preposterous idea that Gaia could hardly process his words.

"You can't take my ovaries," she said. Such a surgery to extract them wasn't possible, and even if it was, she could never have children of her own if they took her ovaries.

Mabrother Iris was smiling his small, cold smile. "We've been practicing."

CHAPTER 17

the sleeper in the tower

GAIA BACKED UP A step and inadvertently bumped into a waiter, whose tray went crashing to the floor. Punch cups and wine glasses scattered in shards and a splash of punch spattered the sleeve of her jacket.

Guests turned to see the commotion, and the Protectorat came forward with long strides, reaching to steady her. "Are you all right?"

"Yes," Gaia said, practically hissing, and flinched away. "Where are my people? Where's Leon?"

The Protectorat's eyes flickered, but he answered with a calm smile. "I'll take you to him." He pressed a handkerchief into her hand and turned to Mabrother Iris. "Ask Sephie Frank to join us at her earliest convenience."

Onlookers were watching the exchange curiously, and the waiter was clearing up the debris as rapidly as he could. Gaia wiped at her sleeve and strode toward the entrance hall.

"Where did you put my scouts?" she demanded.

"They had too much to drink," the Protectorat said. "We found it best to remove them before they disturbed our other guests."

"You drugged them?"

"That, too. This way." He turned up one of the great, curving staircases.

She had been half afraid he would lead her down, to the cellar and the secret passageway that connected to the prison. "Leon's upstairs?" she asked, suspicious.

"He's in his room. Resting."

From the top of the stairs, the Protectorat gestured for her to precede him down a long corridor, and they left the decrescendo of party sounds behind them. The next hallway was smaller, befitting a more private section of the Bastion, and after several more turns, he guided her up a spiral staircase. Unlike the tower her mother had been imprisoned in, this one was lit better, and the triangular landings were clean and broad.

"I saw you talking to Mabrother Rhodeski," the Protectorat said. "Did he outline his offer to you?"

"Mabrother Iris told me. If you think there's any chance I'll let you take my ovaries, you're wrong," Gaia said.

"You should think it over," the Protectorat said. "You might want to consider Leon's perspective."

"He'd never let me take such a risk. Why do you want mine, anyway? I know I have the anti-hemophilia gene, but I can't be the only one. What's so special about me?"

He stopped before a wooden door inlaid with iron scrollwork, and turned to her. "The gene has turned out to be exceptionally rare. We're lucky we ever found it at all. It must be a fairly recent mutation. So far, we've found only nine other people with the anti-hemophilia gene, despite analyzing DNA from thousands of people inside and outside the wall. All nine are women. The problem is, we can't operate on any of the others."

"Why not?"

"One has a heart condition. One is diabetic. Another has an allergy to the narcotic we'd use for the surgery," he said. "The remaining six have families who refuse to let them take the risk, for any price. The chance of fatality is too high."

"You mean the surgery's too deadly? It's essentially a death sentence?"

His eyes narrowed slightly. "No. It's a calculated risk, but not a death sentence."

"Just admit you want to kill me for my ovaries," Gaia said coldly. "Why do you even need my consent?"

"My wife and Mabrother Rhodeski seem to think it's necessary."

With a light tap, he opened the door and gestured her in.

She hesitated on the threshold, wary, but it was an airy, high-ceilinged bedroom with a patterned carpet and tall windows that were open to the night breeze. Sparsely furnished, austerely devoid of personal items, the space was still luxurious in its simplicity. A tapestry of a forest scene lined one wall, a globe of the world was poised to spin in a cherry-colored stand, and a telescope was pointed out the window toward the north. A male nurse rose from behind a desk and nodded respectfully to the Protectorat, who waved him back down.

Gaia came further in. A canopied bed with yellow curtains drawn back in heavy, swooping loops stood in the far corner, and as Gaia saw the figure lying on the covers, her heart dove. Leon lay on his back, sleeping. His left arm was tied to a bar at the side of the bed, and above the bar, a translucent bag hung on a rod, with a line of tubing running down to a needle that was taped into a vein inside the crook of his elbow. His right arm was bent and wrapped securely in an immobilizing splint.

He was dressed in white, and neatly shaven. Two spots of

bright color rode high on his cheeks, and his lips were redder than normal, as if his inner system were working at a fever pitch while outwardly, his chest moved in regular, deep breaths of sleep.

She came nearer still, and she was unable to resist touching her knuckles to his cheek. A blossom of purple bruised his forehead and ringed his right eye, while in the center of the bruise, a small, deep cut had been closed with four stitches.

She turned to look back at the Protectorat. "What did you do to him?"

"We saved his life, obviously," he said, adjusting a lamp so light fell more clearly on the bed. "He was trying to run across a water main between the roofs of two buildings and he fell. Hit his head."

Gaia moved around the bed, scanning Leon's face closely from the other side, and gently joggled his shoulder. "Leon," she said softly. "Can you hear me? Wake up." He didn't move. She drew his fingers into hers, but though they were warm, they were as unresponsive as clay. "Is he in pain? What's in this?" she asked, flicking the IV drip.

"It's hard to know how much he's suffering," the Protectorat said. "You wouldn't know the drug. It's a narcotic we've been developing for various surgeries. We can keep him out indefinitely."

The Enclave didn't have a hospital, and the last Gaia knew, medical care had been limited to setting bones, sewing stitches, assisting births, prescribing morphine and antibiotics, and the occasional appendectomy, yet the Protectorat spoke as if surgeries were now routine.

"You can keep him out for days?" she asked.

He nodded. "He'd get hungry, of course, if we do. There isn't any nutrition there."

She caught the irony of it. The Protectorat had made certain Leon was stitched up after his fall, but he could also keep Leon in a coma and slowly kill him by starvation.

"Perhaps you can see now why I wanted you to consider Leon's perspective on your ovaries," he added. "We would really like your consent and cooperation."

She got it, then. Mabrother Rhodeski wanted a fair exchange: her ovaries for water. The Protectorat was adding his own private twist to the screw: cooperate or Leon will pay.

"It isn't consent if I'm blackmailed," she said. "Wake him up." She reached for the IV.

"I wouldn't do that," the Protectorat said. "It's a delicate process to bring him around. He'll have the devil's own headache. Mabrother Stoltz," he said, turning toward the nurse behind the desk. "See what's keeping Sephie Frank, please."

As the man left, the Protectorat walked over beside the mantel. He nodded toward the bed. "He looks so harmless this way. You'd never guess what he's capable of. That was a nice touch of his with the comic books in the sink this morning. He had me going."

"You lied about helping with water for New Sylum," she said.

"You wasted our time and resources with that farce of a DNA registry," he said. "It will take us forever to figure out the duplications. It would almost be easier to start over."

"You're the one who lied first," she countered.

"So that entitles you to retaliate? To sabotage our water?"

"We wanted to get your attention."

She could feel the Protectorat regarding her closely, even with the distance between them.

"That wasn't your idea, was it?" the Protectorat said, his voice lifting in surprise. "Of course not. That was pure Leon.

Bear in mind that you're accountable for what your people do. There are repercussions, especially when you sic terrorists on innocent people."

"Leon is hardly a terrorist," she said.

"You really don't understand what you're dealing with in him, do you?" The Protectorat lifted a hand in a slow wave. "Look at this room. Leon chose this bedroom when he was ten years old. It's precisely the way it was when he left us to enter the guard. It never looked any different. Is this the bedroom of a normal child?"

Gaia looked around again with new eyes. The lack of personal items took on a different significance now. There were no books or gadgets, no old bird's nests, games, or mementos.

"It's so Spartan," she murmured, absently touching the string bracelet on her wrist.

It hurt to imagine Leon growing up in this sterile place, choosing it. She thought of how gentle he was with her, how deeply he'd craved her trust. Her gaze lit on the telescope, with its implied yearning to see beyond these walls, and with aching insight, she guessed he'd kept himself bereft as a boy because that was how he'd felt.

"He's a cold-hearted boy and he always was," the Protectorat said. "He never kept any comforting little things around him like the other kids. No stuffed animals or favorite books. It's not too late to change your mind about marrying him. I'd think better of you if you did."

But the Protectorat was wrong. Gaia had seen things Leon had treasured as a child, now decaying and chewed in the tunnel where he had played with Fiona. He'd had to keep them safely hidden. She turned her gaze on the man who'd raised him, and who'd beaten him just enough so that he could never be certain when it would happen next.

"He's different now," Gaia said.

The Protectorat paced to the other side of the bed and his mouth hardened into a line. "People don't change that much. He cheated and picked fights when he was in school routinely. By fourth grade, he was stealing from our friends' homes. He broke into a café once and stole enough liquor to get his entire soccer team drunk. They were twelve years old. The very next day, I found him slaughtering chickens for the cook, just because he enjoyed the job."

Gaia shook her head in disbelief. "There had to be explanations. He's not like that. Did you listen to his side of things before you beat him?"

"He could talk, all right. He had his mother and his sisters and half of the staff wrapped around his finger." The Protectorat's voice lifted in false sympathy. " 'Poor little Leon. You're so hard on him, Miles!' " He stopped. "And beat him? I might have slapped him a couple times to get his attention. He's such a liar. I'm the only one who saw him for who he was, and even so, *even so*, I kept trying with him. Kept giving him one more chance." He turned away and gave the globe an impatient spin. "I'll never forgive myself for not protecting Fiona from him."

Gaia felt something go quiet inside as his words caught at her for the first time. She disliked and distrusted the Protectorat, but she couldn't ignore the loss of a heart-broken father.

"I'm sorry about Fiona," she said. "From what I hear, she was an amazing girl. I know Leon misses her terribly."

He glanced back up at her, his face impassive. "Leon wouldn't know how to miss a dog."

She felt as if he'd slapped her. "I need to talk to him. Take him off the drugs." She reached for Leon's IV.

"Don't. You can't just pull that out. He has to be tapered off."

215

A brief knock was followed by Mabrother Stoltz, who held the door for Sephie Frank.

"Let the doctor do it," the Protectorat said. He straightened and checked his watch. "Bring him around for Gaia to talk to, but don't let him get agitated," he said to Sephie. "You can fill her in about how you'll extract her ovaries. I've neglected my guests far too long."

"My answer is no," Gaia said.

The Protectorat paused by the door, a hand poised on his hip. "We can fertilize your live human eggs, let them divide a few times, and then separate them to grow into blastocysts. We'll screen those to be sure they've inherited your anti-hemophilia gene and bingo. I'm not talking about one or two children any-more, here. I'm talking about implanting your eggs into dozens of vessel mothers, maybe hundreds. Anyone who can pay a premium for a child can have one, guaranteed free of hemophilia. That's worth something, don't you think?"

"You're forgetting. There won't be any Vessel Institute when people hear about how you treated Sasha."

The Protectorat waved a dismissive finger. "A blip. She's one failure. We'll triple what we pay the others and screen more carefully. I have no doubts about finding enough new vessel mothers."

Gaia was still trying to grasp the scale of his plan. "The ba-bies from my eggs would all be twins, or quadruplets, or what-ever."

"Some would. Others would be half siblings."

"But why mine?" she asked.

"I already told you," he said. "Your genes are extraordinarily rare, and you yourself are expendable."

"I am not! New Sylum needs me."

"New Sylum needs *water*," the Protectorat corrected her. "Isn't that worth some sacrifice? Let me spell it out for you. Risk the surgery, donate your children to the Vessel Institute, and we'll give you the water you need for everyone outside the wall. Presuming you survive, I will personally dance with you at your wedding to Leon. If you refuse, your people can die of thirst and Leon will remain in our tender care." He hitched his white jacket straight on his shoulders. "Or not so tender. You can probably guess which option I prefer, but I have financial backers to please."

In furious silence, Gaia sat beside Leon, holding his hand, while Sephie Frank adjusted the dosage of narcotic in his drip.

"How long until he's off it?" Gaia asked.

"He'll come around in about fifteen minutes, I expect," Sephie said, and touched him gently on the shoulder.

Gaia studied Sephie's features, remembering how the doctor's serene, wide-spaced gray eyes and little mouth had once made her think of the moon. Now it seemed to her that Sephie's gentleness was nothing more than a tool she could manipulate.

In concise terms, Sephie explained the experiments she'd performed. Efforts to harvest individual eggs, leaving the ovaries intact to produce more, had proven disastrous, and countless animal subjects had died. She had discovered it was better to extract intact ovaries, and her subjects lived. She'd learned to inject her subjects in advance with a boost of hormones to ripen the ovaries. Then a clean cut into the abdomen, a quick extraction of the ovaries, and concentrated doses of antibiotics had resulted in dozens of successful surgeries on pigs and dogs.

"So I'd be your first live human subject," Gaia said.

"Yes."

"And I could die."

"I don't think you would," Sephie said. "It's a risk, though."

"And I could never have any children of my own."

Sephie hesitated. "Not in the normal way, but just think, Gaia. You'd be the mother of hundreds. And consider the other possibilities. With frozen blastocysts, a father could have a family of genetically identical children, triplets or quadruplets born at different times, spaced out over years."

Gaia straightened and pushed the yellow bed curtain farther back, with a rattling of its rings. "What good is that? You won't get genetic diversity that way," Gaia said.

"Genetic diversity is not the problem I've been set to solve," Sephie said. "That can come in time. Getting around the problem of infertility has been my goal, and I've done it. But who wants to go through all the complications of surrogate pregnancy only to have a child that will die soon of hemophilia? If you could see all the children's funerals I've been to this last year. It's awful."

"Then why doesn't the Protectorat work with Myrna Silk? Why not find a cure for hemophilia?"

"There *is* no cure. You don't think we've looked? Myrna's blood transfusions only postpone the inevitable. The real solution is to prevent the hemophilia in the first place. It keeps coming back to you."

"No."

Sephie tilted the lamp shade so it wasn't on Leon's face. "At least think about it. Even your blood type is perfect. With you as O neg, we only need to consider the father's blood type when we choose whose womb to implant the blastocysts in. You're the ideal mother."

218

Gaia wasn't going to argue anymore. "Why is this taking so long with Leon?" Instinctively, she took his pulse, checking the seconds on her locket watch as she counted the sluggish beats of his heart. His chest rose and fell in a steady rhythm, and his eyelids remained smooth in dreamless sleep, like a cursed prince in a fairy tale.

Sephie checked the drip again. "He should be around very soon. Be patient." She faced Gaia. "Incidentally, we could do your surgery anytime, but tomorrow or the next day would be ideal. You were injected with a slow-release hormone when you arrived in the Enclave," Sephie said. "With a kicker, we can have you ovulating within hours. That's when it would be best to harvest your ovaries."

"I said no."

"But wouldn't you do it, for Leon's sake?" Sephie asked.

"Of course I would. But I'd have to trust the Protectorat to keep the bargain, and that will never happen."

"Mabrother Rhodeski and Genevieve can keep him honest," Sephie said.

"What happened to you?" Gaia asked. "When I knew you in Q cell, you were a good doctor."

"I'm still a good doctor. Better than I ever was." Sephie motioned to Mabrother Stoltz. "Give me a hand here and restrain his legs."

"Is that necessary?" Gaia asked.

"He was not the most compliant patient before we put him under," Sephie said. "I don't want him hurting himself when he comes to."

The nurse efficiently wrapped a restraint around Leon's ankles, propped him more upright, and settled a pillow under his broken arm. He checked the restraint on Leon's left arm. Then Mabrother

219

Stoltz and Sephie moved back behind the desk and conferred in soft voices over the computer.

Gaia sat on the edge of the bed and held Leon's left hand, careful not to disrupt the IV. "Leon," she whispered.

Leon's dark lashes were motionless along his cheeks, his eyebrows faintly curving. Tenderness curled through her. She'd seen him sleeping before, but in natural sleep his features were always a ready instant away from mobility, warm with an endearing quality she couldn't identify. Now his stillness seemed too deep.

What if she really had to make a sacrifice to get him free?

Leon rolled his face toward the window, where the night breeze still drifted in.

"Leon," Gaia said, leaning near anxiously. "It's me, Gaia. Can you hear me?"

Leon's eyes blinked heavily, and Gaia gingerly touched the hair over his forehead, careful not to bump his stitches. His gaze met hers for a searching moment. "No," he said, his voice cracking.

Gaia's heart slammed against her ribs. She squeezed his hand and reached for cup of water. "Drink this," she said, trying to smile. "We have to talk." She pressed the end of the straw between his lips. "Please, Leon," she whispered. "Stay with me."

She watched the liquid draw up the straw and then his throat worked in several swallows. He opened his lips to release the straw. Stirring, he turned his gaze to his restrained feet and arm, his other splinted arm, and then back to Gaia.

"Have they hurt you?" he asked.

"No," she said. "But look at you. Did you really fall from a water pipe?"

His was looking past her now, his eyes skimming the room. A soft curse passed his lips. "It's night already. Have you seen Pyrho or Jack? Is Angie safe?"

Gaia glanced over her shoulder, and then kept her voice low. "Angie left the Enclave with Mace's family, and Pyrho's outside the wall, too. I haven't seen Jack since yesterday morning."

Leon nodded slightly. "What time is it?"

"Eleven, why?" she said, glancing at her locket watch.

He frowned at her. "Eleven exactly? You're sure? An explosion is coming in about ten minutes, and when it does, promise me you'll leave in the commotion."

"I'm not leaving you here in an explosion," she said. "Don't be ridiculous."

"This will be a minor one still, but it will cause a distraction. You can escape."

"What have you done?"

Leon gave a tight, grim smile. "A series of explosions has already started by now, and they're set to get worse. The only way to stop them is for the Protectorat to negotiate with us."

"He can't negotiate with us if you're in a coma," she said.

"So tell him to let me go. That can be one of your conditions."

"I'm getting you out of here myself," she said.

He nodded conspicuously at his bindings. "Is that right? You're doing a good job of it so far. What are you even doing here?" he asked. "You're supposed to be outside the wall."

"So are you, remember?" Gaia said. "Things have gotten really complicated."

She reached for the binding on his wrist to untie it.

Sephie left her desk and started over. "I can't have you doing that. Mabrother?" she added, summoning the nurse.

The lights went out and the room was doused in darkness.

Gaia momentarily froze, blinded, then reached into her boot for her dagger and spun to put herself between the bed and Sephie. As Gaia's eyes adjusted, she saw a faint, eerie glow through the windows, but it barely penetrated the room. In the distance, she could hear a commotion of voices, and then there was a bumping noise by the desk.

"What's going on?" Sephie asked. A tapping noise suggested she was trying the keyboard of the computer. "Mabrother Iris?"

"Cut me loose," Leon said quietly. "Gaia. Now."

Gaia was peering toward Sephie, trying to make out where the doctor was. The shadows near the desk were impenetrable. Gaia took a step forward, squinting, and caught a whisper of movement. A pounding weight slammed down on Gaia's shoulder. She rolled instinctively into the blow, ducking her head to dive into her attacker's solid masculine body and shove him off balance. As he fell, she spun around with her dagger, anticipating a second assailant, and her blade caught flesh. Gaia's leg was jerked out from beneath her, but she took Sephie down with her as she fell. Sephie hit the floor hard with a wordless grunt, and Gaia redirected yet again, swiftly slashing out toward Mabrother Stoltz.

Warm liquid sprayed across her hand, and a gurgling came in the darkness. Gaia gave the dagger a savage twist, shoved him off, and closed again on Sephie. The older woman flailed beneath her, but Gaia grabbed her hair and slammed her head against the carpet. The woman's body went stiff, and next began to relax, unresisting.

Gasping, Gaia pushed off from the floor and backed against the bed.

"Tell me that's you," Leon said.

"It's me."

222

"Did you kill them?" Leon asked.

"Maybe. I don't know," Gaia said listening for movement. Her dagger was slippery in her hand.

A wrenching noise came from the bed. "I can't undo my wrist," Leon said. "Hurry. One of them might come around."

By touch, she cut his bindings and helped him off the bed, drawing his good arm around her shoulder. He was heavy and clumsy on his feet, and she could feel him stumbling as they hurried toward the door. She shoved it open to find the stairwell was a void of black.

"I can't see a thing," she said.

"I have the rail," he said. "I know the way."

"But your arm's broken."

When she slid her foot forward, she couldn't find an edge, and she didn't want to catapult down the spiral stairs. He tugged her toward him, pinning her against his left side. "Trust me, Gaia. Hold on," he said, and then she felt his torso twist as he used both hands on the railing. She gripped him around the waist and kept her other arm out before her in the air, feeling the emptiness for a wall or shadow or anything as they descended. Trying to open her eyes wider made no difference at all.

"What happened to the electricity?" she asked.

"I blew up a couple of fuse boxes," he said. "With a timer."

"Is all of the Bastion out?" Gaia asked.

"About a quarter of the city, everything from the Bastion up over summit park."

"A couple of fuse boxes did that much?" Gaia asked.

"They were at a power station. They'll be able to get it up again pretty soon once they find the damage. It was just to give them an idea what we can do. Ouch!"

"What did you hit?"

223

"My toe. Come on."

A moment later, they were down another flight, and hinges squeaked when Leon pushed open a door. Cooler air touched her face as he pulled her into a long corridor with windows arching in the wall to her left. They let in only the faintest light, but it was enough to orient her, and she drew Leon's arm over her shoulder again. He was panting heavily, and she could tell the dregs of the narcotic still lingered in his veins.

A flicker of candlelight showed around the corner ahead.

"Someone's coming!" she said.

"I see. Quick, over here." He pulled her into a small bay that bulged off the hallway, and shoved open a window. He started to climb out.

"You've got to be kidding," Gaia said.

"It's not much of a jump," he said. "Hang by your hands as low as you can go. I'll catch you."

"You only have one good arm!"

She peeked her head back into the hall. The candlelight was coming closer, fast, and a man shouted.

"Hurry!" Leon called.

She stuck her head out and found him already below, waiting with his one good hand up. *Like that'll do much good*, she thought, and scrambled out the window backward, lowering herself down as far as she could with her belly against the masonry. She pushed off the wall and fell toppling onto Leon. He crumpled to the ground, and her elbow jammed into the earth.

"Good?" he asked, hauling her up.

"Never better," she said, cringing with pain, and rolled onto pavement. They'd made it to street level.

He was already leading her away again, moving lightly, and she noticed that he was barefoot. When she turned back for a look at the Bastion, it was entirely dark. Guests, musicians, and servants from the party were swarming in the streets while emergency personnel pushed through. She had no idea where Peter and the others might be. The surrounding houses were lightless, too, but Leon was faintly visible in his white clothes.

He was still panting, and at the end of the street, farther from the chaos, he stopped to brace himself against a building.

"Sorry," he said. "I've got a wicked headache."

"Let me see your arm," she said, tugging at his sleeve. He tilted his head back against the wall. He'd ripped his IV out of his arm, she saw, and there was blood running from the vein inside his elbow.

"You're ruining your pretty clothes," she said. She instinctively searched her pockets and came up with the Protectorat's handkerchief. She folded it quickly and pressed the soft material against his lesion. "It's a little wound," she said. "Hold this here until it stops bleeding." Then she realized his other splinted arm prevented him from holding his own elbow. "Never mind, I've got it," she said, and gently squeezed the nook of his arm.

He put his broken arm awkwardly around her, and she leaned up for a kiss.

"You came for me," he said.

"I don't know. I couldn't think."

She instinctively hugged him closer.

"What did you expect?"

"We can't stay here." he said. "I have a way out. Come on, this way."

"How? Not the tunnels, please."

"I had a day here before I was caught. Enough time to set up a couple escape hatches. You'll see."

Before long, they were sneaking between the rows of the

vineyard and using a ladder to scale the western wall, far from any tower or rampart. They hauled the ladder over and used it down the other side of the wall, to the steep, scabby hillside that dropped into the darkness of the wasteland.

They'd arrived again, back outside the wall.

CHAPTER 18

secrets

GAIA WOKE BESIDE LEON, with her head on his left shoulder and his splinted right arm resting lightly on top of her. As she shifted, his eyes opened, very near, and he smiled.

"Will it always be this hard to get you alone?" he asked slowly.

She curled her fingers into the white fabric of his shirt. "You are such a mess. How's your headache?"

"A little better. You look very nice with sand in your hair, by the way."

As she rolled upward on her elbow, her necklace slid sideways around her neck. His left sleeve was dirty with dried blood, but his IV hole had scabbed over. His stitches looked all right, too, she decided. Sunlight was coming over the edge of the ravine where they'd taken shelter, but half a kilometer to the east, up the ridge, the western wall of the Enclave was still a band of brown shadow. Without rising, Leon reached to pull a bit of something from her hair, sliding it down a long lock.

Dried blood still stained her hand, and she wondered if she'd really killed in the darkness the night before.

"I think I killed Sephie and Mabrother Stoltz, that nurse," she said. Another thought occurred to her. "I didn't throw up after."

"You didn't have time to throw up."

"But I should feel worse," she said.

"I don't see that you had a choice. They attacked you in the dark."

She licked her tongue around her teeth, trying to work up some saliva in her dry mouth. "I'm not sure I like what's happening to me."

He watched her, waiting, his blue eyes steady. She was afraid he'd say something more about how it wasn't her fault. She'd trained to be able to defend herself, to fight if she had to. But this was the first time she'd had to do it so decisively. At the time, she hadn't even questioned it.

But now, she didn't like thinking of the noise Sephie's head had made banging on the carpet. she cringed.

"It's confusing," she said.

"I know." Leon ran a finger down her arm, to her red bracelet. "Would you do it again? The same thing if it happened?"

Slowly, she nodded. "I guess I would."

She studied his features: the faintly arching eyebrows, the straight nose, the set of his mouth and jawline. He had a way of watching her with his intense eyes that reached straight to the depths of her, bringing the truth there without a word.

"There's something else bothering you, too. Isn't there?" he said.

She nodded. "The Protectorat wants me to donate my ovaries to the Vessel Institute. In exchange, he'll build a waterworks system for everyone outside the wall. Mabrother Rhodeski's backing the plan."

Leon sat up. "Say that again?"

She explained about how they wanted her eggs to start a line of anti-hemophilia babies, dozens of them. Taking out her ovaries was the safest way to do it. "Your father threatened to leave you in a coma if I didn't agree."

"But you didn't, did you?"

She shook her head. "I didn't."

He looked at her strangely. "Did you even think about it?"

"Of course," she said, smiling. "I'd give up my ovaries in a second to save your life, but bargains never work that way. I don't trust anything your father says."

"We've never really talked about children," he said.

"I want some someday, don't you?"

"Yes. Definitely. Someday," he said.

He rose to his feet, still shoeless, and held out a hand to help haul her up. "I notice you haven't yelled at me for going into the Enclave."

"I wanted to kill you."

He grinned. "I bet."

They started walking south over the rough ground, heading towards New Sylum.

"So much has happened since then," Gaia said. "What other explosions did you set up? I'm assuming Pyrho helped."

"He was really into it," Leon said. "Jack helped a little, too, but mostly he got in the way. The chimney on Mabrother Iris's house blew last night, and there'll be a fire in the vineyards later today."

"How many bombs did you set?" she asked.

"Enough," he said. "I don't want you to know the details. Pyrho and I can defuse them once the Protectorat starts delivering water for New Sylum. That's all we ever wanted."

"The bombs aren't set to hurt anyone, though, are they? They're just for the power grid and such?"

She watched his bare feet moving over the rocky ground, waiting for an answer that didn't come.

"Leon. This is not okay," she said. "We are not turning into murderers."

"It's possible, if someone's in the wrong place, that they could get hurt from the last bomb. It shouldn't come to that, though."

"You can't be serious," she said.

"It's just one that's dicey," he said. "As long as the Protectorat cooperates with us, I'll have plenty of time to go in and defuse it. But if they arrest you again or something happens to you, I'm going to let it explode."

"We can't do this," she protested. "Where is it? When is it set to go off?"

He shook his head. "I shouldn't have told you."

She took a long stride over a gap between rocks. "I can't believe this. Your father said you were a liar," Gaia said. "I wouldn't believe him."

Leon stopped, his eyebrows lifting in startled surprise. "My father? This isn't a lie, Gaia. It's a secret."

She put up a hand, opened toward the sky.

"You've kept secrets from me, remember?" he said, his eyes narrowing. "Why can't you trust that I know what I'm doing?"

"My secrets couldn't get anybody *killed*," she said.

Leon was silent a moment. Then he started walking again in long strides. She had to skip once to catch up, and then she realized she didn't want to walk beside him. She let him get ahead a few paces and stormed along behind him. He was going to turn them into murderers and he didn't even care. She rubbed her hand on her trousers, trying to get the blood off.

Leon spun around to face her. "I don't get why you're making me into the bad guy," he said. "*My father's* the one who won't give us water. *He's* the one who wants to steal your ovaries for some ridiculous experiment. *He's* the one who'd be happy to let me rot to death in a coma. All I did was set some bombs. They don't even have to go off."

"But they're ready."

"Of course they are." He held up his broken arm. "This isn't a game. People are going to get hurt."

Gaia planted her hands on her hips. "But I don't want *you* to be the one to hurt them."

"Are you going to do it yourself, then?" he asked, his eyes glittering. "Like with Sephie? You need me like this, Gaia. Quit pretending you're morally superior and accept it.

She gasped a breath. Then the truth hit. She'd always depended on Leon to do the hard things for her, the bad things, like holding a knife to a girl's throat way back when they were stealing birth records, or taking Gaia's baby sister from Adele out on Bachsdatter's island. Now he'd set bombs for Gaia. Until now, he'd let her feel like it was never her fault, but she'd always benefited from his cruelty.

She was responsible.

And now she was just like him. She looked down at her hands, at the flecks of blood that stained her sleeve. Leon faced the horizon, then raked a hand back through his hair and peered at her again.

"Talk to me," he said.

"You're right," she said calmly. "I've been unfair to you."

"I don't want it to be like this, either."

"But it is."

She turned her gaze to the south, to where the unlake had come into view with the precarious beginnings of New Sylum huddled below the old, worn homes of Wharfton. What had the

Protectorat said? As a leader, she was responsible for all her people's actions. That included Leon's. And since she knew the Protectorat would never cooperate with the people outside the wall unless he was coerced, that also included bombs.

She could feel a quiet turning inside herself, a certain, final clicking of a gear in a clock that could never go backward.

"All right," she said.

"What do you mean?"

"I accept it. Negotiating is no longer enough. We have to coerce him."

He stepped in front of her so that she was forced to meet his gaze.

"You really mean that?" he asked, and she could hear the relief and hope in his voice.

In a way, it would actually be simpler to fight the Protectorat than try to win him over. They might fail completely. They might all get destroyed, but it would be decided, once and for all.

"He won't give in," Gaia said. "We need a new leader in the Enclave."

Leon regarded her closely. Her fingers found her necklace with the locket watch and the monocle, and she squeezed them both briefly in her fist.

"You're serious," he said.

She felt a last, lonely flicker of idealistic doubt, and then she nodded. "Just as long as the new leader isn't me."

The people of New Sylum began to cheer as soon as Gaia and Leon came down the path, and more gathered, crowding around, as they arrived at the new commons in the center of the new village. Peter wedged past a couple of miners and without preamble, he reached for Gaia, gripping her shoulders.

"Are you all right?" he demanded. "I've been going crazy."

"Yes, I'm fine," Gaia said. She could feel the tight strength of his fingers in his grip, and his searching eyes were near. "We both are."

She took a half step back, gently extricating herself from his embrace, and he opened his hands suddenly as if just aware of what he'd done. She glanced beside her to Leon, who had watched the exchange and said nothing.

"How did you get out?" Gaia asked Peter.

"Malachai got us out when the lights blew," Peter said. "They put something in our drinks, but you were okay?"

"Yes," she said.

Beyond Peter, Will smiled in genuine welcome. His eyes were dark from sleepless worry.

"We were about to go in for you," Will said.

That was when Gaia realized that all of the people of New Sylum were armed, from the archers and scouts to Norris and Dinah, who wielded a bow Gaia had never seen her carry before. They were all prepared to put their lives on the line for her.

Gaia hardly knew what to say.

Josephine arrived then, bursting into tears. She threw her arms around Gaia while little Maya and Junie hugged Gaia's knees. Jack crowded forward next and gave Gaia a bear hug, then slapped Leon on the back. Pyrho lifted a hand in greeting.

"When did you get out?" Gaia asked Jack.

"Last night, during the fuss," Jack said. "We did good, didn't we?" He added to Leon.

"Good enough," Leon said.

Angie pointed to Leon's feet. "Where are your boots?" she asked. Her raspy voice was markedly improving.

"I lost them," Leon answered.

"You need new ones," the girl said.

"I know," Leon said. "Have you been good?"

The girl nodded and touched a hand to her throat. Mace and his family had the girl with them, and Pearl nodded, smiling.

"Come here," Leon said to Angie.

She didn't. He went over to the girl and lifted her up in a big hug, regardless of how gangly she was. She buried her face into his neck and clung to him.

"Mlass Gaia was mad at me," Angie said.

"Gaia's hard on *me*, too," he said. "What are we supposed to do? We still like her."

Jack leaned near to Gaia and spoke confidentially. "Angie's got a little crush."

"I'd never guess," Gaia said, laughing. She scooped up Maya in her arms. "Maya, say hello to our brothers. I don't know them very well myself yet, but Jack seems very funny and deep, and Pyrho likes to blow up things," she said. She realized the four of them, siblings, were together for the first time. It was strange, and delightful, and when Jack did a jogging thing with his eyebrows that was exactly the sort of thing her father used to do, Gaia felt both loss and joy mix in her heart.

"Hello, Maya," Pyrho said politely.

Jack slung an arm around Pyhro's shoulder. "Sort of makes you thirsty for a pint, doesn't it?"

Pyrho smiled. "You read my mind."

Gaia laughed, looking over her shoulder to Leon.

He stood with Angie beside him, conferring with Will, and something in their demeanors put her on alert.

"What is it?" she asked.

"We've just had word," Will said. "It's official. The Protectorat's turned off the water."

Gaia looked around at her friends, sensing the wariness and

fear. They were looking to her now, expectantly. She hugged Maya a little nearer.

"Then we have no choice. It's time to take down the wall," Gaia said.

She was surprised by how little it took to persuade the people of New Sylum to mobilize. The people of Wharfton were even more enthusiastic. They still had two days' worth of water reserved because of constant stockpiling and curtailed use, but Wharfton had endured one backward siege already and had no desire to wait helplessly through another. When people learned of how the Protectorat had tried to bargain for Gaia's ovaries, she received an outpouring of sympathy.

Deep memories in Wharfton recalled decades of stolen children and brutal injustice against anyone who had tried to speak out against the Enclave. Now was the time, people agreed, to put an end to it once and for all.

Wharfton citizens with homes closest to the wall began shifting their valuables to houses farther downhill. Miners and masons focused on fortify walls and roofs against anticipated projectiles. They erected barricades between key buildings to create a protected route connecting every sector of Wharfton. Knives were sharpened and crude weapons readied.

At nine that morning, the Enclave issued a notice via the Tvaltar advising anyone with information about a series of explosions to come forward.

By ten, Wharfton men who worked as guards for the Enclave quietly abandoned their posts and began coming home.

At ten-thirty, an explosion in the mycoprotein plant was audible all the way outside the wall. Gaia looked at Leon.

"There are four more," he said.

"What's the last one? The worst one? When is it set to go off?" But Leon wouldn't tell her.

"I'm committed to your approach. I get it," she said. "You have to let me know."

"Do this one thing for me. Trust me," he said.

Gaia was on edge every second, perpetually listening for another explosion, and she could imagine that for people in the Enclave, the agony of anticipation was even worse. In a countdown with no known time limit, every second could be the last.

At eleven, Gaia received a note from the Enclave:

> Masister Stone:
> Surrender your terrorists and anyone involved with the bombs.
> The explosions must stop immediately. We're prepared to retaliate.
> Yours,
> Miles Quarry
> Protectorat

She replied:

> Mabrother Protectorat:
> Until you give us the water you promised, the bombs will continue.
> Gaia Stone
> Matrarc of New Sylum

She ordered her archers to the roofs of Wharfton, on alert for an attack, and scores of Wharfton people armed themselves with knifes and axes, ready to defend their families.

At noon, the Protectorat sent another message via the Tvaltar inviting anyone loyal to the Enclave to enter promptly through the south gate, ensuring that they would find shelter and hospitality within the walls. No one accepted the offer.

At twelve-thirty, electricity to the Tvaltar was cut off, suspending further communiqués. The south gate was closed and barricaded. The guards were tripled along the top of the wall, and their rifles gleamed in the sun.

The siege was on.

siege

NERVES FRAYED TO THE snapping point as people below the wall waited for the first attack. A sense of barely contained chaos and slow-burning fury ran through the pockets of defenders, with messengers darting behind the line of barricades. Farmers, craftsmen, and merchants were now all turned into warriors. As an hour passed, and then another, Gaia refined her rebels' organization. Decisively, she appointed leaders from each of the six sectors outside the wall, and told them to appoint neighborhood leaders from within their sectors, so that systems of communication and command were established. No one was too young or weak to help in some way. Chaos gave way to dogged determination as thousands of people united around one common goal: end the oppression of the Enclave, once and for all.

"Why doesn't he attack?" she asked Leon that evening. They had turned the Tvaltar into command central, and from the steps, she examined the Enclave guards, face by face, through binoculars.

"I don't know. I'm sure he wants to," Leon said. "He must be talking to Genevieve or Rhodeski."

"He knows he just has to wait until we're out of water," Derek said. "It was like this before, too. He can wait forever."

She lowered the binoculars. "Not this time," she said.

Gaia had a wall to blow up.

She was guided by Pyrho's advice that they focus on three points in the wall that were naturally primed for the most damage: the irrigation pipe; the now plugged smuggler's hole that Gaia had crawled through long before, when she'd first snuck into the Enclave; and the south gate itself. Pyrho used ammonium nitrate from the agricultural fertilizer to concoct the explosives, working with precise, unhurried care into the evening.

Wharfton gradually lay in darkness. The few streetlights that normally burned in Wharfton failed to come on, and archers shot out the floodlights that illuminated the wall. Inside the cavernous Tvaltar, torches had been lit along the walls, and down the length of the sloping floor, swarms of Wharfton and New Sylum people were working together to bolster their arms and refine their defense strategies. The rows of benches had been cleared to the sides, and the screen loomed as a lifeless square of shiny gray on the back wall.

"The explosives are ready whenever you want them to blow," Pyrho said at last.

Gaia was poring over a map of the Enclave with Leon and a dozen other leaders. She straightened at Pyrho's announcement, and found Myrna standing beside him.

"People are going to get hurt," Myrna said. "It's not too late to think this through."

"I have thought it through," Gaia said.

"Think again," Myrna said.

Gaia looked around the packed room at the eager, focused faces in the flickering torchlight. They wanted this. They were willing to take the risks, and Gaia was their leader. She owed them.

"You were a midwife once. Remember?" Myrna said.

"I still am," Gaia said.

"Are you? Think what you're doing."

For too many years, the people of Wharfton had suffered the domination of the Enclave, and New Sylum had faced a bitter welcome. Yet even so, Gaia could still stop the machine if she chose.

Gaia slowly backed away from the table.

"No," Leon said quietly. His splinted arm was in a sling now, useless across his chest. He still wore his white clothes from the Bastion, and she realized he'd never had time to change. "Don't make this more complicated than it is," he said. "We take the wall down, we march on the Bastion, we force the Protectorat to give us what we need."

"And the Protectorat orders his guards to murder us all," Gaia said. With sudden clarity she could see it already: a bloodbath in the Square of the Bastion.

"That's what will happen," Myrna said. "Make no mistake."

Leon reached for Gaia's arm.

"Myrna's wrong. Remember," he said. "We have allies inside. The Jacksons' friends will side with us, and so will the parents of the advanced children, and the advanced children themselves. They won't let the Protectorat mow us down."

"They're cowards," Myrna said. "They'll be afraid for their own families. They'll want nothing to do with your violence. It's too easy for the Enclave to hunt them down and take them out, one by one, after you fail. They know that."

"Could you two quit arguing?" Gaia said. "Just wait."

A silence grew around them, and Gaia realized that people had turned to listen. She had to think, to weigh the possibilities. Her gaze fell on Leon's broken arm, and she had a sharp premonition that he would be the first one killed. How was he supposed to fight with one arm? She could be leading him, leading all of them, to their deaths.

She looked around the table to the people she most depended on for counsel: Leon, Will, Peter, Dinah, Derek, Norris, Bill, Myrna, Jack, and now Pyrho. The other clan leaders were present, too, and Malachai with the excrims, and more friends from Wharfton and New Sylum. Each face caught at her heart as she imagined endangering them.

"We can't go in fighting," Gaia said. She spoke up with new confidence. "We have to change our plans. If we go in attacking, everyone will turn against us. They'll side with the Protectorat. They'll try to protect themselves and their homes and kill us in the process. We would do the same thing if they came down here on the attack."

The others shifted, talking in low voices, but she could see it clearly. The Protectorat was just aching for an excuse to kill them all. Since he controlled the guard, he would order them to start shooting before any unarmed citizens could speak up on behalf of the rebels.

"I knew this before," she said. "How could I forget? Our bows and arrows are nothing against their rifles. I can't lead us on a suicide mission."

"Then what do you want to do?" Peter asked. "We have to decide. Everyone's ready to go."

"We've been cut off from water before," Derek said, stepping forward. "It's only going to get worse from this point, not better. We have to act now, not tomorrow or the next day."

She scanned her gaze over the crowd. The Tvaltar held four hundred people, but there were thousands more outside.

"Come outside with me," she said. "I need to talk to everyone. As many as I can."

"What are you doing?" Leon asked, his voice low.

"The best I can," she said. "Just come."

Turning, she wound her way up the slanted floor and through the foyer to the outer steps of the Tvaltar. Leon and her other friends ranged behind her as she stopped before the central door and looked out over the quad. It was eerily familiar, the scene of upturned faces in the torchlight. More and more people were shifting into the confines of the quad, where an ancient mesquite tree thrust up its dark limbs toward the night sky. In the green commons of Sylum, when she'd faced a similar crowd before, she'd been fighting for justice within her society. Now she was seeking justice against a force far greater than all of New Sylum and Wharfton combined.

"All day, we've been talking about attacking the Enclave," she said.

"We can't hear you!" called a voice from across the quad.

Will overturned a wooden box at the top of the steps, and Leon handed her up. Gaia raised her voice, calling out in a clear voice. "This rebellion has been coming for generations, since the first refugees came here seeking sanctuary from the wasteland and were told to stay outside the wall and survive on cast-offs." She pointed uphill and filled her lungs. "That wall has to come down. I can't wait to see the thing blasted apart."

A cheer rose around her, and in response, more people streamed to the quad. They packed into the doorways to listen and surfaced on the roofs to look down. The windows of the buildings surrounding the quad opened and filled with people, all expectant, all attuned to what Gaia would say next.

Up the hill, the wall hovered as a dark and ominous weight, as if prepared to crush them with its monstrous stones. Just beyond firing range of their rifles, guards were silhouetted along the top, with the pristine, glowing lights of the Enclave behind them.

"I never thought I'd see the people of Wharfton unite this way," Gaia went on. "And the people of New Sylum are proud to join you, uniting our destinies together. But tonight, even as we have our bombs set and ready to explode, I am afraid. I'm afraid that people we love will die. I'm afraid we'll breach the wall only to be killed mercilessly by forces that can overpower us without ever feeling a scratch."

There were protests from the crowd, but Gaia raised a hand.

"I am not questioning our bravery. Or our determination," she said. "But being brave alone does not make us smart. Do you want to see your brothers die? Do you want to see your daughters bleeding and slaughtered?"

"They'll kill us anyway!" called an angry voice from the back.

"They cut off our water!" called another. "Let's take out as many as we can!"

Shouts of agreement echoed the rancor around the quad.

She did not try to yell over them but stood proudly, patiently. She lifted her hand and waited through the chaotic shouts until the buzz quieted once more.

"We will fight," she said calmly. She let her voice lift with urgency. "We *will* fight, but only as a last resort. Only after they've destroyed everything left in us except for our fight. For now, we still have hope. We still want to work out a peace with them."

"They'll never give us peace!" another angry voice said.

Derek pushed forward. "Listen to her. Gaia's taken us further in just a few days than we've come in my entire life. Or haven't you noticed? She deserves some respect."

Laughter and more shouting erupted, and then over that came a woman's voice. "Go on!" she called. "We're listening."

Gaia waited for the last talking to taper off. "Here's what we do," she said. "We blow up the wall. We have explosives in three key places, so we set those off. That's the easy part. And then, when the debris settles, we put down our weapons and walk inside. We round up the friends I know we have inside the wall, and we march with them peacefully to the Square of the Bastion."

Voices rose in amused skepticism, mixed with an equally strong current of frustration.

"They'll shoot us dead," said Bill from the base of the steps. "Any fool knows that."

Gaia turned to him. "How is that any different from what they do if we go in armed with our arrows and swords?"

"At least then we'll die fighting," Bill said.

"We'll be dead, guaranteed, if we go in fighting," Gaia said. "If we go in peacefully, there's a chance, a very small chance, that they won't kill us."

A silence hovered over the quad, and when a new swell of discussion started, it had a different tone.

"We must decide what happens next," Gaia said. "We're the ones who will be going in there moments from now. We're deciding about our own lives, and I don't want us to die."

"She's right!" called a voice in the crowd. "We'd have a chance!"

"It's insanity!" called someone else.

Gaia lifted her hand again and the crowd turned attentive, listening. She could practically hear everyone breathing, like a great, united beast.

"Listen," she said. "The people of New Sylum have already

faced that we could die. We came across the wasteland from a place where our children had no future. It was a risk to come. A terrible risk. But that kind of guts builds strength like you can't imagine, and now we're here with the people of Wharfton." She took another deep breath. "We'll go together into the Enclave, hand in hand. We'll show them what it means to be brave. We'll show them who we are."

A hush passed over the crowd, and with it a kind of grim, determined hope.

"And if they slaughter us all?" called a voice from the back. It wasn't a belligerent question. It was beyond anger.

"Then we'll have failed," Gaia said.

The truth hung in the silent air around them. Torches flickered and snapped, and then the mumbles began to build. Someone laughed. She heard the word *suicide* bandied about, but she also felt the shift. They were with her now. They saw.

Leon was shaking his head, watching her in apparent amazement.

"What?" she asked. "I'm right, aren't I?"

"Yes," he said. "You're right about the part where they definitely kill us if we go in armed. I don't know about the rest of it."

"We have to lead them, you and I," Gaia said.

"I had a feeling."

She smiled, taking his hand from her perch on the box. She looked back to Peter, Will, and the other people from New Sylum. They nodded to her. Derek and the leaders from Wharfton joined her closely on the stairs. Gaia turned to Pyrho.

"I think it's time, Pyrho."

He nodded.

Gaia turned once more to the crowd. "We're blowing up the

wall now. Stay far away from the explosions so you don't get hurt. And then, if you choose to come, put down your weapons and follow me."

Gaia crouched low in the dirt, her weight on her toes, and scanned the top of the wall for guards. She didn't want Pyrho to ignite the explosives until there were no people standing on the parapet directly above the south gate, so they'd planned for a preliminary explosion as a decoy farther down the wall to draw the guards in that direction.

A pop cracked from the distance to her left, in the direction of the spigot for Western Sector Two. Guards shifted along the parapet, then began to run. There was an instant when the top appeared clear.

"Now," she said to Pyrho.

A second blast rent the night, slamming a shock wave of air into Gaia's ears while bright white light exploded out from the south gate. Rock and wood flew thirty meters into the air and soared outward in a brilliant shower of sparks and flame. Farther down the wall, two more explosions followed in rapid succession, bursting light into the night sky. The ground shook with each one, and screams rose from inside the wall.

Gaia's heart charged. She straightened, trying to see through the smoke and flames to the Enclave on the other side. Debris was showering around her. Where the south gate had stood was now a gaping void. A ragged heap of rubble met the raw, mangled edges of the wall. Bits of flaming wood from the door and the upper parapet kept landing everywhere, and fire burned in a shop awning.

"Do you like it?" Pyrho asked.

His happy voice was a shock in her ear.

"It was a lot bigger than I expected," she said.

"That's what it takes," Pyrho said.

Gaia started slowly forward. Voices were calling inside the Enclave. Guards were no longer visible anywhere along the top of the wall. She didn't know if they'd been blown off during the explosion or if they were ducking out of sight behind the parapets.

She reached for one of the torches. A completely new feeling of fear, guilt and vulnerability now ground into her bones. With her other hand, she reached for Leon.

She began up the road, moving slowly, stepping over blocks of debris and around twisted, burning framework. Color seeped away, leaving only black and gray in the night. Behind her came Peter, Will, Jack, and Pyrho. Dinah, Norris, and Derek came next, and then all of the other people she'd grown to love in New Sylum and Wharfton, all but Josephine and the little girls. They carried torches, but no weapons. They held hands, advancing with slow deliberation, and the only threat about them was their numbers.

Gaia made it as far as the huge gap without anyone taking a shot at her. The damage was magnified here, and a tilted, buzzing streetlight still worked, sending long shadows over the macabre scene. Gaia's gaze caught on a wounded guard who'd been blown against one of the shops. He was covering his face with both hands. A woman was crumpled against a curb, her leg at an impossible angle, and other people were negotiating the rubble, digging for others. A man in pajamas staggered by. A shocked woman stood in a doorway, clutching a crying baby in her arms.

Gaia stumbled to a stop, wanting to help.

"You have to come," Leon said quietly.

He was right. "Tell Myrna we need her," Gaia called back. "Tell her to hurry."

Leon pulled her forward toward the main road. They'd gone only a few more paces when a disheveled guard stepped before them, and Gaia recognized Sgt. Burke, the commander who'd arrested her three days before.

"Hold there!" he called.

Another guard joined Sgt. Burke and lifted his rifle.

"Wait, please!" Gaia said, throwing up her hands. "We're not armed."

A clattering came from farther up the street, and a new team of guards ran to surround them. Rapid orders were shouted. More rifles were cocked and aimed at Gaia and Leon.

"You just blew up the wall!" came a shrieking voice from the darkness.

A shot exploded on Gaia's right. Screams followed. She ducked and people dropped to the ground around her.

"Don't shoot! We don't have any weapons!" Leon shouted.

"We're not here to hurt anybody!" Gaia said.

"That's the midwife!"

Gaia lifted her hands, slowly rising again.

"We're not your enemies," she said. "We just want our basic rights."

"I'll give you your rights," said Sgt. Burke, stepping near. He slapped a hard hand against Gaia's face. "That's my brother you just blew up there! You killed him!"

Leon grabbed Gaia, jerking her behind him, and ten other guards pointed their rifles at his throat.

"Leon!" Gaia screamed. "No!"

"Leave her alone," Leon said.

"That's the Protectorat's son," said one of the shopkeepers from the edge of the commotion.

Another one of the guards stepped forward, and Gaia

recognized Marquez. "It's Leon," Marquez said. He faced Sgt. Burke. "It's Leon Grey. You remember him."

"That's right. It's me," Leon said. "And we're here to talk to my father. All of us."

Sgt. Burke looked confused, and then his face contorted with emotion. "You're murdering terrorists, all of you!"

When Marquez put a hand on Sgt. Burke's shoulder, he shoved him off, but he also lowered the butt of his rifle to the pavement with a heavy crunch.

More and more people from outside the wall were quietly, steadily coming in the gap that used to be the south gate, men and women, old and young. They stepped awkwardly around the destruction, picking their footing. Gaia could see they were afraid, but they were also proud, and determined. More Enclave people were coming out of their houses now, too.

"We could use a hand over here," called a woman beside a big pile of debris.

The guards didn't respond. Most still had their rifles aimed at Gaia and Leon. Somewhere the baby was crying again, or maybe he had never stopped. Agonized groans surfaced from the rubble.

Gaia turned to Will and Derek. "Help them."

Will did not hesitate, and within moments, many hands helped to pull broken stones off the trapped man.

Gaia's cheek smarted from where she'd been hit, and her heart beat with dread, but she spoke calmly, and she reached for Leon's hand again. "We're going to the Bastion," she said to Sgt. Burke. "Do you understand?"

Sgt. Burke lifted his rifle again. "We'll take you there ourselves." He swung his rifle wide towards the Enclave people. "Stay back, the rest of you."

None of the Enclave people moved. The guards hustled Gaia

and Leon forward, shoving others with them, until there were clearly more people than the guards could surround, and a massive stream of people from outside the wall followed of their own free will. She held tightly to Leon's good hand, mute, and as they came up the now familiar main road, closer and closer to the square, she began to shake inside.

"You're all right," Leon said, his voice low near her ear. "Remember. They need to negotiate with you."

"How many of the bombs you set are still left?" she asked.

"There's only one left now."

"The worst one?"

"There's time. Plenty of time. I can still defuse it. Don't worry."

Floodlights illuminated the Square of the Bastion, casting it in a pearly, unnatural glow. Armed guards lined the square, more than Gaia had ever seen, and as Leon and Gaia arrived, they were seized and dragged away from the others rebels. Gaia's friends began to shout, crowding the guards to try to keep Gaia and Leon with them, but the guards butted them back. Gaia craned her neck back and saw her people being herded to the center of the square, toward the obelisk, where a row of barricades had been set up to corral them under the watch of the guards.

Gaia tried to stay close to Leon, but at the door of the prison, guards overpowered him and swept him in ahead of her.

"Leon!" she called.

His voice came back to her. "Don't hurt her!"

The next instant, he was gone, deeper inside the prison. Gaia looked around frantically for Marquez, but he was gone. Sgt. Burke gripped Gaia's hair hard at the base of her neck, jerking her. "I want you to pay. Hanging's not nearly bad enough for you."

She winced in pain. "I need to talk to the Protectorat."

250

Sgt. Burke punched her in the gut, and with an "oof," she collapsed forward.

"That's for Ian," he said. "I'd slit your throat myself if they'd let me. How many other people did you kill today? Tell me that."

He shoved her forward, and other guards caught her tight. She collapsed her weight downward and dug her heels into the floor, pushing back to try to get free, but the guards heaved her off her feet and hauled her, resisting, down the halls and steep staircases, until they came around a familiar corner and she saw the dark, heavy door of V cell.

CHAPTER 20

the piglet

UNLIKE BEFORE, WHEN V cell had been illuminated only by the evening light that diffused in the high, barred windows, the room was now lit starkly by two shadeless lamps that stood in two corners. Instead of being damp from recent washing, the floor was dry, and the dangling chains and the whip were gone. A heavy wooden chair now monopolized the center of the room. It was affixed to a platform that concealed the floor drain, and it was positioned to face the lights and a small desk. A wire ran up the back of the chair and crossed the floor to the desk. As the guards dragged Gaia nearer, she saw the chair was rigged with bindings to secure her wrists and others to cross over her chest.

"You can't put me in here," she said, struggling to squirm free. "I need to talk to the Protectorat. Tell Genevieve I'm here!"

The guards clenched her arms and shoved her in, securing her wrists and shoulders tightly. Kicking, she managed to connect hard with one of the guards' legs. He merely leaned over and strapped her ankle down, and then the other.

"You can't do this to me!" she shouted. She looked up, finding the camera in the upper corner of the room. "Let me out!" she yelled to the camera. "We came peacefully! Are you there? Miles Quarry! We want the water you promised! We want to be treated like we deserve!"

"Leave us," Mabrother Iris said quietly behind her.

She heard the door close, and then silence.

Gaia could feel her heart pounding, and she twisted her neck, trying to see him. Her gaze couldn't reach the space behind her to discover where he was. She tried to listen for him over the rushing in her ears, but caught only a faint rustling noise.

"Where's Leon?" she asked.

No one replied. She scanned the desk for weapons or instruments of torture and found a wooden, lidded canister, a flat computer tablet with a keyboard, a box of tissues, and two small clamps clipped to the edge of the table. Wires were attached to the clamps.

"You can't hurt him," she said. "His mother won't stand for it if you hurt him."

She heard a soft noise along the floor and looked down to her left to see a piglet snuffling slowly along the corner of the room. Mabrother Iris moved into view on her right side and leaned back against the wall, rubbing a finger on his upper lip.

"You've never wanted to be friends with me," he said calmly. "Never from that very first day."

"What do you want?"

"Just a few answers," he said.

"You can't hurt me," she said. "The Protectorat wants me healthy. He needs me to be part of the Vessel Institute."

Mabrother Iris smiled sadly, shaking his head. "Let's not start by lying. You know that's not true."

"He wants my ovaries. He told me so. We're working out a deal. Let me talk to him."

"He knows very well where you are right now. But you don't

need to worry about your health. What I do to you won't last," he said.

She twisted her wrists to try to free them, but the cloth bindings only cinched tighter, and she had to relax against the armrests and flex her fingers to try to reestablish any looseness. Mabrother Iris paced slowly forward, studying her, and when he put out a hand to smooth her hair behind her right ear, she jerked her head away.

"What happened to your cheek here?" he asked.

"One of the guards struck me. Sergeant Burke."

She strained her face away as far she could, while he tenderly smoothed her hair back. Then, deliberately, his finger trailed lightly down her right cheek. She grit her teeth, bearing it.

"So sensitive," he said. "And your scar. Is that even more sensitive?"

His touch skimmed her left cheek next, and she tried unsuccessfully to writhe away. Even after his fingers were gone, her skin still tingled.

"You don't care to be touched, do you?" he said. "Not even gently."

"Not by vermin," she said.

"Careful, now," he said. He unclasped her necklace and set it aside on the desk. He touched her red bracelet, then left it. "Whose idea was it to blow up my chimney?" he asked. "Not a bad prank, that. Was that you?"

She licked her lips. "Of course. I sanctioned it."

"It was more in the vein of Leon's thinking, I expect. The fire in his father's favorite grapes, too. That was pure Leon. There's no point taking blame that isn't yours," Mabrother Iris said, and turned from the desk with a U-shaped bit of clear plastic. "Open

254

your mouth. It's for your teeth. So you won't bite your tongue. Try it."

He pressed it against her lips.

"I can shove it in and wrap a gag around mouth if you prefer," he said.

She let him stick it in. It tasted like wax between her teeth, and her mouth began to salivate. Swallowing caused a loud click in her ears.

Next he smeared something on her right pinky finger and attached one of the clamps tightly enough that she couldn't work it off with her thumb. He did the same to her left hand, and then stepped back toward the desk.

"People are very upset about the wall," Mabrother Iris said. "That was going too far. At least one man is dead. We need to be certain nothing like that ever happens again."

She couldn't talk to him with her mouth full. He wasn't even asking her a question.

"I want to give you a sample of what's ahead," he said. "I don't have time for more now, but this will give you something to think about."

He shifted the computer tablet before him and clicked at the keyboard. She waited, fear growing rather than lessening with the delay. She swallowed again around the mouth guard. Mabrother looked up at her, light reflecting off his glasses.

"Ready?" he asked. "Five, four, three—"

Lightning flew through her. The shock was so intense it left every muscle and blood vein seizing after it stopped, and she shuddered, shaking, appalled. Her teeth were clenched so deeply into the mouth guard that they almost met, and swallowing nearly suffocated her.

Mabrother Iris came around the table, extricated the mouth guard from her lips and chucked it into a garbage receptacle. She gasped for air, still trembling, and tipped her head back against the chair while her arms and legs rippled in residual spasms. She was dimly aware that Mabrother Iris had opened the canister on the desktop. He took something out and set it on top: another mouth guard.

"How was that?" he asked.

She couldn't make her throat work to voice any insult harsh enough.

He reached for a tissue and wiped her eyes and nose for her, and when he lightly ran his finger down her cheek again, she jumped in her bonds. Her sensitive skin felt his touch now like feathered needles.

"It's a strange little aftereffect, isn't it? Your nerve ends tend to get more sensitive, not less, as you might think," he said. He stood back, observing her another moment. "I have to go see how your fiancé's doing with his father. Those two have never had the easiest relationship, that's for certain."

She could hear him move behind her, toward the door.

"By the way," he added. "In case you haven't guessed, that camera's live. Leon was able to watch us."

She lifted her gaze and scanned up to the corner of the ceiling where the white box had its red light steady on. Despair for Leon twisted through her. It was the torment he'd once imagined, coming true for both of them.

"You can stay to keep her company," Mabrother Iris said softly.

The door closed. She didn't understand his last words until she heard the snuffling of the little pig on the floor. Mabrother Iris would be coming back. She told herself she wouldn't cry, that it didn't hurt that much, that she couldn't let Leon see her suffering, but she had never been so terrified.

Mabrother Iris came and went, sometimes shocking her, sometimes not. He wanted to know who had set the explosives in the wall, and who had managed the blackout to the Bastion and a quarter of the Enclave the night before. He wanted details about his chimney, the fire in the vineyard, the explosion at the myco-protein plant, and half a dozen smaller bombs that had gone off around the city, disrupting water lines and the electrical grid. He pressed her for a complete list of sabotage targets, but she knew hardly any of them. Leon hadn't told her. She only knew for certain that one bomb remained, but she didn't know what it was or when it was set to go.

She tried to tell Mabrother Iris nothing, but after a point, the shocks were so painful and discombobulating, she no longer knew what she was telling him. Ashamed, broken, she realized she would have told him anything to make him stop.

Once, after a break, when Mabrother Iris didn't even ask her a question before he shocked her, she finally realized that it didn't matter what she said or didn't say. What was being done to her depended on what Leon was or wasn't saying somewhere else while he watched. She lifted her gaze to the camera, confused and hurt. How could Leon let this go on?

Just give in, Leon, she thought.

Slumped, limp in the chair, Gaia was barely conscious when she felt Mabrother Iris touch her cheek once more. He eased out her latest mouth guard. She worked her tongue around her mouth to swallow. Even her jaw was sore.

"There," he said gently. "How are we doing?"

There was nothing she could say.

Mabrother Iris reattached her necklace around her throat, adjusting it lightly over the neckline of her blouse. The cold, delicate metal burned against her sensitive skin. Gaia heard a noise behind her, and then a team of guards came in with a white medical stretcher.

Hands shoved up Gaia's sleeve, and a needle was inserted into the vein in the crook of her elbow. An IV was affixed to the needle and carefully bandaged to her arm to keep it in place. Still confused, Gaia looked up the length of IV tube to find Sephie attaching a bag of fluid like the one that had fed into Leon's arm. She tapped the line and turned a valve.

"One moment, please," Mabrother Iris said.

He produced a short, shimmering, slightly elastic cord. Gaia felt the binding pressure as he wrapped it around her left wrist to form a bracelet, crimping the ends together with a special glittering bead. A soft blue glow illuminated the band.

"It seems fitting you should have this, like the other girls," he said. "You aren't strictly a vessel mother, but since your contribution is even more important, I feel you qualify for the honors."

Understanding brought her horrified despair. "No," she whispered.

Mabrother Iris smiled once more at Gaia. "That's right. Harvest time."

noon

WHEN SHE CAME TO, she was in a small, pale blue room, resting sideways on a bed, with her locket watch ticking softly at her throat. Every millimeter of her skin felt acutely sensitive, while beneath the surface, her entire body felt like it had been shattered and jammed back together. The ends of her pinky fingers were singed and tender. Someone had bathed her and changed her into a white, filmy nightgown with eyelet lace edging the sleeves. She turned her head on the pillow, scanning around the unfamiliar room. A vase of flowers stood on a small table beside her bed, and shear curtains hung at the windows where a breeze of warm air drifted in.

A tap came from the door, and Emily came cautiously in, carrying a white dress and a pair of white loafers.

"How do you feel?" Emily asked.

"Awful," Gaia croaked.

Emily handed her a glass of water, but as Gaia shifted upward to take it, she felt lines of pain along her abdomen. She set a hand over her stomach. A bandage there dumbfounded, then petrified her. She scrambled to pull up the edge of her gown and found a square of dressing carefully taped over her lower abdomen.

"Don't touch it," Emily said gently.

But Gaia nicked free an edge of tape and lifted off the covering to see a new, four-centimeter incision below her bellybutton. Precise, tidy stitches held it closed. *They really did it*, she thought, shocked. *They took my ovaries.*

She lifted her troubled gaze to Emily.

"I'm sorry for what they did," Emily said. "The Protectorat went too far."

It was still more than she could take in. She'd never really believed it was possible. "Where are my eggs now?" She pulled hard at the glowing bracelet that bound her wrist, trying to work it over her hand, but it wouldn't come off. Her red bracelet from Leon was loose by comparison.

Emily handed her the dress. "I don't know. My guess is they've been sold to the highest bidders. But that hardly matters right now," she said. "You need to get dressed quickly. Half of the Enclave is calling for your execution for what you did to the wall last night. A man was killed at the south gate, and dozens more were injured. They're calling you a terrorist. But Mabrother Rhodeski and the rest who back the Vessel Institute cut a deal for your life. They said if you survived your surgery, they would even honor their agreement to provide water for outside the wall."

Gaia struggled up. "Where's Leon?" she asked. "Where are Peter and Pyrho and the rest?"

"That's why I came for you. They're scheduled for execution."

"When?"

"At noon today. The Protectorat wants you to stay away. He says the crowd might still turn against you if you're there, but I thought you should know."

Gaia clicked open her locket watch: 11:47.

"Help me," Gaia said. Adrenaline overrode her pain and weakness. She pulled herself to her feet and hurried to change into the dress. "We have to stop them."

"It's no use, Gaia," Emily said. "Your friends are criminals. They're the scapegoats. The Protectorat has kept the rest of your protestors corralled in the Square of the Bastion. They've been there overnight and all morning because there isn't enough room in the prison, and he'll only let them go after they've witnessed the executions. It's your ringleaders, or everybody."

"We have to try," Gaia said. "Please, Emily, you have to help me." She shoved her toes in the loafers and flew to the door.

"They have my boys," Emily said. "I can't go against the Protectorat. I'm not as brave as you. I never was."

Gaia couldn't wait. She pushed open the door and hurried down the hallway. With her dress still unbuttoned, she clutched her sore belly and ran through the Bastion's upper hallways and down the stairs. She finally skidded across the black-and-white tile floor of the foyer toward the big doors and lunged outside.

Sunlight flooded the terrace, coruscating brightly among the white-clad elite who had gathered for the execution. They were chatting in small groups, and their air was so distinctly at odds with what she expected for an execution that for a split second, Gaia thought there had been some insane misunderstanding and she had stumbled into a party.

She quickly worked the last buttons on the front of her dress and moved forward. Evelyn, with a steely expression, stood silently with her brother Rafael at the far left edge of the terrace. Sephie and several of her fellow doctors stood at the other end, not far from Mabrother Iris. A group of vessel mothers was gathered

261

together. At the top of the steps, the Protectorat and Genevieve stood with their backs to her, talking with Mabrother Rhodeski and his wife.

In contrast to the lighter mood on the terrace, the crowd in the square was sullen and tense. A barricade divided the square in half. To the left of the obelisk were Gaia's friends from outside the wall, contained by a perimeter of armed guards. Strain and weariness were patently obvious in their anxious expressions. On the right, the merchants and working people of the Enclave had gathered, and farther to the side, behind the black fence of the prison, inmates had been lined up to witness the executions.

A cloud shadow dropped into the square, deep and swift, and Gaia blinked upward to where clouds were moving in fat, piled lumps. The obelisk changed from white to gray. Angled to the right stood the hulking structure of the gallows. Two nooses were strung over the high wooden beam. The merchants shifted and then parted to let through a team of prison guards. Behind them came the bound prisoners: Peter, Pyrho, Jack, Malachai, and Leon.

"Stop this!" Gaia commanded, striding forward.

Those near to the Protectorat turned in surprise.

"They're terrorists," the Protectorat said, scanning her from head to toe. "We found explosives planted under the obelisk. Right beneath this very square."

"But we didn't set them *off*," Gaia said. "They were just for a threat."

"A ticking time bomb is more than a threat," the Protectorat said. Leon and the others were being marched up the stairs. Their faces were darkened with bruises and exhaustion. Under his disheveled dark hair, Leon's eyes burned with grim fury, but then, as her gaze met his across the distance, his expression turned to yearning. The guards positioned Malachai and Peter under the nooses.

"We never intended to hurt anyone," Gaia continued insistently.

"Not even Sephie? You killed Mabrother Stoltz yourself," the Protectorat said. "Last night, you blew up the wall and killed another man. You've threatened the lives of hundreds more. It's time for you people to understand, once and for all, that you cannot simply do what you want."

"Then kill me, not them," Gaia said. She took another step forward, shouting toward the gallows. "Stop there! Stop!"

The Protectorat grabbed her arm. "You were convicted, obviously. Your sentence was commuted, thanks to Mabrother Rhodeski. Be thankful now, and be quiet like a good girl." He flicked a finger at her glowing bracelet and shoved her beside a guard. "Watch her," he ordered.

The guard took her arm.

On the gallows, the hangman put a black hood over Malachai's head, and as a second hood was lowered over Peter's, Gaia's heart clenched in panic. *Peter!*

She urgently surveyed the crowd, both halves of it, and was shocked by their cowed passivity. Not one of them dared to speak out. She couldn't find Mace in the Enclave crowd, or Rita, or anybody she knew. On the left side, even the miners held their tongues.

"What has happened to you?" she asked, frustrated and broken-hearted. "This is *wrong!*"

"*You're* the problem, you and your terrorists," said one of the merchants in the crowd. "Things were good until you stirred up trouble."

A woman spoke up beside him. "Mabrother Rhodeski there

can give the new people a little water if he wants, like he says. That's his business. But we want the rest of things to go back like they were."

"The way things were was *bad!*" Gaia said forcefully. She was undeterred by the guard's tightening grip on her arm. "The rich people here are using all of us. They don't even care enough about you to let Myrna Silk run her blood bank inside the wall. They're going to expand the baby factory to buy and sell babies, just for themselves. The Protectorat tortured his *own son*, and me." She clutched a hand to her abdomen, and struggled to find words for what Sephie had done to her. "They've gutted me. I can never have children of my own."

The crowd began to shift then, and voices started up.

"Enough! Remove her," the Protectorat called. "The nooses! Now!"

Guards looped the ropes around Malachai's and Peter's necks, cinching them neatly. A growl came from Malachai on the plat-form behind them, and Leon jostled forward, bumping Pyrho.

"She's right!" Leon called. "My father's promises are lies!"

"Wait! You have to listen!" called a new, high-pitched voice from the corner of the terrace. Sasha, her enormous pregnant belly swelling before her, strode forward beside a man in a cook's apron and lifted the cut band of her bracelet. "They're keeping vessel mothers against their will. Everything Gaia says is true!"

Gaia jerked free from the guard who held her, dodged down into the crowd, and charged toward the obelisk. Despite her sur-gery pain, she clenched her muscles and hauled herself up onto the base to stand tall. "Look at your neighbors and search your hearts," Gaia urged the people. She bored her gaze into face after face. "You know it's time for a change. For fairness. This is about us," she waved her arm toward the square, encompassing all of the people from inside and outside the wall, "against the few of them. Now is the time. We have to stop them!"

"Guards!" the Protectorat ordered.

"I call for the Protectorat to stand down!" Gaia called loudly. "It's time to elect new leaders! Stand down, Miles Quarry!"

A stunned silence immobilized the people.

The Protectorat produced a pistol and aimed it at Leon. His voice came clearly across the square for all to hear. "Drop the convicts. Shoot Gaia Stone and anyone who tries to protect her."

Someone yanked Gaia down off the base of the obelisk as shots smashed into the stonework behind her. The explosion of a gun blasted on her left. Some of the merchants were shooting back at the guards. Gaia realized they'd been armed and prepared, vacillating, all this time.

A corps of guards circled tightly around the Protectorat and Genevieve, firing their guns outward. Men and women screamed, trying to duck and run simultaneously. Many were fleeing in chaos, but a swarm of people crowded in around Gaia at the base of the obelisk. She craned forward, trying to see what was happening on the gallows. Bullets smacked into the splintering wood, and she was agonized to see that Malachai and Peter were still up on the gallows platform, blinded by the hoods over their heads and unable to dodge free from the nooses around their necks. Leon and the others were gone. She had no idea where.

The initial blasts of rifle shots changed to scattered pops of gunfire and the clash of swords. The gallows hatchways opened with a slamming bang. As Peter and Malachai dropped, instead of hitching in the air, caught by their necks, their bodies fell all the way to the ground below the platform. Someone, Gaia realized, had cut the ropes.

"We have to get you out of here!" a man called in her ear.

She turned to find Mace Jackson tugging at her arm.

"I have to find Leon," she said.

"He went for his father," Mace said. "You can't go out there!"

She was already scrambling to push forward between the people that were massed up against the base of the obelisk. Some were holding each other, and many of them were wild-eyed with fear, but they huddled tight around her, people from New Sylum, Wharfton, and the Enclave all together, as a wall of courage, united in protecting her from the Protectorat.

Another explosion of gunfire came from the terrace, and people screamed again, huddling down, and drawing her with them. For an instant, she hunched with them, but her need to find Leon propelled her forward. As she tried again to push her way through, people put out their hands to stop her and pull her low.

"Don't go up there," they said.

She tried to see ahead. The firing stopped again, leaving an awful, expectant noise of moans and crying in its wake.

"I have to get past. Let me by," she said, squeezing through.

Shot people lay slumped on the cobblestones. Others were already trying to help them. As Gaia neared the terrace, looking for Leon, she saw a dozen armed guards, Marquez among them, but now their rifles were pointed inward at a hub of other guards who held their hands open and empty before them. The arrangement made no sense to her until she realized the reversal meant a faction of the guards had rebelled.

Farther within the inner circle, in the place where the Protectorat had stood before, several people were bent over with their backs to her, and as one of them shifted, she saw Mabrother Rhodeski and several others were injured. Leon was nowhere to be seen. Sephie was opening a medical bag.

With increasing fear, Gaia turned again toward the square. More gunshots sounded on the far side, near the prison. Chaos reigned, and though people were running in all directions and dozens were trying to help the injured, the crowd never seemed to diminish.

"Leon!" she called. "Where are you?"

"Over here!" called a young voice. "Mlass Gaia! He's here!"

She peered to her left, under the arches of the arcade, where Angie was waving madly.

Gaia sprinted forward, weaving through the hurrying people. She stepped around the corpse of man with his head shot open. A guard was trying to staunch a woman's bloody arm wound. Another round of rifle shots ripped around her, and she flew under the archway.

Beside the library wall, Leon lay crumpled in a heap, with Angie pressing both of her small hands against his chest.

CHAPTER 22

life first

"I DON'T KNOW WHAT TO do!" Angie said.

"Let me see," Gaia said, shoving nearer.

Leon's dark shirt was covered in blood, so much that she couldn't tell for certain where it was coming from. Angie was holding a saturated bandana to Leon's chest, just below his left shoulder, and when Gaia lifted it to take a quick look, more blood surfaced out of a deep hole. Gaia covered it again, pressing firmly.

"Get Myrna!" she said to Angie.

Angie staggered to her feet, her eyes tormented. "I don't know where she is!"

"I *said*, get Myrna," Gaia said in hard tones. The girl recoiled, and Gaia switched to pleading. "You can find her if anyone can. She was ready for this moment. Run and find her as fast as you can!"

Angie took a terrified look toward Leon and fled.

Leon turned his face weakly, and Gaia pressed the bandana back onto his chest wound. He must be injured in other places, too, she thought, fighting back panic. The splint on his broken arm was gone. When she slid back his shirt from his torso, she found another bleeding bullet wound on his lower right side.

268

"Gaia," Leon said softly. "Just tell me I got the Protectorat."

"I don't even know," she said, her throat tightening.

She tried bunching the shirt against his lower side to apply more pressure there.

"I guess you'll end up with Peter now," Leon said.

"Stop it," she said.

Leon winced. She looked around to see who was near to help and what else she might use as to stop the bleeding. The sandstone pavers were cool beneath her legs, and out of the direct sunlight, the air had a dusty, dim quality that gave a darker tinge to the blood. The only other people under the arcade of the library were wounded, too.

She bit her teeth into the shoulder of her sleeve and ripped the fabric off to ball it up and pack it against his side.

"Are you okay?" Leon asked.

"Of course," she said.

"Don't try to lie. I saw Iris shock you. And they did the surgery," Leon said. "That's what you meant about being gutted, isn't it?"

She couldn't bear the concern in his eyes, as if her problems mattered when he might be dying.

"I'm all right, though," she said. "I survived it."

"I want you to adopt someday," he said. "Hear me? That's what I want."

"Don't say that."

"You're the best thing that ever happened to me," he said.

"Leon, don't," she said, leaning near. "I'm not having this. You're not saying good-bye."

"The best." He smiled, and his eyelids lowered halfway.

She kept the pressure on his wounds the best she could, but she could feel him fading.

"Don't do this to me, Leon," she pleaded.

He didn't reply. Behind her, the noises of battle had diminished to scuffles and cries, but no more gunshots. She glanced briefly through the arch of the arcade to where people were rushing past, paying no attention to the two of them huddled there. She could feel each of his breaths under her hands. *Just stop bleeding so much.*

She wanted Myrna badly, but it occurred to her that even if Angie found her, it could be too late.

She refolded the patch of sleeve and pressed it to his side wound again. "I don't know what to do," she whispered helplessly.

"Get married, raise kids, and grow old," he said.

"Don't try to make me laugh. I'm only doing all of that with you."

He winced again, and then looked up at her, frowning. "Gaia?"

"I'm here," she said.

His eyes closed.

For a moment she couldn't move. She'd seen this before, with her mother, with the Matrarc. It wasn't going to happen now. It couldn't.

"Sephie!" she screamed. She took a desperate look at Leon and stood, lurching toward the sunlight beyond the archway. "Sephie! Where are you?"

She started toward the Bastion, instinctively holding a hand to her abdomen as she ran. Most of the terrace had cleared. A dozen disarmed guards were lined up against one wall, contained there by some of the turncoat guards. Other armed rebels surrounded a collection of white-clad people at the top of the terrace stairs. As Gaia hurried nearer, she found Sephie treating the Protectorat, who was sitting on the steps. He gripped his leg with a bloody hand.

Gaia grabbed the handles of Sephie's doctor kit. "Come with me," she demanded. "Leon's dying. I need you."

"You knifed me last night," Sephie reminded her.

"So? You took my ovaries," Gaia said impatiently. With all her might, she dragged Sephie to her feet. "You have to come with me. Now!"

"Don't you dare go," the Protectorat said.

"Come!" Gaia insisted. Sephie spared a last glance toward the Protectorat, and then she joined Gaia. They hurried diagonally across the square. Even in her terror for Leon, Gaia grasped the significance of Sephie's defection: the Protectorat had lost his power, utterly.

Gaia sped toward the arch of the arcade and flew up the two steps into the shadows. "Leon?" she asked.

He didn't respond, but he was breathing still. She pressed the bandages over his wounds again, and he didn't move. Sephie came up behind her, panting.

"He's been shot twice," Gaia said.

"I know. I saw it happen," Sephie said. "He attacked his father and his father shot him point blank in the chest. That's when your rebel guards were able to move in, but Leon went down. I thought he must be dead already."

Sephie knelt beside her and set a hand under Leon's jaw. Then Sephie lifted Leon's eyelid, and Gaia saw his pupil contract.

"I don't know what you think I can do for him," Sephie said quietly.

Gaia was already rifling through the doctor's bag. "Don't tell me you don't have a—" She pulled up a syringe and a length of IV tube. Then she scrambled for Leon's arm, ripping his left sleeve with one savage pull. The skin in the nook of his elbow from where he'd been hooked up to an IV the day before had already healed with a faint scab over the vein. "We need to give him a transfusion," Gaia said.

"I don't have any fluids here. Besides, it wouldn't—" Sephie began.

"My blood," Gaia said. "Myrna said I was a universal donor. So give him my blood."

For an instant, Sephie frowned at his arm, motionless in thought, but then she took the syringe and quickly rigged the needle to a short length of IV line. She glanced over to Gaia.

"There, sit there," Sephie said, pointing with her chin toward where Gaia could be beside Leon with her back against the wall. "I have to do you first. I can't get a bubble in the line."

"Just hurry," Gaia said, taking her place. She exposed her right arm to Sephie.

Leon's complexion was a mottled gray, and Gaia was afraid any moment he'd quit breathing.

"Make a fist," Sephie said curtly.

Gaia did so, while Sephie lined up the needle along Gaia's arm. Then she slid it under her skin into the vein.

"Hold it," Sephie said. "Here."

Gaia pressed the needle against her arm to keep it steady. Her blood ran down the line, a dark color in the translucent tube, like a freestanding vein all its own. Sephie took another syringe out of her kit, detached the hypodermic needle and fit it to the end of the IV tube. Gaia watched the blood make it down to the needle and begin to come out the end. Sephie doubled over the IV line, pinching it to stop the blood flow. Then she leaned near, clamped the line between her lips to have both her hands free, and lined up the bloody end of the needle on Leon's arm. She let the line fall from her lips so that Gaia's blood began flowing down the line again just as she stuck the needle under Leon's skin. They were perfectly connected, with Gaia's blood feeding into his veins.

Gaia said nothing. She tipped her head back against the wall as Sephie took clean bandages out of her kit, folded them rapidly into fat pads, and replaced the blood-saturated ones from Leon's wounds. Gaia watched closely as Sephie turned Leon's body, and added another thick bandage to a long, oozing gash on his back.

"If he can stop bleeding and stabilize," Sephie said, "I can go in later for the bullets."

"Go in for them now."

"It wouldn't help," Sephie said. "Disturbing him now would make it worse. See if he'll stabilize, and then I can try."

Gaia watched Leon's face, waiting for some flicker, some sign that he was coming around. She touched her right hand to his arm, afraid to move any more than that in case she dislodged the IV line.

"I'm so glad I didn't kill you, Masister," Gaia said to Sephie.

"So am I."

Sephie worked more with the bandages, securing them, and then she straightened backward and shifted on her knees.

"You're not leaving us," Gaia said.

"Do you really want me to stay when others need help, too?" Sephie said. "They need me, and they have a much better chance than he has. I'm sorry, but I can't do anything more for him now anyway."

Gaia didn't want to be reasonable. She wanted Sephie to stay.

Sephie put a hand on her arm. "Don't let the transfusion go for more than five minutes or you won't have enough blood yourself."

"I don't care about me," Gaia said.

"Prepare yourself, Gaia. Are you listening? He's essentially gone already, and I didn't hook you up for a love-sick suicide," Sephie said. "Five minutes. No more. Check your little locket watch."

Sephie pulled the locket watch free of Gaia's neckline for her and pushed the tiny catch. She propped it in a wrinkle in the fabric of Gaia's dress where she could see it. *Life first.* The inscription gleamed inside the cover, and Gaia checked the time: 12:55. She felt a light tingling behind her ears, and leaned her head back against the wall again.

"Thank you," she said to Sephie.

Sephie hauled herself to her feet. "Are we even?"

"I'm in your debt forever," Gaia said, looking up at her.

Sephie met her gaze with a regretful, doubtful smile. A voice called out for a doctor. Sephie picked up her bag and was gone.

Gazing down at Leon, Gaia struggled to accept that at least he looked peaceful. His lips were slightly parted, and his hair was messed over his forehead, covering the stitches there. They'd beat his face. The curving line of his cheek was pale against the background of shadow. She ached with a lost, lonely sorrow.

"You impossible idiot," she said. *Why did you have to go for your father?*

But she knew why. He'd had to watch Gaia be tortured, and that, to Leon, must have been unforgivable.

12:57. She'd lost a minute somewhere. She was getting light-headed and didn't want to move.

"I wanted this to work," she said quietly.

His eyelids twitched, and his gaze blinked open. "You were gone."

Happiness warmed her. "I'm back," she said. Her fingers were already on his arm, but when she tried to touch him more, she seemed to have no strength.

He turned his face to see her, and frowned in confusion. "What are you doing?" he asked.

"It's a transfusion." Her left hand fell heavily to her lap, but her needle stayed in her right arm without being held.

His gaze took in her posture, and traveled to her arm, and then to the bloodline.

"Whose idea was this?" he asked.

"Mine."

"I don't like it," he said.

She smiled. *Too bad.*

His eyes locked with hers, blinking slowly from time to time, and for Gaia, it was enough to be near to him. 1:03. She was supposed to do something about the watch, she knew, but she felt rather sleepy. Foggy.

"Remember the lightning bugs?" she asked.

"By the winner's cabin," he said. "You know I do. I wish I'd gone out into the meadow with you."

She smiled again. How pretty the lightning bugs had been. She could almost see the tiny green streaks of light in the darkness around her, and this time, he was with her and baby Maya.

We should go there again, she said. The words didn't come out, but it didn't matter. She knew he understood what she meant.

CHAPTER 23

under the arcade

"WHAT ON EARTH IS this?" demanded Myrna. Her voice sounded very far away. "Stupid *idiot* of a girl. If she dies of blood loss, I'm going to kill her."

Gaia cracked open her eyes to find Myrna taking the needle out of her arm. Behind Myrna, Angie was anxiously watching. Will had come, too. Still farther back, through the arch of the arcade, sunlight was bright in the square, but here underneath, the shadows were deep and grainy.

"Did we make it back in time?" Angie asked.

"Hard to know. Let me see what I can do," Myrna said.

She pressed a scrap of bandage to the bleeding spot and bent Gaia's arm up. Gaia's gaze flew to Leon, whose eyes were closed. His hand was wrapped in the IV line where he'd pinched it in a crimp to stop the blood flow from her into him.

"Leon," Gaia said, nudging him. "Don't be dead."

He took a faint, visible breath. "Okay," he said.

As Myrna began working over Leon, he opened his eyes with a moan. "Take it easy, there," he said.

"Feel that, do you? Good," Myrna said, and kept working.

Gaia looked up to Will. "Where's Peter?" she asked.

276

Will shifted down beside her and drew her hand into his steady fingers. He kept his gaze on their joined hands. Gradually, she realized that Will was touching her for the first time, and as she studied him, his gentle, wordless silence began to last too long. She tightened her grip, waiting, unable to accept what she started to fear. And then she knew. It had to be Peter. He had to be gone.

Gaia felt a tightness crush all the air from her chest. "It isn't true," she said.

Will nodded. "I should know what to say," he said. "He was my brother, and I have no idea what to say."

"What happened?" she asked, her voice aching.

"He was shot on the gallows," Will said.

"But I saw him and Malachai fall," she said. "They both fell through the trapdoors. They were safe below."

Will slowly shook his head, back and forth. "They did fall. Jack got their ropes free in time, but they were both shot before they fell. Malachai lasted a little while." His voice trailed off. He let go of her and pressed his arm across his face. "My little brother."

Shock and loss stopped Gaia's brain from processing any more. Her eyes took in Will beside her, and Myrna efficiently attending to Leon, and Angie hovering in the background, but her mind stopped understanding. Peter dead. Malachai, too. The words didn't mean anything.

But Peter still loves me, she thought.

"He can't be dead," she said, but as she spoke, she finally believed it, and a crumpling sensation caught her heart. "Will," she said, her voice hushed with grief. "I'm so sorry."

He shook his head, still hiding his face in his arm, but when she tenderly put a hand on him, he leaned his head against her shoulder. A broken, lost sound came from him. Gaia ached for

277

him. She wrapped an arm around him as best she could, while a stubborn, protesting despair rose within her. It wasn't right. It wasn't fair.

"I'm going to miss him so much," Will said.

"Me, too," she said.

She closed her eyes tightly, reaching her other hand to Leon, needing him. From the darkness, she felt Leon's fingers tenderly encircle her own, weak but insistent, and her gratitude that Leon was still alive mixed inextricably with her grief over Peter, fusing deep in the loneliest place within her.

A bullet had penetrated Leon's upper chest and lodged in his left shoulder. A second was buried in his side, lower on the right. A third had gouged a deep streak along his back, but he had sta-bilized, and Myrna was able to extricate the bullets and patch him up.

"He needs more rest," Myrna said the next day, as she checked his pulse again. She'd changed his bandages and was satisfied with his progress. "You think you can manage to keep him quiet?"

"I will," Gaia said.

Gaia longed to take him down to her parents' house on Sally Row where it was restful and quiet, but he was still too fragile to move and she herself was needed here, in the center of negotia-tions. He lay in a small, cream-colored guest room of the Bastion, one with a view overlooking the square and none of the history of his old bedroom. Both windows were open to the echoing, hammering noises of workers repairing damage from the battle of the day before.

If only fixing the society would be as simple as mending a few walls. The Protectorat sat in the prison, officially deposed, and the new jockeying for power had begun. Mabrother Iris had been killed in the fighting on the terrace, accidentally or not Gaia would never know.

She had spent hours that morning working with leaders from New Sylum, Wharfton, and the Enclave, sorting out the chaos of the rebellion and weighing whom to detain in the prison. She had teams trying to reestablish basic services of medical care, water and electricity at the same time that others were drafting a new charter that granted equal rights to everyone.

Elections were scheduled to follow, and from there it would get even more complicated. Gaia was fully aware of the staggering amount of work ahead, considering she had recently gone through a similar process with the people of New Sylum.

She shifted closer to Leon and studied his even features again. He turned his face, licked his lips, and kept sleeping.

"How are you doing yourself?" Myrna asked.

Gaia lifted her hands, examining the singed skin on her pinky-tips where the electrocution clamps had been attached, as if they might provide a way to measure all her other hurts as well. The tenderness in her abdomen was about the same. The heightened sensitivity of her skin had faded, and a foreign quietness had settled over her body like a muffling blanket. It wasn't simple fatigue from grief and blood loss. Neither was it numbness, because she felt as alert as she'd ever been.

"I feel like I'm waiting, but waiting for nothing," she said.

Myrna laughed. "I was thinking more physically than poetically. Why are you still wearing that bracelet?"

Gaia glanced at the glowing blue band on her left wrist. She'd paid enough for it. She held out her wrist toward Myrna, who cut it off with a pointy scissors.

"Let me check your sutures," Myrna said.

When Gaia undid the waist of her skirt and loosened her

bandage to show her the healing stitches from her surgery, Myrna approved.

Gaia slowly retucked her blouse. "I'm glad we have Maya," she said. With all the hurt and losses that others had suffered around her, Gaia hadn't thought much consciously about her own blighted motherhood, but it was beginning to sink in. "There's a chance I could still have my own children, isn't there?"

Myrna folded her arms across her chest. "How so?"

"Sephie took my ovaries, but not my uterus," Gaia said. "If we found some of my eggs, if I bought them back, couldn't we inseminate them with Leon's sperm and implant them in me? I could be my own surrogate mother."

Myrna began wrapping up her extra bandages and salve.

"Couldn't I, Myrna?"

"In theory, with the right hormones, I suppose it's possible," Myrna said. "We've never tried it. I wouldn't give you very good odds."

Gaia leaned a hip against Leon's bed, hugging her arms around herself. "The Protectorat talked about using my eggs to produce dozens of children. It just seems Leon and I ought to be able to have one of them, don't you think?"

"It wouldn't be Leon's child," Myrna said.

"Why not?"

"You really want to know this?"

"Of course. Tell me."

Myrna moved before the window, where the diffused light dropped softly on her white hair. "Your eggs were claimed the minute Mabrother Rhodeski heard someone like you existed," she said. "He had a list of fifty families all privately outbidding each other to buy your eggs. Sephie had everything ready to go as soon as they were harvested. Your eggs have already been inseminated."

"They aren't frozen somewhere?"

Myrna shook her head. "Eggs are more stable after they're inseminated and start to divide. They're being carefully tended in culture dishes. Each one is essentially priceless."

Gaia wanted to see. She wanted to take them all home with her, or else smash them all. Her conflicted, impulsive reaction bewildered her. Heartache was expanding within her so strongly that it was hard to breathe.

"So my kids, mine and Leon's, can never exist?"

Myrna spoke more gently. "I'm sorry about it," she said. "Truly, I am."

"I must be missing something," Gaia said. "This can't be the end." It was such a strange, elusive loss, the vanishing of the hypothetical children she could have had with Leon, like losing a precious dream she'd hardly known she had.

Weary, Gaia eyed the edge of Leon's bed and decided that the space beside him was just wide enough for her to fit in for a nap. "I don't think I'm going to make my next meeting," Gaia said slowly. "Tell Will for me."

"You said yourself that you have Maya," Myrna said. "And you can try to adopt."

"There aren't enough babies, remember?" Gaia said. "Don't try to cheer me up."

"You'll still be a midwife," Myrna said.

Gaia let out a sad little laugh. How hard would it be to tend pregnant mothers when she could never have a baby of her own? "Yes. I suppose I can deliver other people's babies, when I'm not busy with all the funerals we have coming up."

Myrna reached to gently squeeze Gaia's shoulder. "It's always funerals and babies, Gaia. That's what it is."

"I know," Gaia said. "I just never thought they'd be the same thing." She slid onto the bed, curling up beside Leon.

Myrna frowned. "I don't think I like this dark side of you."

Gaia didn't either. She closed her eyes and hoped Myrna would leave before she gave in to her grief. She heard the windows being shut, one after the other, blocking out the noise from the square, and then the door was softly closed.

long shadows

"SHE'S PULLING HER HAT off again," Gaia said.

Gaia itched to fix her sister's hat and tidy up her soft, mussed hair, but her hands were full with a pot of fragrant herbs.

"I've got it," Leon said. "Here, Maya. Let's see you." He crouched down before the toddler and despite his right arm still being in a splint, he adjusted the ties under the girl's chin. "Your hat stays on. See Gaia's hat? And mine? Hold my hand."

When he straightened, the toddler lifted both her hands. "Uppy," she said.

He swung her up in his left arm, and Gaia watched the maneuver closely.

His recovery had been slow, with the setback of an infection that had lingered, and Gaia knew Maya was heavier than she looked.

Leon smiled at Gaia, his eyes amused.

"Enough with the coddling, Gaia."

"I didn't say anything," she said.

"Come here." He pivoted Maya out of the way, leaned near, and angled the brim of his hat to give Gaia a kiss. "All right?" he asked softly.

She nodded, smiling back. "Yes. Of course."

"Good. Maya wants a kiss, too," he said.

Gaia planted a loud smooch on the girl's cheek so that she squealed. Leon did the same thing, making Maya squeal again, and then he aimed a grin at Gaia.

What could she say? He pretty much slayed her.

The three of them were heading toward the Wharfton quad, several weeks after the rebellion, and their late afternoon shadows stretched long before them onto the dirt road. As they came around the corner, the quad opened before them, and Gaia saw people meandering before the Tvaltar. Hammering rang from the blacksmith's shop, and a boy dribbled a red ball around a group of pigeons, sending half a dozen into heavy flight. Up the hill, the dismantling of the wall had stopped for the day. Clear progress was visible in both directions from where the south gate had stood, though the demolition still had a long way to go.

She nodded up at the deserted parapet. "Did you ever patrol up there?"

"When I first joined, I did," Leon said. "It seems like a long time ago. I'm going to need a new job now."

She tried to think what he could do.

"You were good with the excrims," she said.

"I've thought about working at the prison," he said slowly. "To be honest, I don't want to be near the Protectorat."

She didn't blame him.

"We need someone to run the first responders in Wharfton and New Sylum," she said. "Or there's teaching. Kids always like you."

"Could you see me as a teacher?" he asked, his voice doubtful.

She could, actually. Half his students would have terrible crushes on him. "Only if you want. You can think about it."

"Junie!" Maya squealed.

Outside Peg's Tavern, Junie and Josephine shared a table with Norris and Dinah. Others from Wharfton and New Sylum had gathered, too, filling more tables under the brown canvas umbrellas. Leon let Maya down again to run toward her friend, and Gaia's gaze caught on the way he retucked the back of his blue shirt.

"Come join us, Senator," Norris said, lifting his tankard.

Gaia smiled at her new title. She wasn't used to it at all. "We will. We came to see Myrna's new blood bank, but we'll come right back."

"When are you two getting married, anyway?" Norris asked. "We could use a wedding around here."

Leon lifted his gaze, regarding her curiously.

"Norris. Don't be a pest," Dinah said, rising to give Gaia a hug. "Pay him no mind. You just missed Sasha and her grandpa. Let me see you. You're getting your color back. Nice herbs. For Myrna?"

"Yes," Gaia said.

Leon was still watching her, idly pushing his shirt sleeve up a bit over his splint. She could feel herself blushing.

"What?" she asked.

He smiled. "Nothing. Dinah's right about your color."

At another table, with their profiles aimed in concentration over the pieces, Pyrho was teaching Jack to play chess. Angie was curled up in a chair beside Jack, fiddling with the puzzle pieces of an intricate wooden sphere. Derek and Ingrid sat a couple tables over with their daughter, and Derek lifted a hand in greeting. As the piano started up inside the tavern, Gaia glanced toward the open windows, wondering if Will were inside with Gillian. Seeing so many friends, Gaia couldn't help missing the absent faces, too.

"I swear Maya grows bigger every time I see her," Josephine said.

"Can you watch her for us? We'll be right back," Gaia said.

"Are you kidding? I'd be glad to," Josephine said.

With unhurried strides, Gaia started across the quad beside Leon. A light breeze drifted up from the unlake, cool along the back of her neck. She shifted the pot to her other hip, checking her skirt briefly to be certain none of the dirt had spilled on her. When they passed under the dappling shade of the mesquite tree, she instinctively took in a breath of the dry, piney air. Leon slowed to a stop.

"You're not eager to talk to Myrna, are you?" he said.

"I know it matters to you," she said. She didn't care to think about her surgery or how she'd been violated. "It won't change how I feel."

He gently tugged the pot of herbs out of her hands and set it on a bench under the tree. "But what if we could have one of your blastocysts?"

She shook her head. "They aren't mine."

"They're half yours."

"That means they're half *not* mine," she said. "Our children are gone, Leon. They never existed. You can't bring back something that never existed."

"I'd love any babies you carried just as much, no matter who the father was," he said.

"I know. You would."

"And you would, too," he said. "We could push to get one of your blastocysts if you wanted."

She felt a fissure opening inside her. "Why are you doing this to me? There are costs to what we did. Why can't you accept that?"

He ran a hand back through his hair. "I'm just thinking about our future."

"So am I."

His eyes searched hers, and she knew there was no hiding the twisted mess inside of her. Any chance of carrying a baby was so impossibly slim. She didn't think she would ever be ready to open up to the risk and hope of experimenting on herself.

"I'm not trying to make it worse," he said quietly, and pulled her near. "I only want you to know if you ever want to try to get pregnant, I'll do everything I can to help you."

"And you won't be sad if I can't ever try?" she asked.

"Of course not," he said. "You make me unbelievably happy, Gaia. You know that."

"I feel like I'm stopping you from being a father, just because I'm messed up inside now," she said.

He lightly smoothed her hair from her cheek. "I'm Maya's father, in case you hadn't noticed."

It was completely true. Her sorrow softened, easing the darkness within her. She smiled a little. "I've noticed."

A bee skimmed through the shade with a zip of sound, then veered back into the sunlight.

Leon took off his hat and dropped it casually beside the pot on the bench. "There's something I've been wanting to ask you," he said. "Are you feeling settled yet?"

Her heart did a zigzag. "Pretty much. Yes."

"I thought maybe so. Then when should we get married?" He shifted nearer and linked his arms around her.

"Soon," she said.

"I've heard that before. How about tomorrow?"

She laughed. Then she thought about it. Why not? "Okay," she said.

He beamed as he drew her closer still. "That's more like it."

It meant all the more to her that their happiness was built on the genuine, intricate mix of heartaches they shared. She liked the way she only had to lift her chin and his mouth was perfectly near. When he laughed, low in his chest, she could almost feel it under her fingertips. She closed her eyes, leaning into him, and met the light pressure of his kiss.

Being married to him was going to be beautiful.

"We should tell our friends," he said, kissing her again.

"Yes."

She shifted, bumping lightly into his splint as she slid one hand around his warm shirt. He tasted faintly minty, like the warm shade. She tried a new angle and he followed along. When his next kiss trailed to her neck, she ducked her chin and curled her fingers in his shirt. "Um," she said.

"I know," he said, setting another kiss on her cheek and slightly loosening his arms. His eyes were darker when she looked up again. "I've been wanting to do that. You looked so sweet with that pot of flowers."

"Herbs."

"What do you say we forget about Myrna's and head back home?"

She laughed. "We can't. What's happened to my hat?"

"It's there," he said, nodding toward the bench.

She saw her hat on top of his and shook her head. "Smooth."

"A guy has to try."

She laughed again. "I'd like Evelyn and Rafael to come to the wedding. We should notify your mother, too, I think."

His smile gradually dimmed, and he ran his thumb over her red bracelet. "She was ready to stand there and watch me be executed," he said.

Gaia hadn't thought of that. They had talked at length about the rebellion, Gaia's surgery, Leon's injuries, and the torture, which had included Pyrho and Jack, but new subtleties were still coming up, and it seemed like they would never be at peace with all that had happened. Gaia's old nightmares of the Matrarc's death had resurfaced, interspersed now with haunting fragments of the night Gaia had killed Mabrother Stoltz and imagined glimpses of a faceless corpse in the debris of the wall.

Leon was troubled most by memories of Gaia's torture. The first time he saw Mabrother Iris electrocute Gaia, Leon confessed about the explosives under the obelisk, cooperating to make Mabrother Iris stop shocking her, but the Protectorat had not been satisfied. The torture of them both had escalated through stages of questioning as Mabrother Iris fished for every tiniest detail, even when it became clear that Gaia knew practically nothing. Gaia found that Leon was prone to withdraw into a silent rage when he remembered, and it worked best then to set him caring for Maya, who seemed to pull him back to the present.

The vessel mothers had all cut off their bracelets and were regularly visiting their families in Wharfton. Most still planned to surrender their promised babies, but one other besides Sasha was working out a shared custody agreement. Mabrother Rhodeski remained optimistic that the Vessel Institute would thrive, evolving, and he had already hired a second wave of vessel mothers. Gaia couldn't understand, privately, why the mothers would sign on. Neither could she adjust to the idea that she might someday meet her own biological children walking around the Enclave, strangers to her. But she conceded that the vessel mothers had the right to make their own choices, and Mabrother Rhodeski had kept his side of the original bargain for Gaia's eggs by funding a waterworks system for outside the wall. Guilt drove him, she suspected.

The Protectorat remained imprisoned, awaiting trail. He was likely to be sentenced to life in prison. Genevieve was confined to her quarters in the Bastion, under a suicide watch.

"I don't understand Genevieve," Gaia admitted finally. "I thought she sincerely cared for you."

"When it came down to it, she had to choose between the Protectorat and me," Leon said. "I don't want her at our wedding."

She nodded. "That's fine. But Evelyn and Rafael?"

"Of course. And your brothers and the Jacksons. Anyone else from inside?"

She wondered about his old friends. "How about Rita?"

Leon smiled, his expression easing again. "It would be nice to have Rita. Jack will be happy to see her. He always had a thing for her."

Gaia laughed. She wasn't going to touch that.

Leon smoothed a finger along the chain of her necklace. "I wish your parents could be here for our wedding," he said.

"Me, too."

Gaia had taken a walk to Potter's Field the day before, stopping where her parents had matching markers side by side on the dusty slope. Their gravesites seemed so settled compared to the raw, new graves since the rebellion. Before New Sylum ever had a school or a lodge or a library, it had a graveyard. Dozens had been killed during the rebellion, and hundreds more injured. Will had overseen a dozen funerals for New Slyum, saving Peter's for last. The new mounds lay in a peaceful bay of the unlake where grasses grew tall and undulated in the wind, the sister wind of the one that moved in the black rice slue in the marsh they'd left behind.

"Are you missing Peter much?" he asked.

She didn't know how to answer. Thinking about Peter hurt.

"You can tell me," he added. "It won't kill me if you admit you loved him, too."

She lifted her gaze to his, searching. "But I didn't."

"Gaia," he said, drawing out her name.

She didn't know how to explain what she felt. The loss was complicated. She still felt guilty about how she'd treated Peter in Sylum, and sometimes he had really annoyed her. He'd also had a way of seeing her honestly that had mattered. Other times, he had been just Peter, and there was something intrinsically wonderful about Peter. He didn't deserve to die.

"What are you thinking?" Leon asked.

Her gaze had stilled on the warm gap between his collar and his neck, but now she looked up again to meet his eyes.

"I told you I was loyal," she said simply.

Leon smiled. "I never doubted you. I just thought you'd miss him."

"I do. And I will. He was a great guy."

A lilting, merry chortle of laughter came from beyond the shade, and Gaia glanced over as an old woman walked past with a friend.

"How's Will doing?" Leon asked.

"All right. Sad, you know, but all right."

Something had changed there. She didn't know why or how, but the fine, spinning thread of Will's longing for her had snapped. She felt it as a release, a new easiness between them, while, she also knew, they'd always be bound by their common grief for Peter.

Leon slid a hand along her arm to her red bracelet, and kissed her once more. "Let's go see Myrna's new place."

Gaia glanced toward the new blood bank in a storefront

291

opposite the Tvaltar. A new beige awning was outfitted over the window, and a pot of colorful flowers stood by the door. Gaia had heard that electricity had been extended to the blood bank so that Myrna could refrigerate an emergency supply of blood, and she was curious to see it all. At that moment, however, Myrna came out the door, paused a moment on the threshold, and began ambling toward Peg's Tavern.

"I think we missed our chance," Gaia said.

Leon passed over her hat, donned his own, and picked up the pot of herbs. "What do you say we leave these for her, and come back another time for a tour?"

"Sounds good."

They stepped out of the shade. October sunlight slanted brightly on the Tvaltar steps, and more people had gathered at Peg's. Their animated voices created a jovial patter in the square, underscored by the lively notes of the piano. Jack had Maya on his lap now, and she was knocking a couple of chess knights together. It was easy to anticipate how happy everyone would be about the wedding, and Gaia smiled. Norris would make a cake, no doubt. She'd have to find something to wear.

Leon lowered the pot to the side of the door, then straightened, pushing his sleeve up his splint again.

"Let me help you," Gaia said. She reached to do his sleeve for him. Then she folded up the sleeve on his left arm, too, smoothing the fabric neatly just below his elbow. She let her fingers linger on his forearm. When Gaia looked up, Leon's blue eyes were alive with a warm, private smile.

"You are irresistible," he said softly.

She shook her head, smiling. "No."

"Yes."

He leaned near for another kiss, and she touched her hat from behind to keep it steady.

When they finally righted themselves and started across the quad toward the tavern, Gaia was filled with a contagious, generous happiness that encompassed everyone and everything, from the piano melody and Maya with her knights, to the bright angles of the shade umbrellas. Behind her, a wall was crumbling, and down the hill, beyond the swallows that dove and banked, the expanse of the unlake shimmered with distant blue.

acknowledgments

I would like to thank the team at Roaring Brook for their unfailing kindness and for their delight in the details: Nan Mercado, Simon Boughton, Anne Diebel, Kathryn Bhirud, April Ward, Jill Freshney, Suzette Costello, Karen Frangipane, John Nora, Alexander Garkusha, Gina Gagliano, Angus Killick, Allison Verost, Jennifer Doerr, and Rachael Stein. I'm thankful to my agent, the scrupulous Kirby Kim. I'm grateful to Nancy O'Brien Wagner for insights on the messiest draft. Thanks to my children, Michael, Emily, and William LoTurco, for continued understanding of my proclivity for the couch. I can never thank them enough for their inspiration and humor during this four-year adventure of writing Gaia's story. As always, again, I thank my husband, Joseph LoTurco, for everything.

Caragh M. O'Brien
October, 2012